BREAKAWAY

Valentine Cardinale
Author of *One More Dance*

outskirts
press

Breakaway
All Rights Reserved.
Copyright © 2017 A Novel by: Valentine Cardinale, Author of *One More Dance*
v9.0 r2.0

This is a work of fiction. The events and characters described herein are imaginary and are not intended to refer to specific places or living persons. The opinions expressed in this manuscript are solely the opinions of the author and do not represent the opinions or thoughts of the publisher. The author has represented and warranted full ownership and/or legal right to publish all the materials in this book.

This book may not be reproduced, transmitted, or stored in whole or in part by any means, including graphic, electronic, or mechanical without the express written consent of the publisher except in the case of brief quotations embodied in critical articles and reviews.

Outskirts Press, Inc.
http://www.outskirtspress.com

ISBN: 978-1-4787-8331-2

Cover Photo © 2017 thinkstockphotos.com. All rights reserved - used with permission.

Outskirts Press and the "OP" logo are trademarks belonging to Outskirts Press, Inc.

PRINTED IN THE UNITED STATES OF AMERICA

Chapter 1

Ding! Dong!

I can't believe it. I've been in the house for only two days, and someone's ringing the doorbell. In one of the worst snowstorms of the year! I should see who it is, but I'm finally doing some serious unpacking, and emptying these boxes is sapping all my energy. Five boxes done, only twenty-three more to go...

Ding! Dong! Ding! Dong!

Alright, I hear you, I hear you. I wonder who it could be. I'm not expecting anyone, and I really don't know anyone who lives around here yet. Maybe it's a neighbor welcoming me to town. More likely, it's just someone who rang the wrong doorbell. Now I'm curious. Very curious. Like Tess says, I'm too curious for my own good sometimes. I'm coming, I'm coming.

When I open the front door, my face is spritzed with snowflakes. It's starting to get dark and I can't make out who or what is standing in front of me. At first glance, it looks like an alabaster statue of a mail carrier, or is it a creature from outer space carrying some odd-shaped gifts? Oh, come on, Richie. It's just some poor soul blanketed in snow. One hand is clutching the strap of a big, bulging gym bag. The other is hugging what looks like hockey sticks. On the rim of a baseball cap with ear flaps, small icicles are forming, almost concealing these anxious green-brown eyes.

"Oh, hi. Can I help you?" I ask in a neighborly way.

"You mind if I use your bathroom?" the stranger replies in a girl's voice brimming with teenage urgency.

"No, no." It seems like an unusual request, but I've heard stranger ones over the years. "Come on in."

She drops her bag and sticks on the porch, brushes and stamps away as much snow as she can, and walks in.

"Straight ahead through the living room, first door on the right."

She scurries off.

Several minutes later, she's back in the living room, her hat in her hand. There's a ruddiness in her cheeks, a sparkle in her eyes, and a sheen in her long, blond hair that, together, give her a healthy glow. "Whew, that was close," she says, crinkling up her nose. "Thanks."

"Sure."

"Um, my name's Dana, Dana Dvorak," she says. "What's yours?"

"I'm Richard Bianchi."

We shake hands. I feel her energy. "Nice to meet you," I add.

"Same here."

I can't help to ask, "You live in town?"

She waves me over to the front window. "See the little green house across the street, where that Kia's parked at the curb?"

I nod, not so sure of the color of the house or the make of the car under the snow.

"That's where I live with my dad," she explains.

"Oh."

"It doesn't make sense, right?" she continues with a sly smile. "If I live across the street, what am I doing here using your bathroom? My dad doesn't want me home when there's company, and he has company. Her car is parked in the street."

"Aha."

"Not all company," Dana explains. "Only when his friend Mildred Jordan comes over…and, oh, yeah, when he's hosting a meeting of the brotherhood, which is, like, whenever they feel like meeting."

"Please…make yourself comfortable."

She glances across the street one more time, removes her jacket and sits down on the loveseat under the window.

"Here, let me take that." I place her coat on a nearby coatrack that was here when I moved in.

She gives the room the once-over. "Good-looking place you have here."

"It has a way to go...I'm renting." Now why did I tell her that? Would she really care if I paid cash for the place, mortgaged it over a thirty-year period, rented or leased it for a year or two, or borrowed it from a friend?

"I saw when you moved in," she says. "I was watching from my bedroom. It didn't look like you had a lot of stuff."

"You're right, in a way. I brought only a few pieces of furniture with me, but I have a lot of other things I've collected over the years—mostly books, videos, my music collection, souvenirs. And they're all in those boxes."

"Well, the boxes are neatly stacked," she notes.

"That's a start."

"You should see our house," she continues. "Stuff jammed all over the place. I call it junk. My dad says it's all good stuff—antiques, collectibles, treasures."

"Hey, you never know. Some of it could be very valuable."

She shrugged, not agreeing or disagreeing with me, adding, "I liked the way you moved a lot of the stuff into the house yourself. It was thoughtful of you, helping out the movers like you did. It was a cold day."

"It sure was. Most of the items in the boxes are not very valuable, but some of them mean a lot to me. They go back a long way, to my school days and to trips I took over the years, to places like Italy, the Holy Land, Mexico. I carried in those items myself."

"Well, I still think it was thoughtful of you," she says.

"Thanks...I was wondering. Before I became your neighbor, where did you, uh, hang out when your dad had company?"

"Oh, I usually go to my friend Angie's house, or Hugo's. I forgot Mildred was coming today."

My interest in the life and times of Dana Dvorak is hardly quenched, but I decide to go easy on her now. I can come on pretty strong, like a bloodsucker, when my curiosity is peaked.

I got up from the chair. "Hey, I realized I didn't have lunch yet. I'm going to make some pasta. Would you like some?"

She glances across the street one more time. "Sure, if it's not too much trouble. I am little hungry after today's practice."

A little later, we're sitting across a wobbly picnic table in the kitchen and eating rigatoni and salad. By the way she's chomping on the food, Dana seems more than a little hungry. She's enjoying every mouthful. It's far from the three-course dinners I had been used to eating, but it's fine, and filling.

I break the silence. "So, you play hockey."

"Yup, I'm a forward with the Owls, the town's team."

"Any good, the team, I mean?"

"Hard to tell. This is my first year with this team. We've got a new coach, too. He seems pretty sharp. Used to play college hockey in Minnesota."

"Oh, Minnesota, that's an excellent hockey area, isn't it?"

"That's what I hear. We'll see. Next week, we play our first game in a regional hockey tournament for teenagers. We'll be representing northern New Jersey. Do you play any sports?"

"Who me? No, not really." I want to tell her I play chess and I own a pretty decent collection of baseball cards, but I'll save that news for another occasion.

She finishes chewing, closes her eyes, and takes a deep breath. "I love hockey," she proclaims. "I don't think I could live without it. Someday I want to play professional hockey. I'm thinking, when the time comes, I'll sign with the New York Rangers and win a Stanley Cup."

"What about the Devils?" I say. "You're a Jersey girl."

"Well, it's like this," she explains, "Grandpa Gustav, my father's dad, taught me how to play hockey, and he took me to my first hockey game. The Rangers were playing the Canadiens in Madison Square Garden. It was wonderful. I mean it was so noisy and exciting. The Rangers lost, 4-2, but right away I fell in love with them and the Garden."

"How old are you?"

"Sixteen, going on seventeen, in July."

"Oh, you have lots of time to weigh your options. Ever think about joining the women's Olympics hockey team?"

"Yeah, I'd like that, too. I watched the American women win the silver. They were awesome."

I agree with a hardy nod. "What does your father think about hockey?"

"He thinks it's a sport for goons and gorillas."

"Well, it can get pretty violent at times, don't you think?"

"Yeah, but that's only a small part of it, and it's changing," she counters. "To me, it's a beautiful game, fast and physical, yes, but also graceful, exciting, fun to watch. My dad doesn't think it's a sport for girls, but do you realize hockey is one of the fastest growing women's sports in the world?"

"Did you tell your dad that?"

"Sure, many times, but he's stuck in his ways." She taps the top of her head, as if she suddenly got a brainstorm. "Hey, why don't you come see us play? This year, most of the games are being played at the Apple Orchard Ice Rink, about a mile-and-a-half down the road."

"I just might do that." *And get a chance to see what the town is like*, I tell myself.

"Remember…Saturday afternoon, two o'clock. Not this Saturday, but the following Saturday."

"Okay." Barging ahead, I flip her another hot potato. "What does your mother think about you and hockey?"

She takes another mouthful of rigatoni and chews on it, and, after wiping her mouth, she says, "My mother's dead."

"Oh, I'm so sorry."

"Well, she might as well be dead," she quickly adds. "I speak to her once or twice a year. She lives in West Palm Beach, Florida with her new family. My dad says not to bother her with my personal issues. She has her own problems, and she's trying to get her act together."

"Any brothers or sisters?"

"No...I mean, Yes. I have two step brothers or half-brothers, whatever you call them. Two little boys. We share the same mother. Only our dads are different."

"Got it." At this point, I'm beginning to wonder whether I'm getting myself into something I don't want to get into right now, namely another person's life. I was alone in my new home going through cardboard boxes of private treasures and trying to figure out what to do with the next phase of my life, when this smart, dynamic, and determined teenager with at least a half-dozen issues asked to use my bathroom. How could I not want to reach out, or at least learn the facts?

She finishes her pasta and gulps down some orange vitamin water, the only drink outside of tap water on my menu. "This isn't half bad," she says, wiping her mouth with a paper napkin. "Boy," she adds, "you certainly ask a lot of questions. What are you a guidance counselor?"

"No, not really."

"Then what, really?"

"I'm a priest."

By the wide-eyed stare and open mouth on her, I need to explain. "Yes, I'm a priest. I'm a priest on leave of absence."

"So you're an ex-priest."

"No. I'm a priest. No such thing as an ex-priest. Once a priest, always a priest. The bishop has given me time to work through some issues and decide whether I want to continue to do all the things expected of anyone actively involved in the priesthood."

"Or what?"

"Or move back into the lay world, the world of everyday people like you and your dad and Mildred." Why I'm explaining, I don't know. She's a bright girl.

She nods to show she understands. "When did you leave on your absence?"

"About a month ago. After I left, I lived in the city with a friend of mine while I looked for a house to rent in New Jersey."

"Oh." She looks away. "Did you do something bad, like molest some kid?"

"God, no, Dana! One of my favorite jobs over the past few years has been working with adolescent boys and girls, seeing them develop and mature. The last thing I'd ever want to do is add to their problems."

"So…are you gay?"

"What's that got to do with anything? I know some gay men who are excellent priests. But, no…I'm not gay."

"I realize Catholic priests are not supposed to marry. Are you dating someone?"

"Now who's asking a lot of questions?"

She giggles. "Okay, you got me there. One more question. As a priest, you probably know the answer to this one: Is there hockey in heaven?"

"Interesting question. I wish I had a good answer."

"If there isn't, I don't want to go there."

"Who says there isn't?"

"Well, is there or isn't there?"

After stroking my short, scraggly beard in search of an answer, I offer an opinion. "There is, but I don't think the Lord would tolerate the violent part of hockey in His kingdom."

"That's fine with me. I don't like that part, either."

"I'm glad we settled that."

There's a sparkle in her eyes that tells me she liked that little give-and-take. She gets up, puts her dish in the sink, and goes into the living room.

"Company's gone," she announces as she gazes out the front window. Moments later, she removes her jacket from the coatrack and puts it on. "What do I call you?" she says.

"My friends call me Richie."

She opens the front door and walks outside. The wind is spitting out spikes of icy air, but the snow has died down. "Thanks for the rigatoni, Richie."

"You're welcome, Dana. Come again. It was nice to meet you." Frankly, I'm a little sad to see her leave.

She picks up her things and sighs. "I hope we don't get into an argument tonight," she says.

"Why would you?" I say.

"We always get into arguments, my dad and me."

"What do you argue about?"

"You'd be surprised. Everything…homework, boys, girls, being late for this or that, and, of course, hockey."

"If you want me to speak to him…"

"Nah, that's alright." She picks up her bag and sticks and shuffles through the snow to the house across the street.

It's dark now, but I can see enough. After fishing for her keys, she opens the red door and disappears into a darkened room. I linger awhile until I see a light go on upstairs. She must be in her room now. I return to my boxes, but I can't stop thinking of my new neighbor. Nice kid. I hope she doesn't get into a fight with her dad.

Chapter 2

One morning, a couple of days later, I feel the urge to get away from doing all those things that make a house a home, and that includes opening more cardboard boxes and putting away the contents and the memories they stir up—and, yes, priests get cabin fever, too. I decide to visit Tess in the city. As I'm about to enter my car, I spot Dana coming out of her house, and I wave. She smiles and waves back as she lugs a loaded backpack into a pickup truck parked at the curb.

I give the driver, who must be her dad, a quick glance as he nervously taps away on the steering wheel. I can't help wondering what he's like, the man who doesn't want his teenage daughter to come home until the coast is clear. He flashes me a quick smile. Ordinarily, this would be a good time to walk over and introduce myself, but I give him a short wave, instead. Not very friendly, on my part, but I'm afraid I'll say something stupid like, "Why don't you get a room next time instead of locking your daughter out of her home in a snowstorm?" They drive off.

As a practicing priest, I've always been drawn toward families with troubles. I was especially close to younger members of the parish. It's why I organized chat parties for teen groups along with family counseling sessions and I arranged follow-up meetings with behavioral professionals. I like to think I offered some real hope to families, but over time it was emotionally and physically draining.

Dana reminds me of the teens in my group. One in particular, Donny Pfister. A real sweetheart with this big, warm smile. Donny stopped smiling when his family life broke apart. I tried to help, but it was too late. Caught in the middle of a bitter battle between his mom and dad, he became—how can I describe it?—like a toy carelessly flung across the room. He was found one winter night roaming around the Chelsea area, hungry, exhausted, and sick, and he was rushed to the hospital where he died. I never stop thinking I could have done more to help him.

Tess Tessalone looks lovely and comfortable in faded jeans and a scarlet wool sweater when I arrive at her apartment on Manhattan's West Side. Her beautiful hazel eyes tell me she's glad to see me, and she welcomes me with a warm embrace, as if we haven't seen each other in weeks, even though it's been only a few days.

"Did you forget how to get to the West Side?" she says. You never know when she's serious and when she's not, but I'm getting better at reading her. "What took you so long?"

I let out a huge sigh. And explain. "The snow…the traffic…the darn boxes. I never realized I had so much stuff. Sometimes I wonder why I didn't chuck most of it."

"Moving is fun, isn't it? Sit down and relax. I'll make some coffee. How about some bacon and eggs?"

"Sure." I'm not about to pass up a home-cooked meal ever again.

As she steps into the kitchen, I kick off my shoes, stretch out on the sofa, and close my eyes. I've always felt comfortable around Tess. I guess it goes back to when we were kids growing up in a neighborhood west of the theater district known as Hell's Kitchen. I was often invited to Sunday afternoon meals with the Tessalone family, and she frequently came home with me after school for a snack before we did our homework, listened to music, watched TV, and got into arguments over something trivial.

Like many West Side families, when I was ten or eleven, my folks decided to move out of the city in search of that elusive "better life." Our first stop was a rented apartment in West New York, New Jersey, a town just across the Hudson River with a spectacular view of the city. At first, coming from the heart of New York City, I used to think West New York was "the country". In fact, it's more like a small city or city borough—Queens or Brooklyn, for example, only in New Jersey—than a typical suburban town. Later, after three years, we moved into a small, but nice house in a real suburban town in Jersey. All that time, Tess and I stayed in touch through high school and my years at the seminary, and she was right there with a big smile, wishing me well, when I took my vows.

Stretched out on the sofa, I was in the twilight zone, half-asleep, half-awake, when I feel this pressure around my nose and eyes. It's like my face is dough and someone is kneading it. I open my eyes, and there he is, the little baker, holding my glasses in his hand. "Hi, Simon. Hey, give me back my glasses, you!" I sit up and lift the two-year-old onto my lap, and we both start giggling. It happens every time we meet; we make each other laugh.

Tess comes into the room holding a plate of bacon and eggs and a cup of coffee. "Oh, so you found each other," she says, placing the food on a coffee table.

"I was wondering where he was," I say.

Simon spots the food and climbs off my lap and makes a dash for it.

"No, no, that's not yours. Here, this is for you," she says, pulling a Lorna Doone cookie out of her apron pocket. As she bends down to hand him the cookie, she gently removes the eye glasses from his hands and gives them back to me. He takes the cookie and sits down on the carpet and begins eating.

I was one of the first to see him when he was born in the hospital. Weighing less than a good-sized melon then, he was wrapped in a blanket I'm positive was the prop the baby Moses wore in "The Ten Commandments". I was so happy for Tess as she lovingly held the child. Sadly, the father wasn't present for that precious moment.

"He's getting so big so fast," I note.

"And he's fast on his feet. Go on, eat your breakfast, or is it lunch?"

"Both…Mmmm." I quickly start shoveling food into my mouth.

She sits down and watches me eat. "You must be famished."

"Sort of, and I eat faster when people watch me."

"Sorry about that. It's a mother thing."

Eating is better in silence, in my opinion. "That was delicious," I say after my last bite.

"You sound surprised. Want some more?"

"No, no, I had enough."

"How about some more coffee?"

"No thanks."

Moments later, she says, "You alright?"

"I'm fine…why?"

"You look tired."

"Really? I met someone."

"Already?" she says with a sly look in her eyes.

"She's a teenager." I tell her about Dana, how I met her, what she's like, her troubled family life, her passion for hockey. "I can't stop thinking about her. She reminds me of Donny."

"Don't go there, Richie. You did everything you could for that boy."

"Yeah, but…"

"Who else did as much for kids with tough problems in the neighborhood? Others talked, but you reached out and did something, and it wasn't just for kids. You were there for grownups, too, like me."

"I appreciate the vote of confidence," I say. "But there's always more you think you can do."

She shakes her head, remembering something, and starts filling up. "Three years ago, I came to talk to you in the rectory, and, remember, we went to the local diner for coffee, and we talked and talked. I was a basket case. Four months pregnant. I didn't know where to turn. I wasn't about to marry that guy."

I knew Artie well. We were in the same class in grammar school.

"I was so young," she continues, "and he was so sociable and funny, but the last thing I wanted was a child with him." She glances over at Simon and begins to sob. The boy runs to her, and they hug. "That's my boy, that's my big boy," she says, her radiant mother's smile hiding the tears. She turns to me and says, "If it weren't for you…"

"Ah, come on, Tess. You figured it out on your own. Hey, shouldn't you be going to work?"

"I got a late start today." Tess, an NYU graduate, English major, is an editor for an online business news service downtown. "I just need to get dressed and bring Simon over to my mom's. When will I see you again?"

"I'll call you later. I'm going to the rectory now to pick up my mail. Then it's back to the moving boxes. I'll feel better when everything's in place."

"I can't wait to see your suburban mansion." She reaches down and picks up my plate. "Don't forget to eat, Richie. Like my grandma says, *'Mangia, e bone per tu,'* or words to that effect."

"Do I look like I'm wasting away?"

"As a matter of fact, yes." She walks toward the kitchen, stops, and turns around. "Oh, as for your teenage friend, who says you can't try to help her? You've got the training and experience…and the compassion."

Later, as I approach the rectory at my old parish, I'm still thinking about Tess. What a piece of work! Under that tough exterior is this kind, caring soul with a way of making anyone she comes in contact with feel good. I'd been thinking about what she said. I don't ever want to stop helping people, whatever I decide to do in the future.

When I enter the rectory, the receptionist greets me warmly and hands me my mail. Her name is Helen Minerva. I used to call her "Mrs. Mineva", after the movie character played by Greer Garson. She offers to forward my mail to my new address in the future, and I accept her kind gesture. When I ask if Father Logan is in the house, she scratches her head and says he's involved in a liturgy meeting and didn't want to be disturbed right now. I'm sorry to hear that. Father Logan and I have been such good friends. He was upset when he heard I was taking a leave of absence. "Please tell him I was asking for him, and I'm fine."

"I will," she says. "Personally, we all miss you around here...err, Father. I hope you're taking care of yourself. Are you keeping track of your glasses?" (I've always had this tendency to misplace my glasses.)

"So far, so good, Mrs. Mineva. I was thinking of buying one of those chains you put around your neck for your glasses."

"Oh, don't do that."

"Why not?"

"That's for older folks, and you're still a young fella."

"Well, thanks for the compliment."

"By the way, Mrs. Collins was asking for you," she adds. "I told her you were on leave. She sounded disappointed."

"Did she say anything else?"

"Only, to tell you her son, Regis, is doing better."

"I'll call her."

"A few other people asked for you, but I can't remember them all. Oh, Mr. Murphy, the usher, said he had some pictures from his trip to Greece he wanted to show you."

"He finally made it. He's been planning that trip for years."

Before I pick up my car, I decide to pay a visit to the old church next door. This time of day, there shouldn't be many people inside. I'm hoping I won't meet any of the old timers who might start hammering me with questions. *What happened, Father Richard? Why are you leaving us? Who's going to take care of the children? Where do I go now when there's a problem with something the pastor or bishop does? What are you going to do now?*

The church is quiet and peaceful. There are a few candles aglow at the Saint Anthony side altar, and that's where I go. Anthony of Padua is an old friend renowned as a miracle worker who helps people find lost articles. I light a candle and say a prayer for guidance in finding my way in the coming days, then walk to the front of the church and slide into the first pew. How many Masses did I celebrate at that altar? How many couples did I marry here? How many families was I able to console at the funerals of loved ones? How many eulogies did I deliver here? More important, did they make a difference in someone's life?

So many memories, so many experiences, so many relationships. They taught me so much, and I will cherish all of them for the rest of my life. The side door swings open, and about ten women and men enter the church, probably for choir practice or some special prayer service. I recognize a few of them. I want to walk over and say hello, but I decide not to. Not now. I'm not ready.

As I make my way back to New Jersey, I wonder whether my new home will feel as warm and comfortable as my parish residence in the city once felt, especially around the holidays. My mind is made up to meet as many people as I can in my little Jersey town. Going to the hockey game on Saturday should be a good start, and I'll get a chance to see Dana again.

Chapter 3

Turning onto my street, I'm surprised to see a police car with flashing lights up ahead. I hope no one is hurt or injured. The police car, I soon discover, is parked in front of Dana's house, and she's talking with two police officers on the sidewalk. In the doorway of the house next to Dana's, a wrinkly, sour-faced woman is standing with her arms folded across a navy blue pea jacket.

"Hi, Richie," Dana says nervously as I get out of my car.

"Everything okay?" I ask.

"No big deal," she explains, red-eyed. "Just a family argument that got a little too loud, and somebody complained." She turns to the two police officers. "This is my neighbor, Richie Bianchi. He just moved in across the street. He's a priest. He's on leave of absence for personal reasons."

The two officers nod their hellos.

She continues, "There's hockey practice this afternoon, but my dad wants me to stay home and help clean up for a brotherhood meeting on Saturday, the same day as our first game. I tried to tell him we're trying to get in as many practices as possible before the game."

The front door swings open, and this tall, blue-eyed man in a military-white tee shirt bursts out of the house and shouts, "Dana, come in here. Now!" He takes a few steps toward us and stops. Good thing because the two policemen stiffen up, ready for a physical confrontation. A smile breaks across Dana's father's face as he continues to walk toward us. "Ah, it's only a little family matter, for cryin' out loud." Hands on hips, he glances at the house next door. "You'd think people around here never had a disagreement. Come on, Dana, we can work this out. Why don't you all come into the house and have something to eat and drink, a cup of coffee, cocoa, whatever?"

The two policemen exchange glances.

Dana's dad points to me and says, "You're welcome, too." I'm surprised by the invitation. He reaches out and shakes my hand. "Hi, my name is Eddie Dvorak. I heard all about you, Father."

"Richie...Richie Bianchi. Pleased to meet you."

One of the police officers turns to Dana, scratches his head, and says, "You think you can work this out this with your dad?"

Dana nods. They raise their eyebrows. "Well, okay, then," says one of them. "But keep it down. No yelling." They leave. The sour-faced woman with the wrinkles walks back into her house and slams the door behind her.

I follow Dana up the walkway. Here I go, being pulled into something I'm not quite sure I'm ready for now. At the same time, something is telling me this is a chance to help a family in need, something I have the experience and, yes, the desire to do.

Inside the house, I'm overwhelmed by a living room that's obviously well lived in. There is hardly space on the wall for anything else. Some of the hangings are prints of seascapes from various angles around a large black-and-white chart of the New Jersey coastline. A heavy-duty, pale green sofa with a fish hook design and two matching chairs further shrinks the room. Don't ask me why, but I wonder how many people Dana's father is expecting for his brotherhood meeting and where everyone is going to sit. On a coffee table are stacks of unfolded clothes that Dana quickly scoops up and places in a laundry basket.

"They go downstairs, to the laundry room," Eddie instructs his daughter.

"I know where they go, Dad," she says in a slightly sulky tone.

"Well, most of those are my clothes," he notes. "And, remember, I like mine done on the warm cycle."

With a frown, she picks up the laundry basket and storms down to the basement.

"Sometimes you need to tell her three times if you want something done," Eddie says after she leaves the room. "Can I get you something to drink? Beer? Wine?"

"A beer would be fine." A walnut hutch on the other side of the room catches my eye. On the top shelf is a magnificent model of a sailing ship. I move closer for a better look. A small index card tells me this is a model of the USS Constitution, which distinguished itself during the War of 1812. On the shelf below the one showcasing the famous ship, I notice a framed photograph showing three people—a man holding a child of about two years old alongside a pretty, dark-haired woman. They're all smiling. I pick up the photograph to examine it more closely.

As I do, Eddie comes back into the room holding two bottles of beer. "That's me and Dana, along with my ex, Elsie, in prehistoric times. My dad took the picture. What do you think of my ship? I made it myself. "

"It's fantastic. Wonderful detail."

"I visited the real ship in Boston harbor to make sure I got it right. It took me almost two years to build the darn thing." He hands me a beer.

"The sea must mean a lot to you."

"Sure does. Navy all the way! Served on a destroyer in waters near the action areas in the Mid-East. If it were up to me, I'd be still sailing somewhere, probably on some merchant ship, but I got other fish to fry right now, pardon the pun," he says, jutting out his chin toward the basement.

I see an opening and lunge for it. "You must be very proud of her."

"Yeah, but she drives me crazy sometimes, especially with that hockey stuff."

I plow on. "She's so bright and friendly. If her hockey skills are above average, who knows? She could attract a lot of attention in high places, like colleges interested in building their women's hockey teams."

"I think you're dreaming, Father."

"Richie."

"Okay… Richie. Sorry, but I don't believe girls should be playing hockey."

"I felt the same way at one time, Eddie, but the lines of who does what are blurring all over the place."

Dana returns from the basement and reaches for the vacuum cleaner. "If you guys can move into the kitchen, I have work to do."

Eddie takes another slug and says, "Don't you have hockey practice now?"

Dana stops what she's doing and shoots a glance at her dad. "You mean it?"

"Go before I change my mind."

I offer to drive her to the rink, but she says Hugo will give her a ride. With her gear packed and ready to go, she's out the front door in a couple of minutes, leaving an old salt and a transitioning priest to continue their conversation.

I discover Eddie is still close to the sea. He's working at a trucking firm near Port Elizabeth, New Jersey. His company provides shipping services for goods brought in from all over the world by huge container vessels. He's a master mechanic and services the eighteen-wheelers and other vehicles the company uses to truck imported goods to places in the Northeast and other parts of the country. I'm impressed. He likes his job, and apparently he's good at it, but he misses being at sea.

He becomes more emotional when he talks about the Navy, which he served for four years. Initially, he wanted to be a gunner's mate, operating and maintaining guided missile systems and other equipment. "Somewhere along the way, they discovered I was a pretty good mechanic," he explains, "and they put me to work repairing and staying on top of everything and anything that moves except the boat's engine. It was a lot of work and responsibility, but I had fun, and my shipmates were tremendous."

"You should be proud, Eddie, and thank you for your service. I'm not the only one who feels that way. The whole country is grateful. I don't think a day goes by when someone in the government isn't praising our military men and women for all you've done."

The lingering silence that follows is unexpected. Eddie finally says, "I appreciate your personal comments, Richie. I really do. A lot of individuals feel the same way you do. But, sorry, I don't put much weight these days in what the government says and does. Do you?"

"Well, sure. Of course, I don't agree with everything, but…"

"As far as I'm concerned, the government is one of the biggest problems we face today."

"What bothers you about the government?"

"I don't like what's happening in Washington. The bickering, partisan politics, the meanness. For a while there, I thought it was getting better. But problems that need to be solved aren't. It's hurting us, all of us, including military people. We're not blind to what's going on in the country. This government must make an honest effort to change or face the consequences," he warns with reddened face.

I'm surprised by his intense reaction and can't agree or disagree with everything he says. It's best to leave it be, especially since this is my first face-to-face contact with my new neighbor.

I'm also thankful he doesn't ask me a lot of questions about my future plans. I couldn't give him a clear answer right now. I tell him I'd like to have him and his daughter over to my place as soon as I'm more settled. He says he'd like that.

As I get up to leave, I notice this hard, odd turn in his blue eyes, which contrasts with his warm smile and friendly ways. Strange guy to figure. In some ways, he doesn't seem like the kind of father who would lock out his teenage daughter while he entertains a woman friend, and there seems to be a deep connection with his daughter, which was apparent to me in their personal interactions and the photo on the hutch. His love of the sea is also evident and seems genuine, but what was that attack on the government all about? It's puzzling.

Chapter 4

G*ame One—Crowns vs. Owls:* You could feel it in the air. Something special is about to happen, in this case a major regional hockey tournament for teenagers living in the Northeast, and most of the fans are in place waiting for the puck to be dropped.

There are only a few seats left, and they are in the upper reaches of the stands. Making their way to them is a couple dressed in layers of casual winter clothes. Both the man and woman are slightly out of breath when they reach their seats in the last row and sit down.

"Whew! You'd think I just climbed Mountain Everest," the young woman says, gazing down at the whirling skaters in the final stages of their warmup.

Not far from the couple, a group of spectators launch a booming "Go, Owls, go!" chant, drawing a "Let's go, Crowns!" counterattack from a rival group not far away, which, in turn, inspires a muffled but audible coarse comment from a young man sitting next to the couple in the last row.

The couple exchange arched eyebrows. "My first hockey game," she says.

"I know. My second," he says. "This should be fun."

Nearby, a little girl covers her ears to block out the crowd noises while a woman next to the child, probably her mom, leaps out of her seat when a practice puck slams against the back boards. A few seats away, another woman with eyes shut folds her hands in prayer as players on both teams gradually gather at center ice for the playing of the national anthem by the local high school band.

Finally, it's game time. Never mind that another snowstorm is kicking up outside and the weather gurus are promising at least ten more inches of white stuff. *This* is hockey, and the game is about to begin.

The Crowns, the visiting team in royal blue and gray, press the attack right at the start and for most of the first period. The Owls, the home team in orange and black, constantly find themselves trapped in their own zone, fending off their opponents any way they can.

"It's a shooting gallery out there," says an old man behind the Owls bench. "Get it out of there. Ice it! Sit on it!"

Fortunately, most of the shots taken by the Crowns miss their mark, while others accidentally hit players or are blocked by a short, stocky goalie who's flopping all over the place, like a shark out of water. In the midst of the chaos, he's tracking the puck well and doing a remarkable job of keeping it out of the net.

Etched on the young faces of the players on both teams is this look—something between the terror of making a mistake that causes the team to be eliminated from the tournament and the euphoria of making a brilliant play that leads the team to the next round. Their lives and their futures seem to hang in the balance in this one game. After all, this is the first round of one of the most important hockey tournaments for teenagers in the Northeast. Adding to the drama, the final games will be televised on cable and observed by college athletic recruiters and professional hockey scouts, not to mention parents, friends, and relatives.

After two periods, the score is Owls, 0; Crowns, 0.

In the third and final period, the Crowns continue to attack and the Owls keep defending. Players on both teams lose their sense of time, skating beyond their allotted shifts. On both benches, all but one of the players are following the action with laser-beam concentration. That lone player, Number 41 on the home team, sits as still as a sphinx, eyes closed as if in meditation.

The coaches pace back and forth behind the benches, frequently checking the official clock on the scoreboard. Malcolm Butler of the

Crowns team, the more cerebral of the two coaches, is confident his team will move into the next round. If there's a trace of concern on his pale, bony face it's for his team's inability to score up to this point. The Owls coach, Sam Fenda, shouts instructions and platitudes like "Play tough! Play smart!" to his players on the ice, but his words are not missed by the players sitting in front of him. Secretly, he's praying for a whistle to blow to give his team a break. Whistle or not, it's time for a line change.

Finally, the whistle blows. A Crowns player was struck in the thigh by a puck, and the referee stopped play.

"Thank God!" Coach Fenda mumbles. Eyeing the players on the bench, he shouts at the meditative player sitting at the end, "Get out there, Forty-one!" The meditator springs to life and jumps over the boards and onto the ice. Two other forwards on the same line, along with two rested defensemen, complete the change. Forty-five seconds remain on the clock, and the faceoff is deep in the home team's zone.

The old man behind the Owls bench rises, wipes the sweat off his brow, and says to no one in particular, "Hang on, Owls. We'll beat 'em in overtime!"

"Like hell you will!" says a large, boxy woman behind him. "Your team's going down now, old man."

He says something incomprehensible under his breath and gives her a dismissive wave.

The referee drops the puck, and a mad scramble for possession follows. There it goes, hugging the boards behind the Owls net, past players on both teams, and out into the center zone area. Two beefy Crowns defenders take off after the errant disk. Not far away, Number 41 gives chase, too, as the puck trickles into the other end of the rink. With a tremendous burst of speed, Number 41 zips between the two defenders and gathers up the puck and with a curling motion moves it to mid-ice before coming face to face with the Crowns goalie.

A hush falls over the crowd, followed by nervous cries and finally triumphant cheers as Number 41 dekes not once, but twice, and slips the puck under the Crowns goaltender and into the net. The scorer lifts both arms in the air to celebrate and is immediately smothered by an ecstatic band of teammates. "Way to go…way to go, Dana!" yells one. "Love you, baby," says another. "Holy crap, you did it! We did it!"

Solemnly gathered in various poses at center ice are the Owls' mortal enemies for the past fifty-nine minutes and fifty-five seconds. Crowns players glance up at the clock. Hardly time to make a play, but in their hearts hockey players never stop believing in miracles.

As Dana skates to the bench, Owls fans are screaming and laughing and jumping with joy at the turn of events. In the last row, the young couple in layers of winter clothes are hugging each other and anyone next to them. "Wow, what a player!" says the woman. "That's my neighbor," says the man proudly.

Dana is greeted with open arms by Coach Fenda. "Great job, Dana!" he says hoarsely. "I knew you'd do it." Removing her helmet, Dana shakes out her hair and says, "Thanks, coach." Tall for her sixteen years and wiry, she watches the last seconds of the game tick away with a revived intensity in her green-brown eyes.

The buzzer sounds for the end of the period and the game. The Owls players gather at center ice for a victory salute, like the pros do. Dana scans the cheering crowd, but there's no one in the stands she recognizes. She's always hopeful someone she knows, like her dad, will be there.

It's pandemonium in the locker room. But instead of champagne, the players pour bottles of water on each other and anyone within range. "Hey, save it for the big one," says Coach Fenda, who's soaked. Dana, the star of the game, attracts the greatest outpourings of gratitude. It's fun for a while, and she gives as much as she takes. But the first chance she gets she changes her clothes and, with gym bag and two hockey sticks in hand, she makes a dash for the exit.

Hugo, a line-mate, catches up with her. "Hey, where you goin'?" he asks.

"Home. Before I drown."

"I'll drive you," says the newly licensed teenager.

"No. I want to walk," she says, admiring his handsome face. She likes Hugo, a close friend since grade school. He's always ready to give you the shirt off his back, even in this weather.

"In this snow?" he says. "And it's getting dark, in case you haven't noticed."

"It's not so bad, and I can see just fine. It's only a mile-and-half away, according to my wrist monitor." They start walking together.

"You're nuts," he says.

"I know," she says, pulling a Snickers out of her jacket pocket. "Want some?"

"No," says Hugo. "Lenny and some of the other guys are going for pizza. He says he has some good stuff…mood-changers, first rate."

"Yeah, he told me," she says, taking a big bite out of her chocolate bar. "I really don't want to change my mood. I like the mood I'm in."

Hugo gives her a tug to stop. They're standing there, face to face, light snow falling on them. "That was a fantastic goal you scored, Dana. How'd you do it?"

She shrugs. "I guess I got lucky."

Hugo shakes his head. "That's not luck, Dana. It's a gift."

"My grandpa taught me."

"I'll call you later," he says.

"If you're worried someone will attack me or something, don't," she says. "Who'd be dumb enough to be out in this stuff?" She laughs.

"Like I said, you're nuts," says Hugo. He turns around and heads back to the rink. Dana pulls the flaps on her baseball cap over her ears, braces herself against the late-February snowstorm—the ninth or tenth of the season—and plods on.

Chapter 5

The next day, I step out the front door. Halfway down the pathway, I turn around and gaze at the little Dutch colonial I just left. I still can't believe it. That's my place, Richie Bianchi's house! I want to go back and finish the job. But not now. It's Sunday, and I'm on my way to church. I'm also hoping to run into Dana so I can tell her how much Tess and I enjoyed the hockey game yesterday and congratulate her on her big goal, but she's nowhere in sight this morning.

I decide to walk to Saint Albert's. It's cold, but the sun is shining, and it's not so bad once I get going. A new layer of snow freshens the streets and lawns. *Spring is not far away, Spring is not far away,* I keep telling myself.

Coming into view after a twenty-minute walk, the church is a compact, fairly modern, wooden structure, more like a large chapel, with a long slanted roof rising, like praying hands, into the sky. When I enter the vestibule, an elderly gentleman in a dark blue suit greets me with a warm, welcoming smile.

The church is a little more than half filled, and I slip into a pew in the rear overlooking a field of mostly white heads. I think about how hard we tried over the years to increase the number of younger parishioners attending Mass on Sundays. It was a major challenge for us, but I think we made some progress.

Emerging from the back door is a cross-bearer, followed by two altar boys, a couple of lectors, a young deacon, and an elderly priest. I like the way the priest smiles and waves to parishioners as he proceeds down the center aisle. The entrance song is one of my favorites, and something inside me does an emotional flip as the congregation joins a small choir in the singing. *"We gather together to ask the Lord's blessing..."*

The priest prepares for the opening prayers, quietly and respectfully assisted by the young, red-headed deacon.

I'm reminded of another young cleric at his ordination Mass, the culmination of almost eight years of study, prayer, and blood, sweat, tears and reflection. I remember it like it was yesterday. I was wearing the vestments of a deacon, and I was lying prostrate, along with thirteen other candidates to the priesthood, before the bishop. Then we all rose and, two by two, knelt before the bishop who placed both hands on the head of each candidate, conferring the power of the priesthood on each of us. That's when my life took a dramatic, new turn, and, with all my heart and soul, I wanted to make the world a better place in the name of the Lord, the Church, and my family and friends.

I tried, I really did.

I can't help noticing the number of couples in church today, and I think about Tess, sweet, beautiful, funny Tess. I remember her that day. She was so proud of me, as was my mother and father; my older sister Jennifer, who lives in California now with her husband; and my relatives from Long Island and the neighborhood gang.

I wish Tess were here with me today. But it's probably better this way. She's giving me space to think about what I want to do next. You know what? It's a nice gesture on her part, but I miss her.

The elderly priest gives a touching homily about family and mentions that Lent is approaching, which hits a nerve as I recall all the work and preparation that go into that season.

There follow the most solemn parts of the Mass—Offertory, Consecration, and Communion—and the priest finally encourages the congregation to "go in peace." Such a beautiful message! Why don't we share it more openly in our daily lives?

Outside, the sun is hiding behind this huge quilt of clouds. I pull up my collar and begin the trek home when someone taps me on the shoulder. I turn toward the tapper and come face to face with this woman in a navy blue pea jacket, and I immediately know who it is

"Hi, remember me?" she says.

"Of course. My neighbor across the street."

"And you're the ex-priest who rented the old Barnes house."

I don't bother to correct her. Boy, news does travel faster than a hockey puck.

I extend my hand. "My name is Richard Bianchi."

"I guess we were never properly introduced," she says. "My name is Helen Tufts. I'm one of the old timers in town. Been living in that house for nearly thirty years now. Moved in when I got married."

I waited for the rest of the story I knew was coming.

"In case you're wondering, I live alone now," she goes on. "My husband met someone at work and left me after five years, and the marriage was annulled." She turned away and scratched her nose. "I don't know why I'm telling you this."

"I don't mind. After all, we are neighbors now."

She frowns. "Can you beat it, the way those two go at it?"

"Who?"

"The Dvoraks. Shouting and calling each other names. It's disgusting, and I think it's getting worst. That's why I had to call the police."

"What do you think is going on?"

She shrugs. "Maybe he needs to find a good woman."

I think about Mildred, the woman who was visiting him when Dana knocked on my door, but I don't say anything. It turns out I don't have to.

"Oh, he's been seeing someone," she says. "But I don't think that's going anywhere."

Helen seems to know a lot about the Dvoraks, but not everything. I have a feeling vital pieces of information are missing from her story.

She scratches her nose with a pinky, an intense curiosity in her eyes, and says, "I didn't think ex-priests were allowed to go to Mass."

I suppose I should be shocked or embarrassed by her comment, but I'm not. I've met many defenders of the faith over the years.

They're pretty sure about what the church and its parishioners should and shouldn't do.

"There's no reason why I can't continue to attend Mass while I'm on leave of absence. Besides, I love the Mass."

"Are you seeing someone?"

She waits for a reply. I break into a smile and start to walk away.

"Do you need a ride?" she asks.

"No thanks. I need the fresh air. Enjoy the day, Helen."

As I'm about to approach my house, I spot Dana and another girl sitting on the front step. They both spring up when they see me, and I'm anxious to see Dana.

"That was a great game yesterday," I say when they draw near.

"Oh, you were there?" says Dana, confusion in her reddened eyes.

"Yea. Tess went, too. We sat in the last row. Only seats we could get."

"I'm sorry I missed you."

"That was a wonderful goal you scored."

"Thanks."

"What's the matter, Dana? You look so sad."

"It's Dad. He's gone," she says, her voice cracking.

"What do you mean he's gone?"

"I don't know where he went. I got up this morning, and I couldn't find him. I looked everywhere."

"Maybe he went to the store, or he went to see somebody." But then I notice his pickup truck is still in the driveway. "It's possible somebody picked him up, and they went somewhere."

"That's not like him. He always tells me where he's going." She's going to cry but catches herself.

"Calm down, Dana. When was the last time you saw him?"

"Late yesterday, after I came home from the game," she replies. "He was sitting on the couch staring at the ship on the hutch. He had this weird, sad expression on his face. I said 'Hi', and I asked him how his meeting went, and he said 'Fine'. Then I told him we won the game, and he mumbled something like 'that's nice,' and I went up to my room."

"Then what?"

"I hung around after the game, so it was kind of late when I got home, and I was exhausted. I didn't even feel like eating anything. I went to bed."

"Did you hear anything when you went to bed?"

"No. Should I have heard something?"

"I don't know. You tell me."

"I'm sorry. I'm a sound sleeper. I can't tell you how many times my dad said I sleep like a rock."

"Go on."

"When I got up this morning, I went into the kitchen. I expected to find him making breakfast, but he wasn't there, so I went looking for him. I called out for him several times, but he didn't answer. I even went into the garage. I thought he might be working on something, like the snow blower, but he wasn't there, either. I went back into the house, into the living room, and that's when I saw it. I don't know why I didn't see it before."

"What did you see?"

"The mess. Chairs overturned, beer bottles on the carpet…and this big stain."

"Stain?"

"Yes. We think it's a blood stain."

"Show me."

We walk across the street to her house. As we do, she turns to her friend and says, "Tell Richie about your nose, Angie."

"I had a bloody nose once, and once was enough," says Angie, a waif of a girl with big, brown eyes. A thin, bony creature, she looks like a poor, sweet soul who needs a lot of caring and carbohydrates, but when she starts talking, get out of her way. She's loud and she's tough. "Here we are, playing with a whiffle ball in the backyard," she recalls. "My older brother Louie, he's pitching, I'm the catcher, and my little brother Frankie is at the plate, acting like Mickey Mantle. Now he's a little guy, but strong as the Hulk, and he swings hard. This one time, he takes a swing at the ball and misses, but when he brings the bat back he whacks me in the nose."

"That must have hurt," I naively suggest.

"It stung more than anything," she says. "Anyway, I'm bleeding all over the poor lawn. I raise my head and pinch my nose, but it doesn't stop. When I run into the house, I start bleeding all over Mom's new blue carpet in the living room. You should have heard her. I couldn't tell whether she was more upset about me getting hurt or the blood on the carpet."

"What happened to Frankie?"

"He ran and hid in the back of the garage. We couldn't find him for over an hour. We were almost going to call the cops. Poor kid was scared crap. Anyway, I'm no cop, but that spot in Dana's house is a blood stain. Definitely."

When we arrive at the spot, I offer a measured comment. "Let's not jump to conclusions. It looks like blood to me, too, but there's probably a good explanation, and the police need to examine it." Seconds later, I offer another possible explanation. "Could he have fallen and cut himself and had one of his friends drive him to the hospital."

Dana shakes her head. "Someone, I think, would have called me by now."

"Let's check with the police when they come," I say, adding, "Don't touch anything."

The same two policemen who were at Dana's house the other day arrive ten minutes later. They ask a lot of questions, some similar to the ones I had asked earlier. "When was the last time you saw your dad?" "What kind of a mood was he in?" "Did he seem upset about anything?" "Was he angry with anyone?"

And finally, "Did you have a fight with your father?"

"Definitely, no," she says. "We were on great terms yesterday. He kissed me and wished me luck in the game before I left. He seemed excited he was going to be with his buddies in the brotherhood again."

"The brotherhood? What's that all about?" Officer Moseley asks.

"It's just some of my dad's friends. Some of them are people he works with. He meets with them every now and then, and they play cards, tell stories, talk about this and that—you know, guy things. I'm usually not around when they come, but my dad fills me in on what goes on."

"Just for the record," I ask Officer Moseley, "did you check local hospitals to see if they have any record of Mr. Dvorak being brought to the hospital."

"Yes, we checked all three hospitals in our area," he replies. "None of them reported treating or admitting anyone by that name. Mind if we look around?"

"Go ahead," says Dana.

He and his partner, Officer Jablonski, go upstairs first, then they examine the rooms on the ground floor, before they go downstairs to the basement. Outside, they check the garage and the grounds around the property. They check out Eddie's pickup truck, too. I'm not sure what they're looking for. A note from Eddie? I doubt it. The man suddenly disappears, and the signs—the blood on the carpet, the upturned furniture, etc.—now suggest he left, or was taken, after a violent struggle of some sort. I'm getting worried, but I try not to show it.

Back in the house, Officer Moseley says he'd like to go over the story one more time with Dana. With Officer Jablonski poised to take notes, Moseley asks, "so you come home from the game yesterday, and your father's sitting in the chair, looking sort of glum, and troubled. Is that about right?"

"Yes."

"You ask him how his meeting with his friends went, and he says…"

"'Fine'. That's all."

"And when you tell him about the game, that your team won, he doesn't say anything. Correct?"

"No. He did say something, something like 'That's nice,' but I could hardly hear him. Anyway, after that, I went up to my room, washed, changed into my pajamas, went to bed, and fell asleep."

"Right away?"

"I don't remember exactly. I think so."

"Uh…huh."

"I should have heard something during the night."

"But you didn't."

"Correct."

"And you and your father were on good speaking terms yesterday. Right?"

"Right. The best we've been in a long time."

Before they leave, the police officers ask for and receive a photo of Dana's dad, inquire about the names of friends and relatives, get the name of Mr. Dvorak's favorite bar—Barney's in the next town—and ask whether Dana's father has any major medical issues, which he doesn't, according to Dana. "Please make sure, no one touches anything, especially that blood spot. We'll need a sample for the lab," says Officer Moseley.

Discreetly, away from Dana and her friend, I ask whether the police have to wait twenty-four hours before they consider this a missing person's case.

"No, not anymore," says Officer Moseley. "And especially in this case, where there appears to have been some kind of struggle at the scene. We'll get the word out right away. If we move on it immediately, well, we might get lucky and wrap up this case in a New York minute."

Maybe, but we're in New Jersey.

Chapter 6

Mrs. DeLuca, Angie's mom, called Dana immediately after she heard about what happened to her father and invited her to stay with them. "Hey, you're part of the family, sweetheart. You come here until they find your papa. We'll make room," she told Dana. It was a very considerate gesture, and Dana loves the DeLucas—to her they are what family is all about—but the fact is they live in a small, compact Cape, and their family is large, including the three kids and Grandpa DeLuca, who hosts a poker game with his buddies at least once a week.

Two days later, Dana is back home, grateful to the DeLucas for their hospitality but happy to be in more familiar surroundings. I feel the need to spend as much time with her as I can, although she's content just being in her own room with her things, in a place where she can look out the front window and watch for her dad to come walking up the path to the house.

The first person she sees walking up the path is not her father, however. It's Officer Moseley. He has some more questions to ask Dana about her father, including her relationship with him.

My first reaction is that maybe Dana, who's clashed with her dad on several occasions, is coming under some kind of scrutiny, and I ask Officer Moseley about that. "I hope you don't think Dana has anything to do with her father's disappearance."

"Well, not really," he says. "But she may remember something that can help us find him."

"But she's told you everything."

"Hey, you never know," says Moseley. "There might be something, some small detail she didn't think about before, that could be the difference between rescuing her father and, well, we won't go there."

He has a point. Memory is a wonderful faculty for storing things, but some items are more easily accessible than others.

A couple of days later, Eddie Dvorak is still missing, and there's not a clue as to who seized him, and why, and where he might be now. What I do now seems like the next logical step to take. I contact Dana's grandfather in the Bronx, tell him I'm a friend and neighbor of hers, and break the news as gently as I can that his son went missing.

"Missing? What do you mean missing?"

"Somebody abducted him."

"You mean, kidnapped him?"

"Possibly."

"For money?"

"Police are investigating all angles."

"That's terrible."

"Yes, it is."

The silence of someone searching for answers follows.

"I'd like to explain it to you, face to face, Mr. Dvorak, but right now I need to ask you if you'd mind spending some time with your granddaughter."

There's deep breathing on the other end. "Why should I?" he grumbles.

"Because you're her grandpa, and she needs you."

"I haven't been to Jersey in years," he says. "Ever since Eddie and Elsie broke up. I think he thought I was partially responsible for the divorce."

"Why do you say that?"

After a brief pause, he explains. "In those years, after my Lucy died, I used to spend a lot of time at their house. Probably too much time. I was so proud of that boy, serving in the U.S. Navy, living in his own house in New Jersey with this good woman. I mean, Elsie was a little strange, moody sometimes, but she was also sweet and gentle and pretty as hell, and we became good friends. Then there was Dana.

what a jewel! I watched her grow from this tiny thing to this beautiful, funny little girl. We became real pals."

"Sounds like you and the family enjoyed some good times together. Why do you say your son partially blamed you for the breakup?"

"He stopped calling me. Except one time he called and told me to stay away because I was a bad influence on Elsie. I mean, I didn't know she was addicted. She kept that a secret."

"I don't understand."

"I used to bring a bottle of vino every time I visited them, and we used to sit in the backyard, Elsie and me, and hoist a few, laugh a lot, and spot as many birds as we could. Who knew she shouldn't be drinking?" He heaves a long, disgruntled sigh. "I mean, he stopped calling me. The worst time was during the holidays. You think he'd pick up the phone and call his dad. No way."

"Did you try calling him?"

"I was going to a few times, but I have my pride. I had no intention of hurting the poor woman, or being a bad influence. Those were lonely days. If it wasn't for Yank, I don't know what I'd have done."

"Who's Yank?"

"He's my mutt. I think he's part collie and a couple of other things. I found him roaming around a lot near Yankee Stadium one evening."

"So that's where he gets his name."

"Yeah," he replies, adding, "How's Dana?"

"Naturally, she's devastated about what happened to her dad. She's sixteen now and the only girl on an all-boys hockey team out here. They're playing in a big regional tournament now. She's one of their best players."

"One of their best players, aha? I taught her how to play."

"I know, she told me."

"I remember she had a terrific shot for a little kid. I don't know why my Eddie didn't take to the sport. I guess it skips a generation sometimes."

"She wants to play professional hockey someday."

"That doesn't surprise me. She loved hockey." He remembers something, and starts chuckling. "Do you know what she used to ask me? Now this was years ago, she must have been six or seven at the time. She asked me whether there was hockey in heaven. Yeah! Because if there wasn't, she didn't want to go there. Imagine that."

I roar laughing. "Sorry. She asked me the same thing."

"And what did you tell her?"

"I told her hockey is played in heaven but without the violence."

"That's a good one. I said there's hockey in heaven, but no one gets hurt."

Another moment of silence, followed by an audible sigh, and he says, "Do the police have a clue as to where my son might be?"

"No."

"We can only stay for a couple of days, Yank and me. There are some people in the building here I look in on. They look forward to seeing me."

"Stay as long as you can. I think Dana will be happy to see you… and Yank."

The following day, I'm over at Dana's house, keeping her company, waiting. It's a good time to be indoors. There's a chill in the air, thanks to a gloomy, overcast sky. Clearly, winter is taking its sweet, old time about leaving.

Dana seems to be in a trance as she stares out the front window. I think she's on the lookout for two people. One, of course, is the tall, handsome figure of her father striding up the walkway. The other is her grandfather whom she remembers was always a lot of fun and taught her how to play the game she loves.

I walk over and stand behind her. "Anything yet?"

"No," she replies longingly.

"Would you like something to drink? Cocoa? Lemonade?"

"No thanks."

In the stillness that follows, Dana is quiet, pensive. Then she begins, "When I was a kid, I used to stare out the window, like I'm doing now, and wait for my dad to come home from work. This was after Mom left. I must have been nine or ten at the time. Mrs. Newman, who used to watch me after school, didn't like me looking out the window with my feet on the furniture. She was kind of fussy, with this bun in her hair as big as a softball. I used to tell her my dad loves seeing me in the window when he comes home, which was true, and she'd stop bugging me and continued knitting. Mrs. Newman was always making something. Anyway, when I saw my dad get out of his car, I'd run out to meet him, and he'd…"

She stops, chugging back tears, before picking up her story.

"He'd lift me in the air and swing me around with his strong arms. Walking back to the house, I would keep turning around and looking back at the car. It was, like, a little game we played. 'Did you forget something, Dad?' I'd say. 'No, I don't think so,' he'd reply. 'Well, maybe you should check the front seat,' he'd say. And I'd run back, open the car door, and, there, on the front seat, was something in a bag—crayons and coloring book, a set of combs and brushes, a new doll, everything except hockey sticks and gloves and pads, which I really needed."

"What a beautiful memory," I say.

At that, she jumps off the sofa, flies to the front door, and flings it open. As Grandpa gets out of his Taurus and leads Yank up the walkway, Dana runs toward them. Yank pulls on the leash, straining to reach her.

She stops. "Wow, he's a strong one, isn't he?"

"That's one reason I keep him," Grandpa says. "Scares the hell out of people, but he's good protection, and he's really gentle."

"Does he bite?" she asks.

"Only when he's hungry, and usually he prefers kids."

"Really?"

Grandpa laughs. "Nah! Actually, he likes kids. I bet he'll like you."

Dana moves toward Yank and reaches down to pet him, ever so gently. The dog gazes up at her with two bright brown eyes filled with gratitude.

"See, I told you he'd like you," says Grandpa.

Dana reaches down and cradles the dog with both arms.

"Now how about a hug for the old grandpa?"

She obliges with a shy smile.

"Wow, you've grown some since I last saw you," he says. "Actually, you got me by an inch or two."

She nods and grins.

"Hello, Mr. Dvorak," I say, reaching out to shake his hand.

He gives me a firm handshake, holding on for a few seconds longer. "Call me Gustav, for cripes sake. You're old enough."

"Okay, Gustav."

With Dana leading Yank by the leash, we enter the house.

Grandpa Gustav walks into the living room, pauses, and looks around. His eyes seem to drift back to another time. "The place hasn't changed one single bit." He points to the spectacular Constitution ship model on the hutch. "Your dad had just finished building that the last time I was here, five or six years ago. Boats were always something special to him."

Dana sniffles. "Yeah, he's planning on building a replica of the carrier Enterprise next."

Gustav shakes his head in apparent disbelief. "It's not like him to suddenly get up and go. Does he have any girlfriends?"

"There's Mildred," Dana notes.

"The police finally contacted her yesterday," I explain. "She doesn't have any idea where he could be, but she's not worried."

Gustav scratches his bristly chin. "What about the place where he works? Eddie is a friendly guy. Maybe one of his fellow workers knows something."

"I thought the same thing," I say. "That's something the police will want to check, I'm sure, once a detective is assigned to the case."

"What's taking them so long?" he says.

"Protocols, budgets, scheduling," I offer.

"Bull…They'd better get their act together. There are a few politicians in the Bronx who might be able to light a fire under the police out here. I'll call them and see what they can do." He flops down on the reclining chair.

"Anyone hungry?" I ask.

"I could eat," Gustav replies.

"So could I," says Dana.

As I head into the kitchen, Gustav turns to Dana and says, "I understand you play hockey. What position?"

"Right wing."

I stop to listen.

"I hear you're playing in a big tournament. How're you doing?"

"We won our first game."

"When's your next game?"

"Tomorrow…but I don't feel like playing."

"What do you mean? Your teammates are depending on you."

Her eyes fill up. "I want to be here in case Dad returns."

"Nonsense. Your dad would want you to play."

I know what's coming next.

"I don't think so," she says. "He doesn't think much of hockey or of girls playing it."

"Well, I do," says Grandpa, "and I can't wait to watch you play tomorrow."

Will Dana listen to her grandpa and play in this important game? I hope so. It will do her good, maybe lift her spirits. There's nothing much any of us can do now to find Eddie and bring him back home. We need to leave it to the police. I'd like to help somehow.

Chapter 7

Game Two—Cobras vs. Owls: Coach Fenda manages to keep his emotions in check enough to deliver a compelling argument why the Owls should beat the Connecticut Cobras. "This team is good, make no mistake about it," he begins. "It was first, state-wide, and won the New England prelims. They have the best scorer in their league and the lowest goals-against average and the fewest penalty minutes of any team in their division. So, do we have a chance?"

Silence in the locker room.

"You bet we do!" he continues. "We play hard, we play tough, but we play clean. We shake them out of their smugness. We stick to them like pine-tar on a baseball bat, and we do it without drawing a penalty. Knowing this team, we won't get many opportunities to score, but we take advantage of every chance we get, and today we are the stingiest team they ever met. So, once more, do we stand a chance?"

"YEAH!"

Matteo, the Owls goalie, leads the team onto the ice. He's aware of the pressure on him to play the best game of his life. Even Lenny, usually loud-mouthed and brash with a streak of negativity, seems quietly confident today. Little Titus appears to be the most spirited Owl, darting among the players during the warmups like the Pocket Rocket Richard.

Of all the players, Dana seems to be the most detached. She skates in the warmup like someone only going through the motions. Her lifeless demeanor doesn't escape Coach Fenda, who knows what happened to her father. When she comes to the bench, he says, "This must be hard on you, Dana, but we really need you today. Do the best you can."

The best she can do is cause two turnovers in the defensive end, which is not what Fenda had in mind when he called on the Owls to be the stingiest team on the ice. He makes her sit for a couple of shifts, only darkening her mood. Across ice, in the third row of spectators, Grandpa is waving to get her attention, but she doesn't respond. All Dana wants to do is run as far away from the rink as possible. In some dark corner of her mind, she feels largely responsible for her father's disappearance. Maybe if she were more alert that night when her dad was abducted, she might have heard something—a cry for help, the crash of bodies colliding with each other, the thud of furniture being overturned. But she didn't. She buries her head in her folded arms and closes her eyes.

Someone with a heavy hand pats her on the back. "Hey, wake up, girl. We need you out there," says Lenny, sweat streaking down both sides of his face. "Man, those guys are good. I can't move out there. It's like playing in a swamp."

Dana reaches down and picks up a towel and tosses it to him. "You look like a crazy man, Lenny." She glances up at the scoreboard. "Still zero-zero. We're still in this game."

"Yeah, thanks to Matteo. but barely. He stopped twenty shots already."

She turns and gives Coach Fenda an appealing glance. He nods and says, "You're up next, Dana." The first chance she gets she jumps on the ice and joins her line-mates, Hugo and Ernie. Smiles flash across both of their faces when she skates over to them. All three quickly find themselves in the quagmire that is Cobras hockey.

When Ernie ices the puck to relieve the pressure, the referee blows the whistle for a faceoff deep in the Owls end. Dana drifts over to her line-mates for a quick huddle. "Pass it to me at center ice," she says. "I got to get in front of these guys." They nod and take their positions.

After the faceoff, there's a scramble for the puck which winds up at the nearby boards. With his long reach, Ernie outduels two Cobras for the puck and makes a short pass to Hugo, who, in turn, flips the puck to Dana. She shovels the puck between two defenders. Two long strides in the opponent's zone, she takes a high, hard shot that sails over the award-winning goalie's shoulder and into the net.

Score: Owls 1, Cobras 0.

After the period-long onslaught by the Cobras, the crowd is momentarily stunned by the Owls' sudden change in fortune. When they become aware of what just happened, Owls fans break out into wild cheers. Grandpa Gustav hugs everyone within range. "That's my granddaughter," he boasts. "Way to go, Dana!" Fans good-naturedly pat him on the back and shout in unison with other Owls fans. "Dana! Dana! Dana!"

Dana acknowledges the cheers with a fleeting smile. As the horn sounds for the end of the first period, she skates over to Matteo and pats him on the pads with her stick in recognition of twenty minutes of fantastic goaltending. They both understand there are two more hard-fought periods to play.

As expected, the second period is a nail-biter. Leading 1-0, the Owls come out more energized, confident they can pull this one out but aware they are playing a team that is not easily rattled. "Stay on top of them. Don't give them a chance to breathe, but don't sit back on your heels," Coach Fenda urges his team.

Once again, Matteo is outstanding, turning aside one shot after another. Owls fans begin shouting his name. "Matteo! Matteo! Matteo!" His mother and father, immigrants who were recently introduced to hockey, aren't quite sure why they're shouting their son's name, but the smiles on so many faces suggest their boy has done something very good. "He score goal?" Mrs. Bautista wonders. "No, no. He stop goal, like in futbol," says Mr. Bautista. "That's nice also," she says.

Grandpa Gustav keeps an eye on Dana, whether she's on the ice or not. He becomes friendly with a woman sitting next to him, who happens to be Lenny's mother. She continually chastises the referee for not calling penalties against the Cobras. "It's a shame what they're doing to my poor Lenny," she says again and again. She's still complaining after the buzzer sounds for the end of the second period.

Intermission is a welcome break for both teams. Once again, Coach Fenda is brief and to the point. "I like our chances, guys, but we can't be giving them so many shots. And that starts right from the point the puck is dropped. We've got the lead, and that's good, but I'd feel a lot better with another goal or two, wouldn't you?"

"YEAH!"

The coach makes a few suggestions. "Lenny, watch your manners out there. Remember, you're responsible for the stick in your hands. Ernie, don't be afraid to take that good shot of yours. Titus, relax and have fun out there. Matteo, we love you, guy, and we're with you all the way. Okay, now let's go, Owls."

"LET'S GO, OWLS!"

The third and final period begins the way the second period ended. Each team makes sure the other team doesn't have much room to make plays. But clearly, the Cobras, a team not used to losing, are putting on the most pressure. Their big break comes with five minutes left to play. Lenny draws a four-minute high-sticking penalty when he accidentally clips a Cobra player in the chin and draws blood.

Coach Fenda scans his bench. Not a rested soul in sight. "Hugo, Dana, Ernie, get out there. Nothing fancy, just keep the puck out of our zone and don't let them crowd our net. I want Matteo to see where the puck is coming from. If he sees it, he stops it."

By this time, the ice is fairly slushy in spots, slowing down the pace of the game somewhat, but the Cobras are skillful and motivated enough to continue their high-tempo play. Shots come flying at Matteo from every angle, but he manages to stop all of them.

With less than a minute left in the penalty, the Cobras coach removes his goalie and replaces him with another forward. Now the Cobras have six attackers on the ice against the Owls' five players.

BREAKAWAY

Owls fans moan, while Cobras supporters let out thunderous cheers. They're confident their team will pull out a victory. They always have before.

Another faceoff. Hugo manages to win it and sends the puck against the boards. A Cobras forward picks it up and desperately shoots it toward the Owls net, hitting a skate in the crush of players in front of Matteo. By chance—or divine intervention—the puck squirms on to Big John's stick, and the Owls defenseman whacks it down the ice into the goalie-less Cobras net.

Score: Owls, 2, Cobras, 0.

And so it ends. In the pandemonium after the game, Dana spots Grandpa in the stands. He makes a gesture to tell her he'll meet her at the car. She gives him a big nod and skates off with her teammates to the locker room.

Dana decides not to hang around for the Owls victory celebration, and after getting dressed she heads for the parking lot to meet Grandpa. As she's leaving the ice rink, she almost bumps into a man leaning against the side of the building.

"Oh, excuse me," says Dana.

"No problem," the man says. "Fabulous game, Dana."

"Thanks," she says, and stops to get a better look at him. He's stocky, full-bearded, and wearing sunglasses. He's dressed in an army fatigue jacket and jeans, and an olive green baseball cap sits clumsily on his head. He's expressionless except for a slight snarl.

"Your father would be so proud of you."

"Do you know my dad?"

"Yes. He has a message for you."

"What? Do you know where he is?"

He reaches into his side pocket and pulls out a tablet computer. A few finger taps, and a picture appears on the screen. It's Eddie Dvorak, and he's clearing his throat, about to speak. "Hi, Dana, it's Dad and I'm okay. I just need a few days by myself to work out a couple of things. I understand Grandpa is keeping an eye on you, and I appreciate that. Tell him thanks for me. Do me a big favor. Please tell the police to back off and stop searching for me. I'm fine and I'll see you soon. Love you."

Her eyes filled with tears, Dana grabs the stranger by his jacket and cries out, "Where is he? Where's my Dad? Tell me…tell me." The man pulls away, stuffs the tablet in his coat pocket, and makes a dash for the wooded area behind the ice rink.

Dana is about to give chase when Grandpa stops her. He'd been watching the scene unfold from the car. "What's going on here?" he asks.

"He knows…he knows where my dad is," she blurts out.

"Who is that man?"

"I never saw him before."

"Stay here, don't move," he says, and dashes off toward the wooded area. The man in the army fatigue jacket is still in sight, but picking up speed. Gustav summons every ounce of energy left in him to catch up, but he's losing ground fast. The man he's chasing reaches the edge of the woods now and enters a cul-de-sac in a residential area. With whatever is left in his tank, Grandpa makes one more rush toward his prey and stumbles and falls. His large, strong hands save him from cracking his skull. As he reaches a white van, the man in the army jacket lets out a loud, mean-spirited laugh at his fallen pursuer, jumps into the van, and drives off. Grandpa helplessly watches the van spurt out of the cul-de-sac and onto a side road. He gets up, brushes himself off, and limps back to the ice rink, seething with anger.

Chapter 8

Yes, even after seeing the disturbing blood stains on the carpet in Dana's house, I'm confident her father will be found. But with each passing day I become a little more worried for his safety.

Thank God for Grandpa Gustav. He's someone Dana loves dearly, a source of strength and hope at this critical time in her life. And now that he's agreed to stay with her—and he's going to attend the game today— Tess and I are going to enjoy a quiet afternoon at our favorite ristorante in the old neighborhood where we grew up.

"You seem a little more relaxed, Richie, than the last time we met," she says, before taking a sip of pinot noir.

"We should do this more often."

"How about for the rest of our lives?"

"A little pushy, aren't you?"

"I know a good thing when I see one."

I pick up my Amstel Light bottle and bump it clumsily into her wine glass. Not very cool, but I recover. "I do, too."

In the silence that follows, she reaches across the table and holds my hand.

"If you're wondering where I stand in my self-review process, Tess, I really can't tell you. Because I don't know myself. It's still so new. All I'm sure of right now is I love you, and I want to be with you the rest of my life."

"That's good enough for now. Where do you prefer to live? New York or New Jersey?"

"I'm starting to like my little Jersey town," I say.

"How quickly we forget our roots."

"No, the city will always be a part of me, especially the West

Side, but there's something to be said for birds and flowers and trees."

"We've got those things, too," she says. "Only we don't call them birds. We call them pigeons."

At that, Bruno the waiter places our meals on the table. "chicken *francaise* for the lovely young lady, and shrimp *fra diavolo* for the gentleman. Enjoy," he says and walks away.

Tess digs in. I stare at her plate and put on this face feigning concern. "Are you sure that's okay to eat?"

For a moment, she stops eating and gives me a squinty eye. "What?" she asks. Then, breaking into a hearty laugh, she says, "If it's pigeon *francaise*, it tastes great."

As I fork a shrimp, my cell phone rings. "Hello," I answer and cover it quickly. "It's Grandpa Gustav." Tess stops eating, a worried look replacing that glorious smile.

"Hold on a second, Gustav." I get up, motion for Tess to keep eating, and go to the lounge to complete my conversation. In a quiet corner, he relates what happened to Dana outside the ice rink, and I can't believe it. When he tells me how he tried to catch the stranger and fell, I'm stunned. "How are you doing?"

"I'm okay for an old fogey," he replies.

"And Dana?"

"What do you expect? She's very upset."

I ask him whether the police were notified.

"Yes, a detective's coming over later. He said he's been assigned to the case."

"Please, let me talk to Dana."

She comes on, sniffling. Haltingly, she relates what happened. "It was awful, Richie. Out of the blue, this guy comes up to me and shows me a video of my dad, and my dad's talking to me, telling me not to worry, he just needs some time to work out a few things, and tell the police to back off. Seeing him, the way he looked and sounded…At one point, he kept blinking his eyes, and he never does that. I mean, it was my dad, but it really wasn't. Know what I mean?"

"I think so. Maybe he didn't sound or look like your dad, but he was your dad and he was trying to send you a message, the best way he could."

"What kind of message?"

"I think he was trying to tell you he's alright, don't worry."

"But I can't…I won't stop worrying until he's home."

"I know…I know. I'll be leaving here soon."

"Where are you?"

"At a restaurant in the city. With my friend Tess."

"Please don't rush home because of me, Richie."

"Don't worry. We're almost done," I say, which is not exactly true. I'm thinking of the shrimp *diavolo* waiting for me.

When I get back to the table, Tess is anxious to hear what happened.

After I tell her, she says, "I don't understand. Why would Dana's father want the police to stop searching for him?"

I scratch my head. "I'm no cop, but it sounds to me her dad was pressured to say what he said."

"What do you mean?"

"Dana said her father sounded different, sort of stiff, like a robot, and there was something about his eyes."

"His eyes?"

"Yes. At one point, he started blinking, and he never blinks."

Tess shakes her head. "Really strange, the whole thing…Poor Grandpa. Did he take a bad fall?"

"He says he's okay." I push back my chair. "I'd better go now."

"Please, Richie, finish your dinner."

Leaving Tess saddens me. We were having such a good time doing something we don't do often—dining at our favorite restaurant—but it's important I get back home. I'd like to meet the detective. What does he have to say? Does he think the police should back off now, as

Eddie requested in the video? Does he have any ideas where Eddie might be?

I finish eating. Tess looks up forlornly as I'm about to leave. "Call me as soon as you can," she says. I nod and bend down and kiss her. She's smiling now. That's better.

Chapter 9

By the time I get home, I have many more questions swirling in my head. I park the car in my driveway and rush over to Dana's house and ring the doorbell. I'm greeted by a teenager with blood-shot eyes carrying the weight of the world on her sagging shoulders. She barely looks like the girl I met recently, the confident, spirited creature who asked to use my bathroom during one of the worst snowstorms of the season.

"I know, I know, Dana," I say. "I'm so sorry you have to go through this. It must have been so difficult seeing your father on the video."

"It was Dad, but it really wasn't, you know what I mean?" she sobs. "He was different, like a stranger."

"It's going to be alright."

"You think so?"

"Sure. Everything will be fine," I insist. Something I said to Donny, the troubled boy from my parish, a few days before he died, comes to mind. *"Things are kind of rough right now, Donny, but it will all be alright. Hold on. Don't be so hard on yourself and the people around you. Give things time to work out. Be patient, and remember the many conversations we had."*

She nods and, after trying to brush away the tears with the back of her hand, she says, "Come on in. There's someone here who wants to meet you."

I walk into the living room. Grandpa Gustav attempts to get up from the sofa, but sits back down, obviously still in pain from his fall. I walk over to him. "Hi, Gustav, feeling any better?"

"Still a little sore. I would've caught up to that son of a bitch if I didn't trip on that tree stump."

Dana puts her arm around Grandpa's shoulder. "I didn't know you could run that fast?"

"You should have seen me in my prime. I could outrun any kid on the block."

A towering man gets up from a chair next to the hutch and walks toward me, his huge hand extended in greeting.

"Hi, I heard a lot about you," he says as we shake hands. "You mind if I call you Richie, Father?"

"That's fine."

"I'm Vinnie. Officially, I'm Detective Vincent Laszlo."

"Why does that name sound familiar?" I ask.

He smiles, his eyes lit up in his large head like a Halloween pumpkin. "How many times have you seen 'Casablanca'?" he says.

"Hundreds…Oh, I get it. Why didn't your parents call you Victor, like the patriot in the movie?"

"Vincent was close enough. Besides, my father promised his brother I'd be named after him." Looking around the room, he says, "Is there someplace we can talk?"

"You can use the den if you don't mind boxes all over the place," Dana suggests. She points to an area in the rear of the house.

"That's fine with me," I say. Detective Laszlo agrees with a nod, and we head for the back room.

I settle on a small, wooden crate. "So what do you think?" I ask.

Laszlo spots an old trunk and parks his massive frame on it. "Well, on the positive side, he's alive."

"Right…and on the negative…?"

"From what Dana tells me, he seemed to be under a lot of stress in the video, like he was just going through the motions, which suggests he's repeating what someone wants him to say. It's just a hunch, but I get the feeling he's someplace nearby."

"What makes you say that?"

"Our man in the army fatigue jacket comes in a van to deliver a message, and he's by himself. That's not exactly a vehicle you'd expect to see one drive if he's coming, by himself, from a long distance and, say, has to rent a car at an airport. Our man in the army fatigue jacket, I suppose, has to get back as quickly as he can to report in person on the outcome of his meeting. My instincts tell me Dana's father is being held against his will somewhere close by."

"So the search for Eddie Dvorak goes on?"

"Absolutely. Despite Mr. Dvorak's plea to us in that video. I don't like the way he left that day…the blood on the carpet, the upturned furniture, and so on. As I see it, he's in grave danger, and we need to act, and act quickly."

"I think you're right. What do you think about the way the stranger looked and was dressed?"

Detective Laszlo shook his head. "Terrible disguise, a real amateur. He wore everything you'd expect from someone trying to hide his identity—beard, sunglasses, baseball cap. I think the army fatigue jacket was interesting, but I'm not sure what it means."

I couldn't resist asking the big question. "What's this all about? At its core, do you think this is a kidnapping case?"

"Could be, but I don't think so. I've handled a few kidnapping cases over the years. Everyone was a little different. This doesn't feel like one, unless Mr. Dvorak has a hidden fortune I don't know about. Right now, I can't figure out why he was taken from his home against his will."

"Because he needs to work out a few things."

"Yeah, right," says Laszlo.

"How is it that they knew—whoever they are—Grandpa was in New Jersey keeping an eye on Dana?"

"Good question," he says. "To me, it says they've got their eyes on the house and Dana. I'll make sure the police increase their surveillance around here." He takes a moment to gather his thoughts. Finally, he says, "We need to keep digging, so we can get some more leads, some answers. Tomorrow I'm going to the trucking company where Mr. Dvorak works to talk to some people, including his boss."

"You mind if I join you?"

He scratches his nose, pauses in thought, then responds. "It's not something we encourage in the department, but I think it'll be okay in your case. Dana told me all about you before you came. You seem pretty cool, calm, and…"

"And curious about everything."

"With lots of time on your hands right now."

"I don't know about that."

"Maybe you'll spot something I missed," Laszlo finally says. "I'm sure you realize it's all confidential, what we see and hear there. Okay, I'll pick you up tomorrow morning, at seven. I hope you don't mind cigar smoke in a car."

"I can live with it. I hope you don't mind if I crack open my window."

Chapter 10

Detective Laszlo is right on time, a little grumpier than he was yesterday, but so am I on many mornings. I bring him some coffee. It's in a tall, plastic mug I brought back from a trip to Rome three years ago. "Thanks," he says as he places it in the container holder.

"I took a guess. I made it black, no sugar."

"That's fine," he says as we drive off.

I glance at the cup and remember the wonderful parish excursion to Rome. That was my third trip to Italy, but no matter how many times one goes there, the country's filled with surprises. All told, there were almost fifty people in our group that fall. Tess came after I persuaded her to join us. She was going through a rough patch with Artie at the time. She told me later it was the best trip she ever took.

For the next twenty minutes or so, it's quiet time for Laszlo and me except for the heavy sighs of frustration coming from the big guy whenever he's cut off or crowded out of his driving space. "Assholes!" he snaps in a low but audible voice. "If I wasn't in a hurry, I'd pull them over." He turns toward me and says, "Sorry about the language."

"That's alright. Some people are…sometimes."

That seems to break the ice. He lets out a burst of laughter, then takes control again. "I think the roads are getting worse. Some days, I want to chuck it all in and park my carcass on some beach, just me and my bride, Norma."

"How long you married?"

"Twenty wonderful years, and with the same woman."

"Kids?"

"Nah. It's not for lack of trying. Two miscarriages and one stillbirth."

"Sorry about that."

"Yeah. We were going to adopt. But one thing or another, we never did. Too bad. I like kids."

"How long have you been doing this work?" I ask.

"It'll be seventeen years in January," he replies. "I can't wait. Don't get me wrong. I love my job, but my responsibilities keep growing. Everybody wants you to do more with less, and my focus is shifting away from my main areas of responsibility."

"How so?"

"Last week, for example, three towns in New Jersey, including mine, held a nighttime vigil at the local high school for African children in need. We didn't expect so many people to attend and, of course, there are always terrorist concerns, so several detectives, including yours truly, were called in to help keep an eye on things."

"At least, that was for a good cause."

"Yeah," he continues. "In a few weeks, I'll be on duty as Congressional leaders from both parties pass through northern New Jersey on their way to a meeting near Lake George."

"What's that all about?"

"Actually, it's not a bad idea," he says. "They want to get away from Washington to see if they can break the legislative gridlock."

"I hope it works."

"Me, too," he says. "Getting everyone to agree to the meeting was hard enough. From the police's standpoint, it sounds like a simple job, but there's a lot of planning behind the scene, and once again my primary areas of responsibility take a back seat."

As we draw closer to our destination, the conversation shifts to our upcoming meeting. Laszlo tells me what he hopes to learn from the interviews, namely why Eddie Dvorak was abducted from his home during the night and who could have perpetrated such a crime. Not surprisingly, my curiosity about the whole subject of missing persons is piqued, and when that happens, well, I start firing questions.

"How many people go missing each year?"

"One national estimate says more than 800,000 people, nationwide, are reported missing and entered into the FBI's National Crime Information Center each year," Laszlo replies. "That figure includes only those who were *reported* missing, not everyone who actually went missing."

"How many are reported missing in New Jersey?"

"Between 12,000 and 14,000, annually. According to the New Jersey State Police Missing Persons Unit, most are between the ages of 14 and 25. On the positive side, the vast majority of those reported missing are located. I wish I could say there's always a happy ending, but our success rate in the state for locating, recovering or identifying missing persons is pretty high."

"What you're saying is that not everyone is found alive, right?"

"Correct," he says. "Those are the ones who usually make the late news on TV."

A somber pause follows. "Tell me what the police are doing to find Eddie."

"Exactly what we're doing today," he says. "In my opinion, there's nothing more important than good old-fashioned detective work in cases like this. 'Investigate, meditate, activate,' my old boss Mortie Turner used to say. Get the facts, weigh the facts, then get on your horse and act on them."

Laszlo pulls a long, thin cigar out of his shirt pocket and lights it with his car lighter. I crack open my window.

"Of course," he continues, "right off the bat, we need to make sure our missing person is listed in the National Crime Information Center, and that's what we did in Mr. Dvorak's case, especially since he appears to be in grave danger. The NCIC database is a storage base of information available to law enforcement officials throughout the country and could be extremely helpful in spreading the word and obtaining good feedback."

"What's next?"

"We ping Mr. Dvorak's cell phone, if it's not too late."

"Ping his cell phone?"

"Yeah, in other words, try to detect which service tower is getting a signal from his phone, and then narrow down the area where the signal is coming from."

"Do you know if he has his cell phone with him?"

"Dana says it's not home," he replies. "The big question is: Did someone take it away from him and destroy it?"

We finally reach our destination. I don't know what I was expecting. It's a truck company, after all. The facility is enormous. Look at the number of eighteen-wheelers here waiting to load up. Obviously, Eddie Dvorak can't be the only mechanic working here.

The first person we see is a scrawny, pale looking man in dirty jeans. It looks like he's wearing two sweatshirts, the top one bearing a faded New York Giants logo.

"Can you tell us where we can find Wendell Jackson?" Laszlo asks. The man points to a long, enclosed office area lining one side of the building facing the bay. We walk toward it.

I can only imagine how Eddie Dvorak, the mechanic, felt when he started working here, probably like a kid going to a zoo filled exclusively with elephants. Working on these behemoths, he must know his stuff.

As we enter the office, we're greeted by a young, friendly woman who leads us past a row of cubicles, each tended by a man or woman whose eyes are bolted to computers dancing with all kinds of statistical configurations. I can only guess they're engaged in some complex scheduling orders, probably related to the container shippers at neighboring ports.

Our friendly greeter knocks and opens the door to a private office at the end of what appears to be the administrative and logistics section of the huge building. "Mr. Laszlo is here, Mr. Jackson," she says.

"Oh, hello, please come in," says Jackson. We both enter. He shakes hands with Laszlo and gives me a side glance.

"This is Mr. Bianchi. He's assisting me today," Laszlo says.

Jackson, looking well-groomed and polished even without his suit jacket, shakes my hand with a smile that disappears quickly. He gestures for both of us to sit down, while he parks himself behind a large, mahogany desk which, at least on the surface, appears to be neatly kept. There's that smile again in a photograph of Jackson and a pretty middle-aged woman on his desk. On the wall behind him is a large mezzotint style photo of a hunting party with rifles in hand. Jackson is in the foreground holding up the head of the kill, a deer. He catches me staring at the photo.

"Eight-pointer," he says.

"Did you bag it?" I ask.

"You betcha." His dark brown eyes are afire with pride. "In the Adirondacks. Two winters ago."

"What a beautiful animal."

"Sure is. He's on display on the wall in my den." He turns to Laszlo, anticipating he might have a question.

"Thanks for taking the time to see us," says Laszlo. "When was the last time you saw Mr. Dvorak?"

"I guess it was last Friday, before he left for the weekend," Jackson replies. "He came in to say goodnight, I encourage my people to say goodnight before they leave for the day. It's just good manners, in my view." There's a slight twang in his voice, but I can't tell where it's coming from.

"How was he when he left?"

"Fine. He said he was going down to the piers to catch the big ship from Japan docking. I think if he had his druthers he'd been on one of those ships."

"Did he seem angry or discontented or upset about anything?"

"No. He was his usual friendly self. He has this thing about the sea.

He says he's going to hop aboard a tanker one of these days, but it's just a lot of hot air. There's nothing going to tear him away from his little girl."

"Does he have any enemies you're aware of?"

"Eddie? No. Everybody loves Eddie. What's not to like? He's a sweetheart, usually in a good mood, do anything for you. If I had any children, I'd like them to be just like Eddie. Only one thing gets his goat: politicians and government."

"How so?"

"Can't stand them. He thinks the federal government possesses the power to send young men and women off to fight wars, and get wounded or killed, but it can't get its own act together. All of our so-called leaders in Washington are constantly bickering. They can't get the important stuff done. All they do is provide benefits for their special interests instead of meeting the real needs of real people. I can't say I blame Eddie for feeling that way."

I can't sit by and say nothing. "That's a pretty cynical view, don't you think?"

Laszlo snaps a look of quiet disapproval my way.

"Yeah, but it's justified," Jackson says.

I'm about to mention a few accomplishments of our system of government when Laszlo raises his hand and says, "I hear you, both of you. Now, if you don't mind, there's solid information Eddie Dvorak was abducted from his home. Do you have any idea, Mr. Jackson, why that happened and who could have done it?"

Jackson straightens his tie, a crimson thing with something that resembles a serpent in the center of it. "No, not really," says Jackson. "Hey, the way I see it these young people coming out of military service today have a hard time readjusting. It's not unusual for them to want some time alone to work out a few issues for themselves. That's what I think Eddie is doing. A couple of other men working here did the same thing. His job will be waiting for him when he comes back."

"That's very kind of you, Mr. Jackson," I say.

"Well, it's not all altruistic, err…Mr. Bianchi. He's a hell of a mechanic and he knows my trucks inside out."

"What do you know about his friends?" Laszlo asks.

"What do you want to know about them?"

"Who are they? What are they like? Do they have an axe to grind with Mr. Dvorak?"

"All I can tell you is, I'm his boss, but I also consider him my friend. He's close to a few other guys here, including Waldo Cameron, the man you're going to see next. Hey, this is a tight bunch here, just like a family, and like a family, we don't always see eye to eye all the time. Right?"

"Right. Anything else you'd like to share that will help us find Eddie, Mr. Jackson?"

"No. Except, if you find Eddie, please let me know right away. Like I said, I'm not going to hold anything against him. We really value our military personnel, not like our Washington leaders. Melinda Childs, my assistant, will take you to see Waldo Cameron now."

Laszlo and I exchange glances as we get up from our chairs. I get the feeling this interview is over.

Outside the office area, in the wide expanse of the garage, Melinda turns to us and says, "I'm worried about Eddie. He was quite upset the last time I saw him on Friday."

We stop. Laszlo and I look back at the administrative offices. Is that Jackson looking out the window? I wonder, and I bet Laszlo is asking himself the same thing. "Let's keep walking and talking," he says. "What was he upset about?"

"I'm not sure," she replies. "But I know Eddie pretty well. We eat lunch together a couple of times a week, and he's usually easygoing, spends a lot of time talking about Dana, how pretty and tall she's getting. He doesn't like her playing hockey, but at the same time he's proud of her, whatever she wants to do."

"Did you ever meet Dana?" I ask.

"A couple of times. Eddie brought her to the garage for the holidays. She's everything he says she is, and more. A typical teenager, friendly, polite, full of life."

"Don't mind me for asking," Laszlo says. "How close were you and Eddie?"

"If you mean—Was there anything romantic going on between us?—the answer is no. We were good friends. Nothing more," she says, seeming to hold back tears. "I know about Mildred, the sports bar waitress. He didn't talk much about her, but when he did, it was always with a sense of privacy and respect."

I start to form an expanded, new view of Eddie—a loving, caring father; a good friend; a divorced man trying to build a new life for himself; a top-notch mechanic with a deep love for the sea; and a man with strong views on how the country should be run.

We walk into a building on the other side of the garage, past a special dining area for the drivers and mechanics, and down a narrow hallway lined by a row of small offices. We enter one of them, where Waldo Cameron is waiting for us. His flannel shirtsleeves are rolled up his tattooed arms, and he's sitting with his head in his hands in one of the folding chairs set up around the meeting room. He stands when we enter, and we greet each other.

Laszlo wastes little time. "How do you know Eddie Dvorak?"

"We're both mechanics here," he replies. "I consider him my buddy."

"How would you describe him to someone who never met him?"

"Wow, that's a tough one," says Cameron, a tall man in his mid-thirties with slumping shoulders. He seems nervous, tired, like this is not a place where he wants to be right now as he searches for the right words. "Let me try...let me try. He's all-Navy, a sea lover. He's a good friend who'd do anything for you. He'd rather talk about his teenage daughter than anyone else. He's a considerate, friendly guy, but don't ask him anything about politics."

I make a note to myself: *That's pretty much what Jackson told us.*

"Are you married?" Laszlo asks.

"Yes. Two kids, ages two and four."

"Did you and your wife ever go out with Eddie and Mildred?"

"Yeah, once or twice. She seems nice, outgoing, friendly. They've been going out for a couple of years, on and off"

"Been working here long?"

"Four…no, five years."

"Do you enjoy the work?"

"Oh, sure, I consider myself one lucky guy, especially these days. Mr. Jackson has been very good to me."

"Why would anyone want to abduct Eddie Dvorak?"

He pulls a tissue out of a nearby Kleenex box and wipes the sweat off his forehead. "Don't have a clue, and I'm not convinced he was abducted. It could be he needed some time to sort things out, alone, away from everyone."

That also sounds familiar.

"Anyone angry with him?" Laszlo asks.

Cameron scratches his cheek. "Not that I'm aware of. Eddie's a likable dude. He enjoys gambling. He plays poker with some guys from time to time. What happens there I don't have a clue."

"Is he a winner?"

"Well," says Cameron with a nervous laugh, "he's still working here. Not that the pay is so bad, because it ain't."

The ride back home is time for reflection and a chance to compare notes. We agree on much of what we heard, and we both think Melinda Childs should be contacted for further questioning, away from the office. I also apologize for engaging Jackson in a debate about big government. I couldn't help myself.

"It's okay. You got back on track fast enough," says Laszlo. "The only time you want to debate someone in an interrogation is if you hope to draw something specific out of the person."

"I'll try to remember, sir," I say, grinning.

He laughs. "Okay."

We hit a stretch of road with less traffic, and we move along at an even, monotonous pace, not saying much to each other. Finally, I want to share something I had observed. "Did you notice the serpent tattoo on Waldo Cameron's arm?" Laszlo's shakes his head. "It's exactly the same as the serpent on Jackson's tie?"

"Interesting observation," he notes.

Chapter 11

***G**ame Three—Owls vs. Mongrels:* Of all opponents, the Mongrels from South Jersey are the team the Owls most look forward to playing. The Owls skated against them twice earlier in the season, each time winning by big scores, 6-2 and 7-1.

Most of the Owls can't believe the Mongrels managed to come this far in the tournament. Coach Fenda has a different view. "Hey, give them their due," he tells the players. "Doesn't matter how they got here; they're here. On any given day, any team can beat anybody."

Lenny doesn't say anything, but by raising his eyes and hands skyward and transforming his mouth into a silent scream, everyone has an idea what he's thinking. It's hard to say whether the other players agree the coach is, well, just being a coach, but Lenny's antics get a big laugh from his teammates.

From the moment the puck is dropped to open the game, the Owls prove their superiority over the hapless Mongrels. In less than five minutes, the Owls get goals by Gussy Grant, a defenseman, on a dazzling pass from Titus, and by Big John Mason, another defenseman, on passes from Ernie and Hugo.

Score: Owls, 2; Mongrels, 0.

So far, Dana has been kept off the scoring sheet, which is not surprising. After the meeting with the stranger in army fatigues, she has felt creepy and nervous about coming to the rink. "I just want to play this game and go right home," she confided to Hugo before the game. "Grandpa said he'll be waiting for me outside the dressing room."

"Don't worry. I'll walk you and Grandpa to the car," said Hugo. "And if I bump into that creep, I'll cross-check him in the face."

"No, don't bother, Hugo," she said. "Get me to Grandpa's car and go straight home yourself. Promise?"

"Promise."

Another goal, this one by Ernie late in the second period, gives the Owls a commanding but not an air-tight lead.

Score: Owls, 3, Mongrels, 0.

Could this be an easy afternoon for Coach Fenda's team? He has some thoughts on the subject between the second and third periods. "Don't underestimate this team," he warns the players. "You know what they say about three-goal leads in hockey. You give up one goal, then two, and pretty soon the score is tied. Twice before in the tournament, the Mongrels came back after being down. They're a hungry and desperate team. Play hard, play smart, and don't take them for granted. Okay?"

"OKAY!... LETS GO, OWLS!"

Now, Coach Fenda's interest in the team goes beyond the rise and fall of his players on the ice. Over the past two years, the retired high school teacher and former collegiate hockey player lost his wife to a rare form of cancer and was crushed when his son, an aspiring actor, moved to California. Fenda is not unfamiliar with, or insensitive to, life's more painful experiences.

As the Owls players file out of the locker room, he taps Dana on the shoulder and says, "Got a second?" She gives him a short, nervous nod. When they're alone, he says, "What's going on, Dana? You seem so down today."

"I'll be alright as soon as my dad comes home."

"I know you will. But what do you do in the meantime?"

Dana shrugged. "I don't know. This has been going on for too long a time."

"Can I make a suggestion?"

She nods.

"Why not go on doing the things you've always done?"

"Like what?"

"Like laughing, having fun with the guys, playing hockey, making fun of your coach, things like that."

She laughs. "I'd like that"

"And if you really want some fun, I'll let you play goalie sometime."

"No thanks," she says, a big grin on her face.

"Good. Nothing makes me happier when all my Owls are happy. Not even winning."

"Yeah, right," she says with a twinkle in her eye.

"C'mon, let's go play some hockey."

As the third period begins, the Owls are confident this game is all wrapped up. Lenny is talking about having a victory party later at his house. Ernie asks if he can invite his girlfriend to the celebration.

The Mongrels, embarrassed and angry after the first two periods, have other plans. After some early back-and-forth play, Jordan Elroy, their burly, barrel-chested captain, steals the puck away from Lenny and lumbers into the Owls zone. With Owls defender Big John Mason practically draped over him, Elroy continues moving forward and finally, six feet away from the net, lets loose a low, hard shot past Matteo.

Score: Owls, 3; Mongrels, 1.

Fifteen minutes left on the clock. Still plenty of time to score two goals and tie this thing, a reenergized Mongrels team is thinking. Most Owls are not worried. It's only one goal, they tell themselves; we'll score again and restore our three-goal lead.

With renewed determination, the Mongrels press the attack, shooting from all angles, most of the time missing the net. In one stretch, they don't score but they cause so much havoc the exhausted Owls are forced to ice the puck and, crucially, the Owls have to remain on the ice without making a line change. The result is catastrophic.

After putting fresh players on the ice, the Mongrels win the next faceoff and briskly pass the puck around, as if they're on a power-play.

The vise tightens. The Mongrels converge on Matteo, who's desperately trying to keep sight of the puck through the logjam of players. He stops one shot, two shots, three shots, but the puck is still loose somewhere. Coach Fenda is shouting at the ref to blow the whistle and stop play, but the whistle is never blown. A tall Mongrels winger, Dante Politto, finally sticks his long stick into the pileup and shoves the puck forward and into the net.

Score: Owls, 3; Mongrels, 2.

On the bench, Coach Fenda is still screaming at the ref for allowing the play to continue when the puck got lost in a swarm of players. A good argument, but the goal stands.

Nine minutes to go, the Owls are still leading but feeling very uneasy. The tide, it seems, has turned in favor of the Mongrels. "Defense! Defense first!" Hugo urges his teammates with a trace of desperation in his voice. "Stay cool, guys! Let's take it to them," says Dana with a little more confidence.

As the clock ticks away, the Owls hold the line against the onrushing Mongrels, who continue to play like a team on a mission. The Owls fall back into a defensive posture, with only an occasional foray into the other team's zone. Dana's instincts tell her that getting a goal now would deflate the Mongrels' bubble, so, while she's defending hard, she's looking for an opportunity to score.

Six minutes to go, five, four... Desperation is showing on the faces of all the players. The Mongrels defensemen are joining the attack at every opportunity.

Three minutes to go, two... A bad Owls pass allows the Mongrels to seize control of the puck. The play is carried into the Owls zone. Earlier than expected, the Mongrels pull their goalie and replace him with another forward. Jordan Elroy, the Mongrels captain, shoots, and the puck hits the edge of the net and skips around and out to the blue line.

Less than a minute to go... A Mongrels defender lines up the puck for a shot, but in his haste he misfires, and the puck trickles out to center ice. Using her speed, Dana seizes the puck and carries it into Mongrels zone. Less than fifteen feet from the empty net, she slides the puck into the goal.

Score: Owls, 4; Mongrels, 2.

Despite Coach Fenda's best-intentioned advice, Dana hardly feels like celebrating with her teammates and friends when the game is over. After she and Hugo meet Grandpa outside the locker room, she is again reminded of that awful encounter with the stranger in fatigues as Grandpa limps back to his car. It's a memory she'd like to forget, but can't. It's a memory that makes her anxious, fearful, and angry.

Chapter 12

I made up my mind yesterday when I dropped by to see Dana after the game. Asked if she were excited about being so close to the championship round, she said, "I suppose so." That would have been enough, but seeing Grandpa hobbling around the room, I decided we need help. So here I am, next morning, at Newark Liberty Airport about to board an early morning flight to Florida.

This trip will serve a double purpose. First, I'll get a chance to visit my folks. The last time I saw them was during the Christmas holidays when I was still a practicing priest. I hope they're still talking to me. Second, I'll try to persuade Dana's mother, Elsie, to spend some time with her daughter. She really needs her mother these days.

When I told Tess of my plans, she was supportive but I sensed disappointment in her voice. She said if I had given her more time, she might have been able to rearrange her schedule and join me. I told her this was a spur-of-the-moment trip I needed to take and I'd be home the following day. I began wondering whether Tess thought I was spending too much time trying to solve Dana's problems. At the same time, Tess told me she understands what I'm trying to do and hopes my visits go well.

To be honest, I'm a little uneasy about both visits. I can handle Dad, I think. He tends to be quiet, less emotional than Mom, although he blasts off when he can't find something he lost or misplaced, like his fiberglass hammer or his newspaper. Mom, on the other hand, always wears her emotions slightly below the surface, and she feels deeply about a lot of things, especially her faith. She's often said that the proudest day of her life was when I became a priest.

As for Dana's mom, I don't know what to expect. She's a woman carrying a heavy burden, including her addiction, which she's still fighting. Who knows what happened between her and Eddie? They were young, and so many of us in our earlier years say and do awful things. Now she's trying to put her life together again with this new family, but I'm hoping the ties between mother and child from an earlier union are still there.

After landing at West Palm Beach International Airport, I rent a car and drive, first, to my parents' home in Port Saint Lucie. The weather is delightful, sunny in the mid-seventies, and now I wish Tess came with me.

I ring the bell at the one-level, pale yellow house, which my parents bought three years ago, and I pray. Edna Bianchi, my mom, opens the front door and lets out a strange welcoming cry, and we embrace. I'm feeling better already. "Come in, come in, before you let all the hot air in," she says. (Spoken like a true Floridian.) "Your father will be along in a bit. He went for the paper and buns. I hear you had some more snow."

"Yeah, I lost count of the snowstorms."

"You want something to eat?"

"No, I'm good. Maybe something to drink."

"Beer?"

"Fine."

Cat-like, she goes into the kitchen, retrieves a beer for me and a bottle of water for herself, and she's back before you can say Bud Light. *Not bad for someone in her late sixties.*

"How's good old Jersey?" she asks.

"Jersey's Jersey. My place is coming together, slowly. You have to see it."

"Sure…when it gets really hot. But now's the best time of year down here." She sits down on the sofa next to me. I have the feeling the conversation is about to take a more serious turn.

"Have you talked to Jennifer lately?" she asks.

"No, not really." I love my sister Jennifer, but she's my big sister and she never lets me forget it. Besides, we live so far apart. She lives in the San Diego area with her husband, Raymond. No children. "How is she doing?"

"Not so good these days."

"What do you mean?"

"Ray lost his job—I'm never sure what he does. I think it's some kind of engineer."

"Systems engineer. How's Jennifer doing?"

"She's still teaching, but she's worried they won't be able to make it over the long haul. And she's worried about you."

"Me? Why me?"

"She doesn't think you should leave the priesthood."

"I haven't left anything yet, Mom. I'm still thinking about it, and I don't think she should worry about me. She has her own problems right now."

"Well, you can't blame the people who love you for worrying about you."

"No, but…I'll give her a call."

"Don't bother. She's coming to New York in a few days."

"Oh? Why?"

"A national teachers' conference or something."

The front door opens. It's my dad, Bill Bianchi, a small bakery bag in one hand and a *New York Times* in the other. I get up and give him a big hug.

"Easy…you'll crush my crumb buns," he says with a big smile. "So, to what do we owe this honor?"

"Just a visit. No announcements. It's been a while since I saw you guys."

"You're always welcome here, son. Right, hon?"

My mom nods and, as expected, starts filling up.

"Later, I plan to visit the mother of a teenage girl who lives across the street from me with her father. Her mom lives in West Palm Beach. I hope to persuade her to visit her daughter. She needs her mother badly right now."

Dad places the bag and the newspaper on the end table and flops down on a recliner. "Well, once a priest always a priest," he says.

"Now where have I heard that before?'

The door to a deeper conversation is finally flung open.

"Oh, I'm still sick about the whole thing," my mother says. "I can't understand why you want to give up something you've worked so hard to achieve."

"Like I told you, Mom, I haven't done anything yet."

"You were such a good priest. You did such wonderful work, the parishioners loved you, and I've always been so proud."

"I know, Mom. I'm proud of my work, too. I love many things I did during my ministry, and I plan to continue to help others…but my personal life is changing."

"Whatever you decide to do now can never measure…"

Dad steps in. "Easy, Edna. Richie's got a good head and a good heart. He'll figure it out, whatever he wants to do with his life."

"I know. I'm sorry."

"It's okay, Mom. Like I told you before, I love Tess, I love Tess with my whole being, and I want to be with her, like you and Dad are together. I don't know how it happened. It just happened. Over time, she became a part of my life, and I became part of hers. Right now, she understands what I'm going through, so she's not pressing me and I'm not pressing her, but the love between us is growing. Does that make sense?"

"Yes…Tess is a good woman," says Mom.

"She sure is, and she's from the neighborhood," Dad adds.

"Tell me about your teenage neighbor," Mom asks after a pause. A genuine curiosity has long been her trademark. I guess that's where I get it.

I tell them in broad terms, concluding, "She needs her mother now more than ever."

"I think you're right," says Mom. "If there's anything we can do…"

"Not really, Mom. I hope I can persuade her to spend some time with Dana."

"Well, we're here, if you ever need us to help. West Palm Beach is not that far away."

"Thanks, Mom. If it's alright with you guys, I'd like to spend the night here before I head back tomorrow."

"No problem," says Dad. "In fact, why don't you spend a few days here? We have plenty of room."

"I appreciate that, Dad, but I need to get back."

"Sure, I understand."

What distinguishes this two-story condo complex from the ones I've seen up north is the palm trees lining the entrance way. I check the registry. The closest name to "Elsie Mendez" on the list is "A. Mendez—211". I ring the bell, and I'm buzzed in. So far, so good. I assume 211 is on the second floor, but rather than take the close, run-down elevator, I take the stairs.

At apartment 211, I take a deep breath and knock. The door opens creakily, and I'm greeted by this tall, graceful woman with a child in her arms.

Her eyes blinking, she waits for an introduction.

"Hi, I'm Richie Bianchi, and I live across the street from your daughter in New Jersey. I'm here because I have an important message for you."

"Is everyone okay?"

"That's what I want to talk to you about. May I come in?"

"You're not going to bop me on the head and steal whatever I own, are you? If you are, you're in the wrong neighborhood."

"No. I've nothing to bop you with except these two delicate hands."

"My husband will be home soon anyway. Come in." She leads me into a small, congested room. I assume it's the living room despite the fact that a baby's crib shares space with a sofa and easy chair. She points to the easy chair. "Please sit down. My name is Elsie Mendez."

"I'm Richie Bianchi."

"I know, you told me. Please sit down." She puts the baby in the crib.

"Boy? Girl?"

"Boy."

"He's beautiful, and so well-behaved.""

"Thank you."

'What's his name?'

"Alexander, same as his father's." She sits on the sofa, obviously anxious to hear the "important message" I came all the way from New Jersey to deliver.

I tell her the story, completely, leaving nothing out. Several times, she's about to cry, but she manages to contain herself.

"Why didn't someone call me and tell me what was going on?" she asks when I'm finished. "Does Dana know you're here?"

"Yes. I told her I'd like to stop by and see you after visiting my mom and dad. She gave me your address."

It sounds as if someone is turning the lock in the front door. The door swings open. A wiry man comes bounding into the room, with a toddler on his shoulders.

"Hi, Alex," says Elsie.

Looking like he's having fun with the boy on his back, he leans over and gives Elsie a kiss before he spots me.

"This is Richie Bianchi," says Elsie. "Richie, this is my husband, Alex, and that little guy in his arms is my other boy, Francisco. He spent today with my in-laws."

Alex stares blankly at me.

Elsie jumps in. "Richie came all the way from New Jersey to

visit his parents in Port Saint Lucie. He also has some important news about Eddie and Dana. He lives across the street from them. Sit down, honey. Let Richie explain."

After we shake hands, I proceed to lay out the facts slowly, carefully. I catch a little hesitation and mistrust in Alex's demeanor—Who wouldn't be suspicious in a situation like this?—but I keep talking. I feel the need to reveal I'm a priest on leave of absence and I only recently moved into this house in New Jersey and met Dana and her father quite by accident. "I went to see Dana play in this big hockey tournament, which is still in progress. What a player! But ever since her father's abduction, she doesn't want to do anything except stare out the window and, hopefully, catch a glimpse of her dad coming down the path. I can't get over how much she's changed in the short time I've known her."

Francisco makes a run for his father. "Stop, Cisco. Not now," he says calmly. Turning toward me, he asks, "How can we help?"

"I was wondering if Elsie can come up to New Jersey and spend a few days with Dana. She really needs her."

Elsie takes a deep breath, then lets it all out. "Oh, Richie, or is it Father?"

"Richie's fine."

"Believe me, I wish I can help, but does it look like I have a lot of time around here with these two little guys?"

"I understand."

"On top of that, I work three nights a week in an emergency care center. I just started there three weeks ago. Then there's my sobriety meetings."

"Oh, I didn't realize…"

"I wish I could help, Richie. But I can't…I really can't. I'm sorry."

"Really, I understand." I get up to leave.

"No, wait, please sit down," she says.

"Can I get you something to drink, Richie?" asks Alex. "Coke? Lemonade?"

BREAKAWAY

"Lemonade's fine."

As Alex goes into the kitchen, Elsie asks me if there's a chance Dana could come down to Florida and spend a few days with her.

"I don't think so," I reply. "She's determined to be home when her father returns, God willing, and there's school, plus the tournament and her friends."

"She sounds like a busy young woman."

"She is."

"Please tell her I'll call her."

"I will."

Alex returns with the lemonade. "Have you a place for the night?" he asks.

"Yes. I'm staying with my parents in Port Saint Lucie tonight and going home tomorrow."

"You're welcome to stay here anytime you're in the neighborhood."

"Thanks, Alex."

Elsie is shaking her head now. "I can't believe this is happening. I wish there was more I could do. Thank God for Grandpa and neighbors like you, Richie!"

"Take care of yourself. That's the main thing. When you get a chance, give Dana a call. I'll call you, too, and fill you in on what's going on."

"That would be great. Boy, life takes some crazy turns sometimes, doesn't it?"

"It sure does."

Here I am in Florida, talking to someone I never met before—the mother of two young children—about coming to New Jersey to spend a few days with her sixteen-year-old daughter, whose father was abducted from his home—and I'm doing this while I'm trying to figure out what to do with the rest of my life. Is that a crazy turn of events or what? I can't wait to see what happens next.

Chapter 13

As the plane whirs north toward Newark, my mind is focused on the past twenty-four hours. My mom and dad seem to be enjoying their retirement and fitting in with the Florida lifestyle. That's good. While I think they'll always be there for me, whatever I decide to do, part of them will always think of me as a priest, and I can live with that, too. As for Elsie, I was disappointed she won't be able to spend some time with Dana, but the woman has her hands full, with the two little guys, and there's her new job along with her commitment to her sobriety meetings. They may be excuses, but they tell me she's trying hard to build a better life for herself and her family.

Dana's probably anxious to hear from me, so I dial her on my cell. She immediately picks up the phone. "Hi, how did it go?" she asks.

"It was fun, too brief, and I'd like to go back for a more extended visit," I reply.

"I bet you were glad to spend some time with your mom and dad."

"Sure was. They're real Floridians now. They're obviously adjusting well to life down there, and they look great. They'd love to meet you someday."

"Tell me about my mom."

"She's doing well, busy looking after the two little guys, and she's working hard, just like so many other folks. Naturally, she was shocked and sad to hear about what happened to your dad, and she told me to tell you she'd be in touch with you. And, of course, she wanted to know all about you and how you're doing. She was especially excited when I told her you're playing hockey, and you're the star of the team."

"Oh, Richie."

"Well, you are. I saw you play."

"Still…"

I'm reluctant to mention her mom can't get away to spend a few days with her in New Jersey, but Dana can read between the lines.

"I guess I won't be seeing her anytime soon," she says.

"Hey, you never know. Right now, she has a lot going on, especially with the two boys."

"Oh, it's okay. I understand. Like my dad told me many times, my mom has issues she needs to keep working on, one day at a time. Tell me, Richie, is she still pretty?"

"I don't know what she looked like before, but I think your mom's a lovely looking woman. What's more important, she seems to be doing well as far as her sobriety is concerned, and she's working three nights a week at an emergency care center."

"Did you get to meet Alex?"

"Actually, I met both big Alex and little Alex. Big Alex seems like a nice guy. He offered to put me up for the night, but I already made plans with my mom and dad. Little Alex is a beautiful boy, looks a lot like his dad."

"And what about Francisco?"

"Huh, he's quick and a bundle of energy…How's Grandpa?"

"Grumpy," Dana replies. "He's itching to get back to the Bronx."

"I think the neighbors miss him. I have the impression some of them are very old and sick and live alone. He keeps an eye on them, and they look forward to seeing him."

"I'll miss him when he goes."

It's dark when my plane lands in Newark and I pick up my car. Instead of going straight home, I drive into the city to see Tess. Hopefully, I didn't hurt her feelings by not encouraging her to come along with me. I wanted to make this a fast trip, do what I had to do and come right back home.

I wonder sometimes whether Tess thinks I'm spending too much time on Dana's problems. But Tess has been my partner, confidante and friend, encouraging me to use my talents to help Dana any way I can.

Truth is I miss Tess and her beautiful smile so much, even though it was only an overnight trip. Seeing Elsie and her young family made me wonder how Tess and I and the little guy, Simon, would be together, and I think we'll do fine. We may not start off like other couples, but we have life experiences they don't have. I get excited thinking about it.

I park my car and walk three blocks to Tess's apartment. The city is getting ready to swing into its night-life mode. Life is always changing in New York. Now that I don't live here anymore, I miss watching the city transform itself from a center for big business, with each corporate entity fighting for survival, into a city of neighborhoods, with each family struggling to scratch out a living for itself, and, finally, into a hub for a restless subset of individuals of the night looking for the pleasures only this town can offer.

I knock twice, and the door barely opens, and eyes scrutinize me from a short chain. "Oh, it's you," she says, and swings open the door. I grab her before she turns away, and the startled expression on her face tells me she doesn't expect the enthusiastic hello she's getting from me. After we embrace, she says, "For a minute there, I thought you were Richie."

She hasn't lost her sense of humor.

"What's up? You alright?" she says.

"Yeah, I missed you."

"Yeah, right. You sailors are all alike," she says, hands on hips. "You go away, live it up in some exotic place for a couple of days, then drag yourself back home."

"That's not exactly what it was like."

"Then what was it like? Tell me."

"Where's Simon?"

"He's sleeping."
"Good. Make me a cup of coffee, and I'll tell you all about it."

The coffee is strong, but I don't care if it keeps me up all night; it tastes delicious, and I'm with Tess, who's all ears.

"I think it was a good idea to spend the night with my parents," I begin. "They had a chance to tell me what's on their minds, and I was able to explain why I decided to do what I'm doing."

"And?"

"Obviously, they're disappointed, especially Mom. But they know now what it's been like, living two different lives, like I had been living. They understand what I want to do now."

"And what's that?"

"Find a life for us."

"I couldn't have said it better, Richie. Did they ask for me?"

"Of course. They always do. I don't want to give you a big head, but they said some nice things about you. Above all, they think you're a good woman."

Her eyes fill up. "Sometimes I feel so bad, Richie. I wish...I wish..."

"Shh, shh...don't talk like that, Tess. We'll find a way."

"Your sister called me yesterday."

"What did she want?"

"She said she was calling to see how I was doing, and she went on to tell me her real reason for calling. She said it would be a mistake for you to leave the priesthood and I should do everything in my power to encourage you to stay. I told her the decision was yours, not mine."

"Did you tell her how much we love each other?"

Slowly, after taking a couple of deep breaths, she says, "Honestly, Richie, it wouldn't have made a difference. She was on a mission to say what she had to say...nothing was going to stop her."

"That's my big sister."

"Oh, Richie, I feel like crap," Tess says, trying to control her emotions.

"I feel like this desperate, single mom trying to snare a husband for myself and a father for my child. It's not that way at all, Richie. I think you know that. I will not do anything that will block you from continuing your ministry, if that's what you choose to do… I just won't."

"I know, Tess. Jennifer can come on like an 18-wheeler sometimes. She's arriving in New York in a few days for a teachers' conference. I'll meet her in the city, have lunch or something with her, and talk to her. This is my life. It's time she minds her own business when it comes to something I need to do for myself."

"Only, I hope you don't mind if I don't go with you. I might toss my chicken *francaise* on her head."

"Oh, that would be a lovely sight."

"Tell me something else about the trip to Florida."

"My parents wanted to know what I planned to do if and when I leave the priesthood. I told them I don't know for sure, but I'd be working with people, helping them, doing many of the things I've been doing as a priest."

"Right."

I reach across the table and hold her hand and tell myself, *Come on, lighten the mood, Richie.*

"My parents are really into this retirement thing," I say, changing gears.

"What do you mean?"

"They got it down to a science," I explain. "The day starts early for both of them. Dad goes out for bagels or buns and the newspaper, and Mom tidies up while she watches her favorite morning TV show. Later, they take a dip in the community pool and catch up with friends. Then, after showering, they head off to their favorite buffet for the early bird special. What they can't eat they wrap up and take home for the following day. Talk about having a system."

Tess breaks out into that beautiful smile. "Good for your mom and dad… And how was your visit with Dana's mother?"

"Elsie was very welcoming, friendly. So was her husband, Alex. I told them all about Dana and what happened to her dad."

"Did you tell them she's a hockey star?"

"Yup. They got a big kick out of that."

"And what did they say when you told them about Eddie?"

"They were dumbfounded. They couldn't understand why anyone would abduct him."

"That's the big question. Did you ask Elsie about spending some time with her daughter?"

"Yes…but unfortunately she said no. They've got a lot going on in their lives now with the two little boys, Francisco and Alexander. I was disappointed. It would have been good for both Dana and her mother. But I understand."

"You tried, Richie."

"Hey, you know me. I don't give up that easily. I'll call her in a few days and tell her what's going on. Maybe she'll change her mind."

Tess gets up from the table. Under the overhead light, I could see her face more clearly, and there are dark shadows under her eyes. Now I wonder whether I should have come here and burdened her with all this stuff.

"You alright?" I ask.

"I'm fine. Why?"

"You look tired."

"Now why do you suppose that's so?"

"Tell me."

"It's called life, Richie. Don't worry about me. I'm fine."

I check my watch. "Wow, it's late." I get up

"Want some more coffee?" she asks.

"No thanks. I better go. I almost forgot you have a job to go to in the morning."

"I'm more worried about you on the road. Why don't you stay the night?"

"Thought you'd never ask," I say, smiling broadly. "Thanks, Tess. It's been a long day."

She puts her arm around my shoulder. "It'll be a nice surprise for Simon if you're here when he wakes up. He always lights up when he sees his pal." *And I always light up when I see the boy. Maybe I can draw some vitality from him for what lies ahead.*

Chapter 14

After pulling into my driveway next morning, I take stock of the Dvorak house across the road. All seems quiet there, and it occurs to me Dana is probably in school now. I'll drop by later.

The last three moving boxes I had planned to open but never did greet me when I enter my house. I guess it never ends, but who cares? I'm home, sweet home.

In the living room, I flop on the love seat, reach for my phone, and dial Detective Laszlo's number.

He answers right away. "How was your trip?"

"Florida is beautiful this time of year. You and Norma should be there."

"Tell me about it in three years after I retire."

"Anything new?"

"Well, we did get a signal from Mr. Dvorak's cell for a little while, but we lost it or we got cut off. Anyway, it didn't last long. We weren't able to pinpoint the exact location."

"Did you get anything?"

"Nothing I could take to the bank. Only, that it wasn't far away, as I suspected. I'm sure someone got to his phone before we were able to trace the signal."

"Too bad. Talk to anyone else?"

"Yes. I had an interesting conversation over the phone with one of Eddie's Navy buddies, Brewster Bennett. He used to live in New Jersey. He's in North Carolina now. He said he hasn't seen his friend in about a year. The last time they met, Eddie was talking about quitting his job at the trucking company. Too much politics. He said he refused to suck up like everyone else in the company. He said if it wasn't for his daughter he'd might even reenlist. Mr. Bennett said he never saw his friend so down in the dumps—and he was drinking more than he'd ever seen him drink. He said he couldn't understand it. Eddie was always a pretty upbeat, easygoing guy except when he's talking about politics. He said he's got this bug about the government and how it's screwing up this great country of ours. Sound familiar?"

"Yes, echoes of Wendell Jackson and Waldo Cameron. They both made similar comments about Eddie."

"Right. I'm not sure how it all fits together."

"And you know what? The first time I met Eddie he went into a brief tirade about the Washington establishment."

"Hmm."

"How did you find out about his Navy buddy?"

"Mildred Jordan mentioned him when I spoke to her," Laszlo replies.

"I think she has a lot more to say. Mind if I went back and talked to her?"

"No problem, Richie. I think you're ready for a deputy badge. Just be careful."

The last time I was at a sports bar I was in high school. Two of my classmates and I were celebrating our coming of age with our dads. My father was quick to remind me we were there "to see what it's like" and that includes a light lunch and a non-alcoholic drink. I don't know about the other guys, but I was a bit overwhelmed by the variety of sports attractions on TV, along with the table games, the noise, and, of course, the pretty girls.

I walk into The Honey Comb today, a different person, armed with whatever maturity I gained from my contact with the life experiences of my parishioners. I'm on a mission, to find out what Mildred Jordan knows that may help explain why Eddie was taken from his home. She must be privy to information that could be crucial to the investigation.

Thanks to a friendly greeter at The Honey Comb, I'm quickly led to Mildred's station, which is quiet right now. When I introduce myself, she says, "Oh, I know who you are. Eddie told me all about you. You're the ex-priest who moved in across the street. Come with me." She leads me to an empty table, and we sit down.

"Well, I thought I could ask you a few questions," I say.

"How's Dana?" she snaps back. "She's never home when I'm there."

"Oh..."

"She must be worried sick about her father."

"She is."

"Tell her not to worry."

"Yeah, well..."

"I'm sure her dad will be back soon, and I'm positive..."

"Can we slow down, Ms. Jordan? I realize you have to get back to work, but this seems like a good time to talk."

"Sure." She pulls a makeup kit out of her side pocket and dabs her cheek. Blonde and brown eyed, she has a pretty face under thick eye lashes and heavy makeup. "What do you want to talk about?"

"Eddie. Why would anyone want to abduct him?"

"I don't think Eddie was abducted. He probably needs some space and time to work out a few issues in his life."

"What makes you say that? Has he ever done anything like that before."

"Sure. There were times he wanted to be alone. He just tuned me out for days, even a week or two. Then he'd call and tell me not to worry, he just needed some time for himself. I'm sure he'll contact Dana to let her know he's alright."

Amazing! Coincidence or what? The stranger at the ice rink...the video message from Eddie telling Dana not to worry... and now Mildred Jordan reiterating his message.

"Eddie can be a moody guy sometimes," she concludes.

"Interesting. When he 'tuned' you out, did he also tune out his daughter, leave her in the house alone."

Her eyes narrow. "Well, that was a slightly different situation. The fact is she's a pretty mature young lady. She's perfectly capable of taking care of herself…for a week or two."

"Mind if I ask you a personal question?"

"Sure, why not?"

"How close were you and Eddie?"

"Very close, at one time. Right now, I'm not sure where we're going in our relationship, if we have a relationship anymore, Father."

"Richie."

"Okay, Richie. We even talked about getting married at one time."

"And what happened?"

"He wasn't ready. He said he needed more time. Like I said, he could be a moody guy sometimes. Lately, we haven't been seeing each other very much."

"I know. Does he have any enemies you're aware of?"

"Eddie? No. He was, is, very likeable. Ask the people where he works."

"We did. They said the same thing you did. One more question: Do you have any idea where he might be now?"

She makes a fist and gently bites into a knuckle. "No. He's pretty secretive about where he goes when he takes one of his breaks. It wouldn't surprise me if he boarded one of those ocean liners at Port Elizabeth. I'm only kidding, of course."

"Sure."

"More likely, he went to a place like Atlantic City. He likes to gamble."

"Could be…I appreciate your taking the time to talk with me, Ms. Jordan."

"Mildred."

"Right, Mildred."

"I never met an ex-priest before. I hope you find what you're looking for."

"Right now I'm looking for Eddie Dvorak."

"Well, if you're ever looking for a good time…not with me, of course…just give me a holler. I know some friendly people here who'd love to show you a fun time."

"Thanks."

I go away trying to find something useful in our conversation. It sounds as if she and Eddie were drifting apart.

When I call Detective Laszlo and fill him in on my meeting with Mildred, he says, "I hear you. Her comments open up more questions than answers, and there are some gaps that need to be filled in."

"Like, how can she be so sure Eddie was not abducted?" I wonder. "She seems to believe he merely needs time to work out a few issues alone. I should have mentioned the blood stains in the carpet, but I didn't."

"Do you think that would have made a difference?"

"Probably not…And what about the comment she made that Eddie would probably contact Dana and tell her not to worry, he just needed some time alone?"

"Odd comment, especially since Dana was just shown a video from her dad telling her the same thing."

"That's what I thought."

"But never mind what she said or didn't say. What's your overall impression?"

"My impression is there's no great love lost now between Eddie and Mildred," I reply. "Maybe there was at one time, but not now. It's all so odd. They've been going out for…what?…two years. You'd think there'd be a stronger emotional attachment to him, and she might be a little more concerned about his disappearance."

"It sounds like the relationship has gone sour," Laszlo says.

"I think you're right. The whole relationship is strange."

"Yeah. Listen," he continues, "I got a call from Melinda. She'd like to meet with me—you, too, if you're available. She's got something important to discuss. Want to come along?"

"Sure. When?"

"Today, for lunch."

"Where?"

He mentions a restaurant in Bayonne.

"I'll meet you there. This could be very interesting."

Chapter 15

Laszlo is seated in a booth in the rear of Tre Soldati when I enter, and I join him. Melinda Childs has not arrived yet. Fifteen minutes pass. A half-hour. It's a good time for a quiet chat with the man across the table. I learn Vinnie Laszlo and his wife, Norma, are Jerseyites, born and raised in Paterson. No children, as he already told me, but they've made a good life for themselves without them. They love to travel whenever they get a chance. One of their favorite vacation spots is Paradise Island in the Bahamas. Growing up, Vinnie aspired to be a professional football player and was a linebacker in high school. That dream morphed into a career in law enforcement when he finished community college. He's looking forward to retiring and traveling to sights unknown to him and Norma.

Suddenly, this beautiful, young women bursts through the front door and sweeps past the maitre d'. Her dark blue eyes nervously dart all over the place while her rich auburn hair gently bobs around her. She finally spots us. We both get up and welcome her, smiling, as she approaches our table. She's seems dead serious, all business.

"I think I need a drink," she says, collapsing into a chair

"Waiter! What would you like?" Laszlo asks her.

"I don't know. Some wine...yes, red wine."

"Pinot noir? Cabernet sauvignon?"

"Cabernet."

Laszlo and I are glued to every expression and movement she makes.

"It was hell getting out of the office, and it was hell getting here," she explains. "I took a late lunch. I just had to come. For his sake."

"You mean Eddie Dvorak?" says Laszlo.

"Yes. I knew something was wrong the last time we had lunch together. He was quiet. He had this pained expression on his face. He was not the cheerful, fun guy I know. I asked him, 'What's wrong, Eddie?' He shook his head. I kept asking him, and he kept shaking his head. I finally said, 'Look, Eddie, I thought we were friends. How many times did I open up to you? Don't you think it's time you told me what's bothering you?' He stared at me, like he was going to cry. 'I can't,' he said. 'My life's in danger, and I don't want anyone else to get hurt.'"

Both Laszlo and I squirm in our chairs. I reach for my beer in a show of casualness. I'm lucky I don't knock over the bottle.

"Did he say why his life's in danger?" Laszlo asks.

"No. That's it. He wouldn't tell me anything else, no matter how many times I asked. All he said was, 'It's my own fault. I should have known better.'"

"Known better about what?" asks Laszlo with this intense, penetrating look.

"I don't know," Melinda replies. "He wouldn't say. I asked him if he was in debt. He chuckled a bit and said 'Isn't everyone?' Did he have a fight with someone? He shook his head. I asked him if he had a falling-out with Mildred, he just waved his hands, as if he didn't want to talk about that. When I asked whether there was a problem with Dana, he started filling up again and said, almost in a whisper, 'She's the least of my problems.' I finally suggested he talk to the police if his life's in such grave danger. He just waved me off. 'Too complicated. Too much trouble,' he said."

Laszlo let out a deep sigh, probably the frustration of a detective being so close yet so far to a key piece of information. "Want to order?"

"I guess I'd better eat something. She picks up the menu. "I'll have a Caesar salad," she says, hardly examining the choices.

"What about you, Richie?"

I'm staring in space. "Same thing."

"I think I'll have the fish and chips," says Laszlo. He places the orders and reaches for something, probably a cigar, in the inside pocket of his suit jacket but decides against it. "So, Ms. Childs, tell us something about yourself."

"What's to tell? I live in Elizabeth with Czar, my Lab."

"Family?"

"My parents live about a mile away from me. My Dad is an old Army man, retired as a major two years ago. My mom is a high school teacher, or at least she was. She's semi-retired, works part-time in the school now. I have two sisters, both married. One lives in Vermont; the other moved to Seattle last year."

"Do you get a chance to see them?"

"Sometimes. Around the holidays. We try to stay in touch."

She seems like a considerate person, Melinda does. I'm wondering if she's the self-designated caregiver in the family, choosing to live near her parents because she wants to keep an eye on them as they move into their retirement years.

She takes a sip of wine and slowly places the glass on the table. "Enough about me," she says. "I wish I could help you more, but my relationship with Eddie is pretty much confined to the work place. I'm aware of what he does around the garage. He's an excellent mechanic, well-liked by the other employees and the bosses. He gets together with some of them once in a while, maybe once a month, and plays poker, sometimes at his house. In the summer, he even goes on vacation with a couple of them, and once a year all the boys go up to the boss's place in the Adirondacks to hunt. Although Mr. Jackson runs a tight ship, I think everyone gets along fine, on the surface. Like I said, I know Eddie mainly through work, but he's my friend, and I love him for being my friend." Holding back tears, she adds, "I'd hate to see anything bad happen to him."

"We feel the same way," says Laszlo, "but we need more information, and we need it fast. Please call me if you hear anything else that may be useful." We exchange phone numbers as the food arrives.

As she gets ready to dig into her salad, her eyes widen with alarm. "What is it?" I ask.

"It's just a guy I know from work, one of our suppliers."

She waves, an obligatory smile on her face, and the man leaves his party and comes walking over to her. Melinda, muttering something under her breath, gets up to greet him.

"Hey, Melinda," he says, "how're you doing? What a surprise to see you here. I didn't think they let you out."

"Hi, Mr. Cartwright. Hey, even lowly associates have to eat once in a while."

"Why not?" he says with a hearty laugh. He glances at Laszlo and me.

Sensing an awkward moment in the making, we both get up to introduce ourselves, but Melinda beats us to the punch. "Meet Vincent Laszlo and Richard Bianchi, friends of mine," she says with reddened face.

"A pleasure to meet you," I say. Laszlo jumps on board. "Same here."

Cartwright returns the greeting. Looking down at our table, he says, "Oh, goodness, you guys haven't even touched your meals. So sorry for the intrusion."

"No problem!" the three of us agree.

"Listen, Melinda, nice to see you again, but I've got to run. I'll see you back at the office next week," he says.

"Sure, Mr. Cartwright," she says. "Say hello to your lovely wife, Linda."

"Enjoy your lunch." He leaves, grinning from ear to ear and waving.

"Whew," Melinda mumbles as we sit back down.

"Is that a worried 'whew' or a relieved 'whew'?" I ask.

"Both," she says. "I don't like to share what I do in private with the whole office, and Mr. Cartwright is a bit of a gabber, if you know what I mean."

"I sensed that," I say.

"Damn, I shouldn't have used your real names," she says. Somehow, we quietly finish our meals.

After Melinda leaves us, we stay to confer on what, if any, progress is being made in the case. I ask Laszlo the million-dollar question, or series of questions, "Based on your investigative experience, are we making any progress? Are the pieces coming together into some kind of coherent, plausible story?"

He rubs his forehead and sighs. I'm expecting this long, reasoned reply. He says, "Yes and No. Yes, I think we're making progress. There are no great secrets to success in this business, in my opinion. It's good, old legwork, and I think we're doing that, but there's still a way to go. Of course, we have to talk to all the right people, follow the leads wherever they take us, and ruthlessly review the facts."

I'm struck by the word "ruthlessly". I think I know what he means by that, but I'm not sure. "Okay, so are the pieces coming together or not?" I ask once more.

"Again, Yes and No," he replies. "Yes, the pieces are starting to come together, but a coherent story, no, it's not there yet. Something's going on here, but I don't know what. Any ideas?"

I'm a little uncomfortable sharing my views with an expert, but they may help put things in perspective. "Everyone we talked to agrees Eddie is a lovable guy with no real enemies. But except for Melinda no one seems to be worried that he's missing. In fact, most of the people we interviewed say Eddie was not abducted, but just needs some time alone to work out a few things and will be back home soon. If I didn't see the blood on the carpet and his pickup truck in the driveway I might believe them."

"So what are you saying: They're lying?"

"It's not for me to call the shots. I'm only a priest on leave of absence."

"Personally, I think you're on to something, Richie. Of all the people we spoke to, I'd say Melinda is the most believable. As for everyone else, they're all on the same page on most things, and that makes me a little suspicious. It's like they're all trying to buy some time. For what, I don't have a clue."

Chapter 16

***G**ame Four—Owls vs. J-Drones:* There's a nervous buzz in the Owls locker room, which turns into cheers when Dana and Hugo finally arrive.

"What took you so long?" says Lenny, his nose and chin angled sharply at his two teammates. "Late for practice yesterday, late for the game today."

Dana shakes her head, slightly annoyed, and goes to the girls' dressing area.

"We got here as soon as we could," Hugo explains.

"Think we have a chance today?" Ernie, a tall, thin right winger, asks.

"Of course. I guarantee it," Hugo responds with a sly grin as he hurriedly begins putting on his uniform.

"You want my opinion?" says Lenny.

"No," several players reply.

Lenny shrugs. "I'll give it to you anyway. We're dead ducks. The J-Drones are the toughest and dirtiest team in the tournament."

"That's the spirit, Lenny," Hugo says with obvious sarcasm.

"Yeah, Lenny. We'll kill 'em," says Titus, the smallest member of the team.

"Way to go, Titus," Hugo says.

"They just like to bully the teams they play," says Matteo, the goalie, from across the room.

"Yeah, and they do a good job of it," says Lenny.

"We got to stick together," Matteo says with quiet determination. "We can beat this team."

The players abruptly stop talking. It's their quiet time before they go onto the ice. Some use the time to say a prayer, others to put on their game face. As Hugo finishes lacing his skates, Coach Fenda walks into the room. "Where's Dana?" he snaps.

"Right here, coach," she replies in full uniform.

"Good. Now listen up," he says, addressing the entire team. "Don't fall for their dirty tricks. You don't have to respond whenever they do something stupid, and they *will* do something stupid. Keep cool! Be smart! Let them take the penalty. We'll take the power play anytime. Let's go, Owls!"

"YEAH!" everyone agrees, including Lenny. They file out of the locker room and onto the ice for their pre-game warm-up.

Less than a minute after the puck is dropped to start the game, a fight breaks out when a J-Drone player drills Dana against the boards. An Owls teammate retaliates, and a J-Drones player quickly grinds his glove into the face of the retaliator. Soon, players are throwing punches at anyone within striking range, while other hockey players turned wrestlers are practicing holds on the ice surface. A referee's whistle is shrieking somewhere, to no avail. It would be laughable, like a routine by clowns at an ice show, were it not for the fact that someone could get hurt.

Somehow Dana manages to wiggle out of the pile and glide over to the bench, holding her side. Finally, probably out of sheer exhaustion, the combatants stop fighting, pick up their gloves and sticks, and return to their respective benches. One player, the one who slammed Dana against the boards, is thrown out of the game, and the retaliator and the glove grinder are each assessed a five-minute penalty along with a ten-minute misconduct, which means they can't play for a total of fifteen minutes. The referee gives a stern warning to each bench. "One more outbreak like that, and this game is over. Play hockey, or go home!"

They finally start playing hockey, but the J-Drones have gotten their point across. Thereafter, at least through the second period, the Owls are tentative in the pursuit of the puck. They fall into a defensive shell that keeps them pinned in their end of the ice most of the time. By the time the horn is sounded for the end of the second period, the Owls find themselves at a serious disadvantage.

Score: J-Drones, 3; Owls, 0.

The Owls clump into the locker room, a whipped and battered flock of birds. After several minutes, Coach Fenda walks to the center of the room to address his players. They sit on benches all around him, holding their heads in their hands, trying to rub their aches away, or just staring into space.

The coach finally smiles slightly and begins to speak, "Okay, guys, we got 'em exactly where we want 'em." The players snap a look of disbelief at him. "Yeah, I know. You feel pretty crappy right now. What do you say I go to the ref and tell him we quit? We've had enough. These guys are too good for us. In less than an hour we can be back in our nice, warm houses drinking cocoa and enjoying our I-Pods."

"NO! We can beat these guys," Dana says "I know it. You know it. They're just a bunch of goons pretending to be hockey players."

"Yeah," Titus says, "we can beat 'em."

"I can play better," Matteo chimes in.

"Me, too," says Lenny.

Hugo gets up. "Okay, let's go out there and show them how to play this game."

Coach Fenda jumps in. "So, you think you can beat these guys?"

"YEAH!"

"So do I. Let's do it!"

Period three. The boys in gray are grinning from ear to ear as they wait for the puck to drop. They seem so cool and confident. They fail to notice the calm determination in the eyes of every Owl player. However, although they're gaining increasing possession of the puck, the Owls don't break though until fourteen minutes into the period on an unassisted goal by Hugo.

Score: J-Drones, 3; Owls, 1.

Six minutes to go now. The Owls continue to go on the offensive. Dana picks up the puck behind the Owls net and zig-zags up the ice into the opponent's zone. As a defender comes charging toward her, she flips the puck to Hugo who, in turn, passes it to Ernie, positioned in front of the J-Drones goalie. Ernie doesn't waste any time shooting.

Score: J-Drones, 3; Owls, 2.

Less than two minutes to go. The Owls appear to have their opponents on the ropes. As the players bunch up in front of the J-Drones goalie, Owls defenseman Big John Mason takes a slap shot which is accidentally redirected by two players before the puck finds its way to the back of the net.

Score: J-Drones, 3; Owls, 3.

Owls fans, or at least those who remained after the second period, go wild, and the stands are rocking. Only thirty seconds left in the third period. The J-Drones on the bench are crushed, but at least they can redeem themselves in overtime, or so they think. The unexpected then happens. A J-Drones defender tries to make a cross-ice pass, but the puck never reaches its intended target. It kicks off the skate of a teammate and onto Lenny's stick. The Owls player instinctively heads toward the J-Drones zone. He's all alone, in a classic breakaway. His long legs can't move fast enough, but he manages to position himself about ten feet from the J-Drones goalie. As he rears back to shoot, a J-Drones player catches up with him and jams his stick between Lenny's legs, sending the Owls player crashing into the boards. Lenny never got off a shot. Owls fans groan, but their disappointment is short-lived. The referee blows his whistle and points to center ice. Lenny is awarded a penalty shot.

A silly grin on Lenny's face clashes with the terror in his eyes as he skates over to the Owls bench. Lenny, the last person anyone on the team would want to take a penalty shot, goes directly to Dana, who's seated on the bench. "What do I do now?" he says, his eyes blinking furiously.

"Just relax, Lenny," she says. "Don't try to do anything fancy. Be yourself and take your shot, like you do in practice."

"You think?"

"I know," she replies.

"You can do it, dude!" says Titus, providing additional support.

Lenny takes his position at center ice. When the referee blows the whistle, Lenny cradles the puck and skates, slowly and easily—as if he were in a free skate at a skating rink—toward the J-Drones goalie. About five feet from the net, he picks a spot high in the top corner over the goalie's glove and shoots.

Score: Owls 4, J-Drones 3.

When the game ends, Lenny, the unlikely hero, is carried off the ice by his ecstatic teammates. Dana is proud of him, but once again she doesn't stay for the celebration. She just wants to get home, her hopes for good news about her dad waning.

Chapter 17

I'm sorry I had to miss the game. Jennifer had called that morning, and I'm on my way to meet her at some fancy restaurant on Manhattan's East Side. Nothing's too good for big sister.

On the way, I'm reviewing the reasons why I'm leaning toward leaving the priesthood. To me, it all boils down to one thing: I love Tess with my whole being and I want to spend the rest of my life with her, but I can't do that without leaving the priesthood, which has been so much a part of my life until now.

Obviously, I expect Jennifer to start firing away as soon as I meet her. I'm wrong. That's not what happens. As it turns out, I'm greeted by this lovely woman who seems genuinely pleased to see me when I meet her at the restaurant.

"Oh my God, Richie, you look great," she says.

"Thanks. So do you, Jen."

"Come here, let me look at you up close." Then she does something she used to do when I was a little boy. She pinches me on both cheeks.

"I hated when you did that when I was a kid. You know what? I still hate it."

She gives me a loving jab on my arm and a big hug, and we sit down at our table.

A waiter in a tuxedo immediately comes over. "May I serve you something to drink?" We both order some merlot.

"You look terrific," I tell her again. Perhaps a couple of pounds heavier since I last saw her more than a year ago, she has this smart, professional air about her in a gray skirt and matching jacket and rose-colored blouse. If Ray's job loss has upset her, I don't see it in her face. Her light brown eyes are clear and bright. In fact, she seems well rested for someone who's traveled cross-country to attend an academic conference after learning her husband was fired.

"Thanks. I'm glad to be back in the old city. I can't believe I lived here once and roamed these streets as a girl."

A slight correction. "Only, it was probably a little farther west where you roamed," I remind her.

"Yeah, I guess," she says, grinning.

"How's Ray doing?" I ask as our drinks arrive.

"Mom probably told you. He's changing jobs. In fact, he's lined up a couple of interviews for today."

"Good for him." I toast the news with a tap of my glass against hers. "Here's hoping he finds what he's looking for."

We settle into an easygoing conversation about San Diego; her job as a university professor; my move to New Jersey and the rigors of setting up house there; and my recent visit to Florida. During one pause, we order our meals—a salmon salad for Jennifer, chicken *francaise* for me. I let out a big grin when I place my order.

"What's so funny?" she asks.

"I thought of something. It's nothing," I say, wondering how my chicken *francaise* would look on Jennifer's beautiful, perfectly quaffed light brown hair.

I also mention my new neighbors, the Dvoraks, but in a general way. "Lovely people. Right now, these are really tough times for them. I'm trying to help them any way I can." I want to eat the words I say next. "Like Dad says, 'Once a priest always a priest.'"

The door is wide open now.

And she comes charging in. "Listen, I need to talk to you about that," she says. "I don't want you to leave the priesthood, Richie. It's been your whole life ever since you were a teenager."

I try to collect my thoughts. "Like I told Mom and Dad, I still haven't fully decided what I want to do one way or the other. I'm still thinking on it. Anyway, thanks for sharing your view. It's not that I didn't know where you stood. I know you've talked to Mom and to Tess, and you're right. The priesthood has been my whole life, and it's served me well in so many ways, but I want Tess to be an integral part of my life, but that won't happen if I continue as a priest."

"But you've been such a good priest."

"Thanks for that, Jen. To be honest, sometimes I think I could have done a better job here and there, but overall I'm proud of what I've been able to accomplish, and I'll continue to reach out and help others no matter what I do."

"Yeah, but…"

"I'm well aware the priesthood gives me something special… what's the word?"

"Leverage? A broader platform?"

"Right. Yes, the priesthood gives me the platform to do good works for a whole bunch of people, rather than just a few, but who says I can't do some good in this world as a layman?"

"What about your parishioners? Are you going to walk away from them?"

"That's a tough one. My parishioners were always special to me. Still are." Once again, it's time to collect my thoughts. "You know, parishioners are used to having priests come and go in their lives. I'm not saying they like it, but it happens. The bottom line is I don't think I can be a good priest if I can't have the love of my life beside me. I'm not saying celibacy can't be a part of the priesthood. It's just not for me anymore. Please try to understand where I'm coming from, Jen."

"I'll try, but I'll miss Father Richard."

"So will I."

There are tears in our eyes as we hold hands across the table.

By the time I get home, I'm emotionally drained. I'd like to call Tess and fill her in, but I'll talk to her later. I'd also like to know who won the game, but I'll wait a bit to find out. I'm looking forward to some quiet time now.

I'm sitting on the edge of the bed, contemplating my next move—Should I check my e-mail? Should I shower? Should I take a nap? That's when I hear it. It's a shriek, but not like one I ever heard before. It's a high, piercing cry for immediate attention, and it's coming from somewhere nearby. I hurry down the stairs, open the front door, and zero in on the figure crouched in the doorway across the street.

There's Dana, covering her mouth, tears streaming down her face. As I approach her, she looks up at me with terrified eyes.

"What's wrong?" I ask.

"It's Grandpa," she says. "He fell over while he was talking on the phone. I think he's dead."

I help her to her feet and rush into the house. Grandpa is lying face down on the carpet in the living room. Next to him is a cell phone, its dial tone barely audible. I pick up the phone, dial 9-1-1, and request emergency help.

Gustav is out cold, but he's alive. Yank is sitting on his haunches nearby, watching everything with canine concern. Don't ask me why I did what I did next—some family member in a distant memory probably did it—I ask Dana to get me a cold, wet towel, and I apply it to the back of Grandpa's neck. He's stirring now, a good sign, and I lean over and whisper in his ear. "Gustav, Gustav, wake up. It's okay, you're okay, wake up." Yank's barking helps.

He starts moaning and blinking, then mumbling; finally, his eyes snap open now. "The phone…where's my damn phone?" he says before grabbing it out of my hand. "Is that creep still on? Hello, hello. He's gone…he's gone."

"Who, Gustav? Who was on the phone?"

"That man from the ice rink. The man with the video," he says, almost shouting.

"I hear you, Gustav. Calm down. What did he say?"

"He says he's sending another video to show us, but …but he doesn't want me to fall and hurt myself again, so he's sending it to Eddie's computer here."

I shoot a look at Dana, and she nods and runs upstairs, no doubt to her father's room and his computer.

Gustav continues, "I told him never mind the video. Just send my son home. Now! That's the last thing I remember."

The doorbell rings. It's the police, closely followed by an EMS team of four people. "What's going on?" Officer Jablonski asks. I tell them about Grandpa, who's still on the floor, but sitting up. "I found him lying on the carpet here, unconscious, when I came in."

"I'm alright," Gustav says.

The emergency squad immediately goes to work, checking his vital signs and getting some medical history. Seems this is not the first time Gustav blacked out.

"What do you want to do?" says this young woman in a blue uniform, apparently the leader of the EMS team.

"I'm fine," Grandpa says.

"I think he should be checked out," I say.

"I think that would be a good idea," says the leader.

Gustav shakes his head. "I passed out for a second, for cripes sake."

"Sir, it's only routine, but it makes sense to have the hospital check you out. Your numbers are a little high," she says. ""They'll probably send you home later."

"You think so, young lady?"

"Yes, sir."

"Okay, let's do it."

In less than two minutes, the first responders set up the flexible stretcher and roll Gustav out of the house and into an ambulance. It's amazing how quickly and smoothly they work.

As soon as everyone is gone, I go upstairs in search of Dana. As expected, she's sitting at the computer viewing the new video, probably for the second or third time. When she spots me, she says, "Let me start it from the beginning."

As the video opens, Eddie is in front of a huge, stone-faced fireplace. He looks older than his years. There are shadows under his eyes. His hair is slicked back and neatly combed, not in his usual easy and natural style. He's wearing a black jumpsuit, which Dana is quick to point out as something he'd never wear if it was his decision. He speaks slowly and deliberately, and there's a gravity in his voice that contrasts with the energy and quickness I recall when I first met him. His words speak for themselves:

"By now, you're probably wondering why I'm not back home. The answer is simple. I'm not ready to come back. There's still a few issues I need to deal with before I can assume my role as a man and a father. I hope you'll be patient with me. In the old days, when a man reached a critical stage in his life, he just got up and went out for "a pack of cigarettes" or "a cup of coffee." I have no excuses except to say I need to do what I'm doing. I hope you respect my honesty and need for seclusion.

The camera never strays from Eddie against the backdrop of the huge fireplace. From this point on, he seems to be speaking with more feeling as he addresses Dana. She seems overwhelmed. I gently put my arm around her shoulders as we watch the rest of the video.

I love you, Dana, with my whole heart and soul. We may have had our differences in the past, but they're nothing compared with the respect and pride I have for you as a young lady with a bright future, whether it be as a hockey player or something else. Please be patient, and forgive me for putting you through this ordeal. It will be over soon. Tell my dad I love him, and thanks for taking good care of you. Also, tell Richie I appreciate the way he's watching over you, but tell him he needs to spend more time on his own issues, instead of mine. So, Dana, be brave, be strong, your dad will be coming home soon.

Dana is in tears. His words at the end seem to come straight from the heart, and I never expected him to mention me the way he did. I check my watch. Detective Laszlo is probably gone for the day, but I'll call his office anyway and leave a message about the new video. I follow that with another call, this time to Tess. It's been a long day. I tell her all about it. She has three words for me: "Get some rest."

Good advice, but who knows what else is in store? "I'll try," I tell her.

Chapter 18

Rest doesn't come easy on the sofa in Dana's house. Grandpa Gustav is spending the night in the emergency room because the doctors need to do more tests on him and the admittance department couldn't find a regular room upstairs for him. In Grandpa's absence, I don't think it's a good idea to leave Dana alone in the house and, after the events of the past twenty-four hours, I suggest she stay home from school. She needs a good night's sleep.

So do I, but it's not meant to be. After a restless night that seemed longer than most nights, a bright sun is breaking through the front window and jabbing me in the eyes. I turn away from it, but it's no use. I can't get comfortable. Why can't they make sofas that fit the shape of full-sized humans?

The doorbell rings, and that's it for the restorative powers of sleep. I spring to a sit-up position and try to unscramble my brains before getting up to answer the door. It's Detective Laszlo. "I understand you have a new movie to show me," he says as I let him in. He's talking but it seems like he's yelling. I haven't adjusted to the human voice and the daylight yet. I call up to Dana, and we all converge at the computer in Eddie's bedroom.

As the video begins, I keep one eye on the screen and the other on Laszlo's reactions. The detective is a difficult read. "Well, what do you think?" I ask him when the video ends.

"Convincing, very convincing…in spots," he says. "It's like he believes what he's saying, especially when he's talking to Dana. I'm sure he meant every word he said at that point. I have trouble when he's talking about why he can't come home now because he has to deal with a few more issues. What issues? Why can't he deal with those issues when he's home? How complicated can they be? I mean here's a top-notch master mechanic who deals with very difficult and intricate problems every day. I just don't buy it. I still think he's being coached, and badly coached at that. What do you guys think?"

I agree. "It doesn't make sense."

Dana offers this strange observation: "That fireplace looks familiar to me."

"What?" snaps Laszlo.

"I've seen that fireplace before. It's big and it's old, and it made an impression on me when I first saw it."

"But where did you see it?" he asks.

"I don't remember."

"Was it on a trip you took?" I ask.

"Could be. I don't know."

"Recently?"

"No…maybe…I don't know for sure. But I did see it. I was standing in front of it, and I remember it as being tall, very old, and like something out of a scary movie."

"Try to remember where you saw it. That's very important," says Laszlo. "If you remember where the fireplace is, that might tell us where your father is."

"I wish…I wish…" She's sniffling now.

"It'll come to you," I say. "Sometimes when you don't try so hard the memory comes back to you."

The doorbell rings again.

"I'll get it," says Dana as she dashes down the stairs. We follow her, but at a slower pace. "Oh, hello," she says after opening the front door.

"Hi," says the visitor. "I don't know if you remember me. I'm Tess Tessalone, Richie's friend from the city."

"Oh, hi."

Spotting me coming down the stairs, Tess says, "Ah, there you are. I figured you'd be here."

I greet her with a hug and a peck on the cheek. "What a surprise. Aren't you supposed to be working today?"

"I took a discretionary day off," she says. "I thought you guys could use some help."

There's a somewhat bewildered expression on Dana's face.

"Tess, meet Detective Laszlo." They shake hands.

"Gee, I hope I didn't interrupt anything," she says.

"Not at all. I was just about to leave," says Laszlo.

"And who's this guy?" says Tess.

"That's Yank, my grandpa's dog. He's a little mopey today."

"Come here, boy." Tess gives him a gentle pet and hug." Yank responds with a wag of his tail and a lick.

Laszlo makes his way to the door. "Catch up with you later, Richie. You, too, Dana. Call me right away if you remember anything. Nice meeting you, Tess." He leaves.

"Where's Simon?" I wonder.

"In good hands, Grandma's."

"You should have brought him."

"I was going to."

The confusion in Dana's face grows.

"Simon is my two-year-old," Tess explains. "He loves trains both big and small, any kind of food, and kids of all sizes. You're right, Richie. I should have brought him along."

Dana warms up with a smile.

Hands on hips, Tess assumes a take-charge pose. "I brought a few things. First, for breakfast, fresh New York deli bagels, cream cheese, and orange juice. Later, I thought I'd make lunch or something. Do you like pasta, Dana?"

She nods.

"Especially rigatoni," I say.

"Well, I didn't bring rigatoni," says Tess with mock testiness. "I was going to do some basic spaghetti and meatballs."

"I like spaghetti, too, and meatballs."

"Good. I hope you know how to roll meatballs, Dana."

"Sure. My dad taught me."

The morning is spent eating New York deli bagels and getting acquainted. Tess shares stories of what it was like growing up on Manhattan's West Side. "If you ever saw the movie 'West Side Story', well, that's not exactly how it was," she explains, deadpanned. "We didn't spend a lot of time singing and dancing in the streets. If we did, we'd probably get run over by a car from Jersey heading for the theatre district. Right, Richie?"

"I'm not sure, Tess," I finally say, coming up for air. "A lot of it was a blur to me. All I remember was going over to your family's apartment every Sunday afternoon for lunch. Lunch? Huh. It was more like a wedding feast."

"It was fun, wasn't it?" Tess says. "No one ever leaves the Tessalone house hungry. That was our motto. Kidding aside, growing up in Hell's Kitchen was something special. I still get together with many of the old gang, like this guy. What about you, Dana? What's it like growing up in New Jersey?"

She pauses to gather her thoughts. "It's quiet. It's small. And comfortable. People are friendly. I sometimes wonder how they all got here."

"Amazing, isn't it?" says Tess. "How do people wind up where they wind up?"

"Yeah," Dana agrees. "I'm so glad Hugo and Angie live a few blocks away from me. They're my best friends. I can tell them anything, or mostly anything, but I have to be careful with Hugo. He's a boy, after all."

Tess raises her hand as if she has a question, which she does. "What do the kids at school think about your playing hockey on an all-boys team?"

"Um, a few kids have a problem with it," says Dana. "Most don't. They know I'm playing hockey because I love to play hockey. I happen to be playing with boys now. Someday I might be playing on an all-girls team. We'll see. How do you feel about me playing hockey on an all-boys team?"

"I love it. I just wish I knew more about the sport. I saw you play a couple of weeks ago, and that was the first hockey game I ever saw.'"

Before we know it, it's time for lunch. Inevitably, after hunting for the appropriate pots and pans, after getting the meatballs into shape, and after eating a delicious meal, we settle into some friendly chit-chat about this and that, including the hockey tournament, before the conversation turns to Eddie Dvorak's disappearance. We're sitting in the living room now, and Yank has found a warm, comfortable spot on the carpet.

"Why would anyone want to take my dad away from his home?" says Dana, fighting back tears.

Tess sits down next to her and puts an arm around her shoulder.

"I mean, it's just the two of us in this little house," says Dana, "and he's just a good mechanic and a pretty nice man most of the time."

"It doesn't make any sense," says Tess.

"Like, we've had our disagreements from time to time, but everyone likes my dad. He's a friendly guy, he'll do anything for you, and he's got this great smile." Dana points to the hutch. "He made that ship."

"It's beautiful," says Tess.

"Would you like to see the video of my dad we just got?" Dana asks Tess, who glances at me for a reaction. I give a barely noticeable shrug.

"I think not, Dana. That's for you and Detective Laszlo to examine. But if you have some old family photos…"

"Sure."

I leash Yank and take him out for a walk. I need some time to let my mind go blank for a while. We covered a lot of ground today. At the top of the hill, someone in a white van revs up the engine and comes roaring down the hill toward us. Crazy kid! I'm thinking, but that doesn't make the van stop. I freeze for a moment before my instincts for preservation kick in, and holding onto Yank's leash for dear life, I tumble onto the sidewalk. I drum up a profanity I hadn't used since I was ten as the van passes by. I don't know what Yank is saying but he's barking mad.

Chapter 19

Later that day, after Tess returned to the city, I pick up Grandpa at the hospital and drive him back to Dana's house. On the way, he grumbles about his overnight stay. Not that anyone did anything terrible to him. He doesn't like hospitals, although the nurses I saw had taken a liking to him.

"The next time I pass out, pay no attention to me," he pleads. "I'll come out of it on my own sooner or later. After a lot of tests, the doctors in the hospital told me I have a heart murmur and my pressure's too high. Big deal! I could have told them that in the ambulance."

Sometimes no response is the best response.

He sighs and continues, "So, what did I miss while I was away? Any news on my son?"

"We viewed the new video. Again, Eddie says not to worry; he'll be home as soon he works out a few issues, whatever they are. I found it hard to believe part of what he had to say, and he seemed tense, not himself. Detective Laszlo saw it, too. He believes Eddie was coached in some of his remarks."

"How's my mate, Yank?"

"We took good care of him, but he probably hasn't felt this lost since he was roaming around the lot near Yankee Stadium. I'm sure he misses you... And, oh, Tess, my friend from the city, came by for a visit and spent some time with Dana, and they made spaghetti and meatballs together."

"I love spaghetti and meatballs."

"We saved you some."

By the look on his face, I get the feeling life is good sometimes.

My cell phone sounds off, jarring me like a school bell notifying the class the test is over. As a curious observer and willing participant in the events surrounding the Dvorak family, I suppose that's to be expected. I answer it quickly.

"Detective Laszlo here. I got some news, but I don't know what to make of it yet."

I catch a nervousness in his voice. "What's up?"

"It looks like Melinda Childs is missing now."

"What?"

He explains. "I tried reaching her at home—I wanted to ask her a few more questions—and her phone just kept ringing. I also tried calling her at work, and this woman in Wendell Jackson's office said Melinda never showed up for work today, never called, and Mr. Jackson is worried sick. She said it's not like her; she has an excellent attendance record."

"Strange."

"Yeah, it sure is. I was going to call her parents—I found their phone number and address—but I thought I'd wait until I get more information."

"That's a good idea."

"I'm going to take a ride to her apartment now."

"I'll come along if it's okay with you."

"Pick you up in fifteen minutes."

The apartment where Melinda Childs lives is in a three-story building that's part of a row of residential/commercial structures on the main drag in town. A Cantonese restaurant occupies the lower level of her building. Fortunately, the superintendent is home, and when Laszlo shows him his badge, he reluctantly agrees to use his pass key to open her door.

"I don't like to barge in on anyone, especially when it's someone with a dog," says the scrawny, unshaven man in his late fifties. "He's been barking all morning. Can't even hear my TV. I was going to call her on the phone, but a couple of times the barking stopped. Get what I mean?"

"Yeah, yeah, I get you," says Laszlo as we climb the stairs. "I hope the young lady is alright."

As the super turns the key in Melinda's door, we can hear scratching on the other side. Upon entering the apartment, we are greeted by this hairy, tan animal about the size of a medium-sized suitcase. The dog's jumping on us and licking us and pawing us like this is his first encounter with humans. I don't get the sense this animal is trying to do us harm. This is a dog desperate for company right now.

"See, I told you," says the super. "This animal's gotta go. He's a menace to the tenants and visitors of the building."

Laszlo, obviously a dog person, leans over and pats the Lab with his huge hands. "Do you know his name?"

"I think she said it was Czar," I recall.

"Right. Hi ya, Czar. Good boy. He's alright. He just wants to say hello."

I love all of God's creatures, but my personal experience with dogs is limited. The one that stands out the most is my first dog, when I was a little boy. His name was Dipsy. He was a nervous mutt, only a little thing, but we were warned not to get too close to him or else he'd bite our noses off. One day Dipsy ran out of our apartment in the city and got hit by a car and died, and that's all I remember about Dipsy. Later, my encounters with dogs got better. I'm now ready to give Czar a few pats of my own. "I think he's glad to see us," I say in a classic understatement.

As we move through the apartment, I don't like the feeling coming over me. If Melinda left to go on a trip or something, she left in a hurry. Her belongings are visible everywhere, and there are dishes and a frying pan in the sink.

When we enter the bedroom, I brace myself for what we may find. And there she is, lying face-down, fully-clothed, across the bed. Laszlo calls her name and gently turns her onto her back. She's a bloody mess. Her face is battered and splattered with blood, which has trickled down her neck and knotted her beautiful hair. I can't tell whether she's alive or dead. Laszlo searches for a pulse, then shouts out to me, "Call 9-1-1." I make the call on my cell.

If she's breathing, it's on a very shallow level. I don't know if she's dying, and I'm not taking any chances. I reach into my inside jacket pocket and pull out a small bottle of anointed oil, which I carry around for instances such as this. "Excuse me," I say to Laszlo.

"Go ahead, Richie."

With a drop of oil on my thumb, I anoint her forehead and say, "Through this holy unction may the Lord pardon thee whatever sins or faults thou hast committed. In the name of the Father and Son and Holy Spirit."

We both say "Amen".

After Melinda is taken to the hospital in critical condition—she was repeatedly struck in the head and appears to be in a coma now, according to one EMS member—Laszlo starts taking notes and cell-phone photos of the apartment. Objects like lamps, chairs, plants, and clothing are scattered like fallen soldiers everywhere, but mainly in the bedroom. A tremendous struggle must have taken place here. I give Czar some water and find some food for him, and he's quiet now. The super left us alone and went back down to his TV, and that was a wise move on his part. Laszlo is still seething that the super didn't act sooner and check out Melinda's apartment when the dog started barking.

Our work done in the apartment, I leash Czar and we head off to see Melinda's parents. When we arrive at their small colonial about a mile away, the only one there is an elderly man, apparently Melinda's father. The gray-haired man, who seems fit enough in his jeans and gray sweatshirt, is raking the lawn where the snows of winter had melted away. He seems surprised to see these two men walking toward him with a familiar dog.

"What's going on? What's happening?" he asks in a voice crackling with anxiety.

"Mr. Childs?"

"Yes."

"I'm Detective Laszlo and this is Richard Bianchi, who's working with me. We have some bad news to tell you." I wonder how many times Laszlo had a conversation like this one. He proceeds to tell him what we know happened to his daughter.

"I knew something was wrong when I saw Czar," says Mr. Childs. "Nancy, my wife, isn't here now. She's working today."

"Would you mind if we asked you a few questions?" says Laszlo.

"No, not at all, but I'd like to call my wife and go to the hospital as soon as possible."

"I understand. When was the last time you talked with Melinda?"

"Last night. She called us about seven o'clock."

"How did she sound? Did you pick up anything different in her voice?"

"No. Obviously, she was tired. She works hard, and she's always on the run."

"Has she been having trouble with anyone lately?"

"No, not that I'm aware of, and I know my girl. Melinda lives a pretty simple, basic life focused around Nancy and me, her dog, and her job, which, I understand, she loves."

"Did she ever mention someone named Eddie Dvorak?"

"Oh, yes, she's mentioned him many times. They work together. They're good friends. Poor guy! I hope they find him."

"We're working on it. If you or Nancy remember something that might be of interest to us, call me. Here's my card. Thanks for your time."

I hand him the leash. He leans over and gives the dog a big hug, and the animal returns the greeting with a generous lick on Mr. Childs' cheeks. The old man seems like a real gentleman, which says something about the kind of person Melinda is, or was.

Chapter 20

On the way home, I can't stop thinking of Melinda Childs. *Who could have done such a terrible thing to that lovely, caring woman? Why? Was what happened to her tied in any way to Eddie's abduction? If so, how? What would have happened to Melinda if we didn't go to her apartment when we did?* I think I know the answer to that one.

The bright sun is pouring through the windshield, suddenly brightening my spirits. I turn to Detective Laszlo and ask him with a smile, "Maybe we should head down to the Shore."

"Yeah, sure, that would be fun, but I forgot my suntan lotion."

"I'll lend you mine."

"Okay," he says with a snicker. Then, quickly changing his tone, he asks, ""Hey, do you think what happened to Melinda is connected to Eddie's abduction?"

"I was wondering about that myself. Yes, I think so, but I don't know how. They're friends, work buddies, but they live separate lives."

"That's true," he says, "but she had personal information about him no one else had. He was obviously very worried lately and he told her his life was in danger."

"Yes, he felt close enough to her to tell her that."

"Another thing," he says. "She seemed really nervous at lunch the other day. Like she was telling us things she shouldn't be. I mean, what was she so worried about?"

"And what about when she saw that supplier, Mr. Cartwright? She really got tense." "What was it she said? She doesn't like to share what she does in private with the whole office?"

"Yeah, she said that. But, you know what, a lot of people feel that way."

"Hmm."

At home, I've got to get busy. I need to unload a couple of more boxes and place their contents away in order to stop worrying about Melinda. At least, she's in good hands now. Later, I break for something to eat, I check my e-mail, I watch the news on TV. Finally, I put on my jacket and walk over to Dana's house.

Grandpa is stretched out on the recliner, napping with the *Daily News* across his chest, while Dana is on the sofa doing her homework. On the coffee table in front of her is a pile of old photo albums she had taken out to show Tess, but never had the chance to go through them all. I don't know whether I should say anything about Melinda for fear it would upset them. I decide not to say anything about that now.

"Did you have a good time with Tess?" I ask.

"Oh, yeah. She's a lot of fun."

"Too bad she didn't bring Simon with her."

"She showed me pictures. He's so cute."

"Did Grandpa like the spaghetti and meatballs."

"Are you kidding? I think he's dreaming about them now."

The doorbell rings, forcing Yank to respond with a couple of barks that awaken Grandpa. I open the door. There's a woman standing there with a suitcase in one hand and a carry-on in the other. At the curb, a taxi cab is pulling away.

I can't believe it. "Oh, my God, it's you, Elsie. What a surprise. What a wonderful surprise." I give her a big hug. "I'm so glad you changed your mind. Come on in." I grab her bags.

"Thanks, Richie. I spoke to my boss, and she gave me as much time as I need, and Alex's mom is watching the two kids."

She reaches down and gently pets Yank. "I didn't know Dana had a dog."

"Actually, it's Grandpa's."

Dana is standing a few feet away, frozen, apparently not sure what to do or say. Elsie walks over to her and gently folds her arms around her, and Dana gingerly returns the hug. Both have tears in their eyes

"Wow, let me look at you," says Elsie. "You're beautiful."

"So are you," Dana says.

"And you've grown taller since I last saw you. I hear you're playing in a big hockey tournament now. How are you doing?"

"We're in the finals," she says flatly.

"That's wonderful."

"Yeah, but…" Dana shrugs, lopping her thought. Obviously, playing hockey in the championship series is not the most important thing on her mind right now.

"I know," says Elsie. "This must be hard for you."

Grandpa rubs his eyes, as if he can't believe Elsie is here. "Remember me?" he says.

"Sure do. My old buddy."

"C'mere and give me a hug. You're still as lovely as ever. How are the kiddies?"

"Oh, they're fine. Alexander's the baby, and Francisco, his big brother, is two years old," she says with a proud smile.

"How's… umm… excuse me, your husband?"

"The other Alex is doing well. Working hard."

"And how's Florida these days?"

"Perfect, not too hot, not too cold."

"Just like me," Grandpa says.

The laughter that follows is welcome in this house of pain.

I'm privileged to have a front-row seat to this family reunion. Dana and Elsie are like old friends who haven't seen each other in years. Dana doesn't show any smoldering animosity. Nor do I sense any feelings of guilt coming from Elsie. Can anyone accept or place blame for what happened? I think not. In my experience working with addicted adults and teens, the devil is in the disease itself, and it takes a long time, sometime years, for both the addicted and non-addicted to come to that realization. It's amazing Dana is so understanding of her mom's battle with addiction.

Something else is bringing mother and daughter together. It's the shared experience of having a father and former husband violently taken away from his family. Right now, they're not sure they'll ever see him again, and it hurts both of them—yes, Elsie as well. She must have many precious memories she shared with Eddie.

Sitting in the living room, Elsie asks a lot of questions about what happened, and we bring her up to date on what we know, including the events surrounding the actual abduction, the people we interviewed, the stranger at the ice rink, and the videos. When Dana decides to show her mom the latest video, she's struck by how different Eddie looks. "I realize that's Eddie, but that's not him," Elsie says. "It doesn't even sound like him. Something's missing. Are you pleased with the way the police are handling the investigation?"

The nods signal general approval with how it's going.

But Grandpa adds, "I like Laszlo. I think he's working hard, and he keeps us informed. But I'd like to see more action. I think we should have had an arrest by now."

I challenge that idea. "I've been tagging along with Detective Laszlo on several interrogations. It's not that easy. Something about this case. It's different, bigger, than, say, a simple ransom case. I don't think money or some kind of treasure is involved."

"What do you think is involved? Why was he taken?" Elsie asks.

"I don't know...yet. I can't tell you what the people we interviewed said, but I think we're starting to draw some conclusions."

"Conclusions are nice," says Grandpa, "but I'd feel a lot better if the police started taking some action, you know, made some arrests and asked some tough questions."

"Oh, Grandpa!" says Dana. "Don't you think the police would like to do that?"

"I don't know what they'd like to do, honey. I know what I'd do."

"What's that?"

"I'd search every nook and cranny for anyone with an axe to grind with my Eddie and wring the truth out of them until someone confessed."

"Don't you think that's a little harsh, Grandpa?"

"No. Absolutely not. That's my son someone stole."

"And that's my dad."

"Yeah, I know," says Grandpa in a more commiserating tone. He glances up at the magnificent ship on the shelf and shakes his head in frustration.

"I remember when he started building that model," says Elsie, shifting the conversation. "But tell me, now that I'm here, what can I do to make life easier for you guys?"

No one replies at first. Then Dana says quietly, "Just be my mom."

"I'd like that," says Elsie. "For starters, maybe we could look through those photo albums on the table there sometime. I need a refresher."

Obviously, it's good for Elsie to be with her daughter, but how long can this Floridian mother of two stay here? The search for Eddie may take weeks, months, even years.

Oh, shut up, Richie. One day at a time.

Chapter 21

The Finals— Ice Storm vs. Owls: It's a little less than an hour before the start of Game One of the championship series, and Owls are everywhere. Some are perched on the porch of the Dvorak house. Others are clustered in twos and threes in the driveway. A few are hanging out on the lawn.

Inside the house, Coach Fenda and two of Dana's teammates, Hugo and Ernie, are trying to persuade Dana to play in the first game of the two-out-of-three series with the dreaded and talented New York Ice Storm. The coach lays out three reasons why she should play: Dana is the best player on the team, drawing nods of agreement from both Ernie and Hugo; her teammates are counting on her; and a lot of people are pulling for the team to win.

"I can't, I don't think it's right," says Dana, sitting on the sofa between Grandpa and her mom. "Someone comes, beats up my dad, and takes him away. Why? I don't know what they're going to do to him, and, like, you want me to play a stupid hockey game."

"You're right. It's only a hockey game," the coach responds, "but it's not a stupid hockey game. It's important to our town, it's important to the area. But mostly it means a lot to the players. For some of them, this is a chance of a lifetime and could help determine their future."

"We need you out there if we want a chance to win," Hugo adds.

"C'mom, Hugo, give yourself more credit."

"Who's going to keep Lenny under control?" Ernie asks.

"Nobody. Lenny's Lenny," Dana says. "You guys better get going if you're planning on playing today."

Coach Fenda walks over to the front window. "Come here, Dana. I want to show you something." She slowly rises and walks over to him.

"Recognize all those guys out there?" he asks. "They're your teammates, and, you're right, they should all be down at the rink getting ready for the game. All of them insisted on coming here with me today. They want you to play, too. I'm asking you one more time. Please, Dana, come join your teammates and play some hockey with us today. Help us get off on the right foot… Just this once. I won't ask you again."

Then a voice not heard from before: "Go get your things and go play the damn game," Grandpa urges her. "Do it for me, your father's father. I know he's not much of a hockey fan, but you won't find a bigger fan of Dana than your dad. And this is your day, Dana. This is your time."

"I think Grandpa has a point, Dana," Elsie adds, "and I'd love to see you play. But this is your choice, honey. I think we're all with you whatever you decide."

The nods all around showed they agreed with Elsie.

The game is about to start, and the noise level is incredible, thanks mainly to the Owls fans. On hand, front and center, is Mayor Midge Larkin, proof of the importance of the game to the town and to his political career. In a pre-game interview with the cable TV team covering the games, he announced he made a bet with his counterpart in New York State: The mayor with the losing team would sing, record and distribute a karaoke song for charity. Other local celebs on hand for the big game include Renee Latour, ex-beauty contestant and pilates body instructor, and Josh Cimmaron, one-time junior hockey coach and an original Owl. Phyllis Gurth, a popular librarian in town, was asked to sing the national anthem, and she rocks the ice rink with her rendition. As the teams line up for the opening faceoff, the Ice Storm players are bigger and more imposing than the Owls, conveying an aura of confidence and dominance in their gray and white uniforms and shiny black skates. The Owls, in their familiar orange and black jerseys, come in different sizes and shapes, a spirited bunch that plays as much with their hearts as with their sticks. They are definitely the underdogs in this series.

Before the puck is dropped, Dana steals a glance at her opposite winger, Mario Cane. His teammates call him "The Dog" because, on the ice, he's as a ferocious as a pit bull. An exceptional skater with weightlifter legs hidden behind pads, he's known for his fast breaks into the opposing zone and his heavy shot. Dana feels helpless as he peels away from her and picks up a pass from his center and plows toward the Owls goalie. Less than fifteen feet from the net, he slaps the puck past Matteo.

Score: Ice Storm, 1, Owls, 0.

The crowd, or at least the Owls fan base, is stunned. What a comedown from the pre-game hype, and the game is not even two minutes old.

As Dana, Ernie and Hugo skate off the ice for a line change, Hugo turns to Dana and says, "Did you see that?"

"No, not really," says Dana.

"Somebody's got to stay with that guy," Ernie bellows.

"That's not a bad idea," Dana calmly responds, "but let's win the faceoff first."

The Ice Storm sends in its second line, with another of its star players, a lanky center called Percy McBride, whose father owns a tools company upstate. He wins the faceoff and immediately shoots the puck behind the Owls net and gives chase. With deceptive quickness, he beats everyone to the puck and passes it to one of his forwards streaking toward the net. He taps it past Matteo, who doesn't stand a chance.

Score: Ice Storm, 2, Owls, 0.

Before the first period comes to an end, the Ice Storm almost score again, but Matteo makes a couple of outstanding saves. No doubt, the early goals hurt, but the Owls are beginning to find their legs and are skating better, something that doesn't go unnoticed with Coach Fenda.

"Keep it up, keep going," he tells the team later in the locker room. "Look, guys, their skates didn't cost more than yours, and I notice they don't have better sticks. You can play with these guys. Believe it. Don't quit."

The Owls manage to play the Ice Storm evenly for most of the second period, thanks to the continued strong play of their goalie. Their only glaring mistake is a four-minute high sticking penalty by one of the Owls forwards, Leroy Campbell, near the end of the period. Leroy recently moved to New Jersey from Toronto, Canada. A hardworking player, he's yet to score a goal and is devastated when he draws a major penalty for accidentally clipping an Ice Storm defender.

There's a ferocity to the Ice Storm's game now that the Owls did not see before. They're shooting from all angles. They're crashing the net. They're hitting anyone in their way. And the Owls are responding by blocking shots, giving and taking hits, and keeping their heads. Matteo is stronger than ever. The buzzer sounds, and the period is over. Finally.

Dana glances over her shoulder into the stands as she heads off the ice for the break. She has this odd feeling. *Could that stranger with the video be lurking somewhere around the rink?*

"Are you expecting someone?" Hugo asks.

"No," she says, slightly embarrassed.

"Grandpa's behind the bench."

"I know," she says, quickly adding, "Listen, we've got to get some more shots. They're all over me."

"I'll try to get into the clear for a pass."

"Okay."

After some quiet time and a short pep talk, the Owls return to the ice, a little more confident. While they feel good about holding the Ice Storm scoreless in the second period, they're aware they still have a big hill to climb. Before the third period starts, Coach Fenda decides to shake up the line combinations. He puts Leroy on the line with Dana and Hugo and moves Ernie to the line with Lenny and Titus.

Once again, the Ice Storm force the play early, but the Owls withstand the pressure. In one sequence, after Matteo makes a tremendous save, Titus picks up the rebound and, with lightning speed, skates past two Ice Storm defensemen. He can't believe there's room. He sees an opening. He shoots.

Score: Owls, 1, Ice Storm, 2.

Titus is congratulated by the players as if he just scored the winning goal, but Coach Fenda is a little more subdued. "Good work, Titus," he says. "Keep it going, guys!"

A few shifts later, Dana, Hugo and Leroy jump on the ice, energized by the deafening cheers of Owls fans after the Titus goal. When the puck springs loose during a clash of warriors at center ice, Hugo picks it up and sends it skidding behind the Ice Storm net. Using her exceptional speed, Dana pursues the puck and catches up with it as it's coming out from behind the net. Leroy, in the slot in front of the goalie, taps his stick on the ice. He wants the puck. After making two lightening moves, Dana passes the puck to Leroy, who slaps it past the goalie's shoulder.

Score: Owls, 2, Ice Storm, 2.

The Ice Storm coach calls a time-out, obviously to help his team regain its composure. When play resumes, the action moves quickly from one end of the ice to the other, each team taking turns to go on the attack.

Two minutes to play. Now ninety seconds. With less than a minute to go, Dana is holding the puck and skating in a wide circle in front of the Ice Storm net. Time's running out. There's a narrow opening, and with 3.2 seconds left on the clock she shoots the puck.

Score: Owls, 3, Ice Storm, 2.

On that score, the first game of the championship series ends. With the cheers of her teammates and fans, including her mom and Grandpa, ringing in her ears, Dana is enjoying the moment. Still, she can't help stealing an anxious glance into the stands for a man in an Army fatigue jacket.

Chapter 22

The following day, Grandpa is getting ready to return to the Bronx to catch up with his friends and neighbors. Elsie and Dana are settled down for some quiet time together. I think this is an ideal time to spend a couple of hours off on my own someplace. It would be like I'd be going on a short retreat, only without the talks and seminars.

As I pull away in my Passat, I glance back at Dana's house. I'm sure she's excited about having some one-on-one time with her mom.

It's another spring-like day, and the sun feels warm and comforting. New life is sprouting up everywhere. Where should I go? The thought occurs to me— Don't ask me why or how? Maybe, it was something I saw on TV. I've never visited the Statue of Liberty. That's not unusual for anyone growing up in the metro New York area. I sometimes think tourists are the biggest supporters of our most treasured attractions. Thank God for out-of-towners!

I turn on the radio, which is pre-set to a news station that satisfies some of my curiosity about what's happening in the world, and this story coms on:

Two women were abducted after terrorists invaded an office building in Berlin and killed a prominent business executive. Police are looking for a green van which is believed to be holding the hostages and heading East. The slain business executive was the leader of a group calling for limitations on immigration to Germany.

A little later, there's this news over the same news station:

BREAKAWAY

For the fourth straight day, Belgium police forces are fighting terrorist cells operating throughout the country. The terrorists were believed to be planning another major strike in neighboring France...

I change stations, but the news has a familiar ring.

Machine guns were on display on Broadway as police and home security officials combed the area in search of a terrorist who announced plans on social media to blow up an undisclosed building along the Great White Way...

I switch to a public talk radio station on my "Favorites" list. It's in the middle of a discussion of another type of terrorist attack.

Host: *"'So what are you saying, that we spend too much time worrying about attacks from foreign sources when we should be focusing more on domestic threats?"*

Guest: *"The threat from foreign extremist terrorists is real, and we can't take our eyes off of it. At the same time, we can't overlook the hundreds of anti-government groups and militias, based here in the U.S.A, some known, some without names. These groups are not necessarily engaged in violent or criminal activities, and some are supported by political leaders in their areas. But let's be clear about this: Some are capable of inflicting terrible harm, as was done in Oklahoma City..."*

I let the program run its course. I can't believe there are so many active anti-government groups in the U.S.—a total of 998 in 2015, including 276 with militias, according to the Southern Poverty Law Center. The total number of anti-government groups has fluctuated wildly in the past couple of decades, but it's still considerable compared to the 149 anti-government groups in 2008. A couple of other trends catch my attention: More people with strong anti-government views are turning to cyberspace to express their views, and instances of lone-wolf attacks are on the upswing.

I finally arrive at Liberty State Park in New Jersey, where I buy the fare for the next ferry to Liberty Island and the Statue of Liberty. Across the Hudson is the famous skyline of my old home town. My eyes drift to lower Manhattan and the majestic new One World Trade Center building towering, they say, higher than any other structure in the Western Hemisphere. The entire World Trade Center complex, but especially the Memorial, is a fitting tribute to all the people who lost their lives on 9/11. I remember that day like it was yesterday, when four planes hijacked by terrorists changed the way Americans live and view the world.

After a short ferry trip that was over before I finished my diet cola, I arrive on Liberty Island at the foot of the magnificent statue of the lady with the torch. Security is high, and it's evident everywhere as watchful and friendly National Park Rangers patrol the grounds.

Actually, security begins before one steps onto the island. It starts with a screening when a visitor boards the ferry. A second screening is carried out at the entrance to the monument for those holding reservations to the Crown and Pedestal areas. Among the items not allowed on the island—besides weapons, of course—are sharp instruments, tools, suitcases and other large parcels and packages, and, believe it or not, facemasks and costumes that could conceal one's identity. Anything surrendered is retained by U.S. Park Police and not returned.

Yes, the world has changed since 9/11, but I think the lady in the harbor is as beautiful and welcoming as ever. She makes the trip to see her worthwhile despite the inconveniences that are now part of our lives. I stare up long and hard at Lady Liberty. I think of the millions of immigrants, like my father's parents, who sailed across the sea and observed the stature for the first time. What were they thinking? Did their hearts feel her grace and hospitality after a long, rough journey? Did she make the trip worthwhile for them?

BREAKAWAY

Driving home, I feel a little richer and wiser for my trip. Do I now have answers to the problems I had before I left, especially as they relate to the abduction of Eddie Dvorak? Maybe. I have some ideas, and I'm anxious to share them with Detective Laszlo.

Chapter 23

Later that day, after my excursion, I dial the first person on my to-call list. "Oh, hi. Richie here. How's everything?" I inquire after Elsie answers the phone.

"Everything's good. Quiet. No news, except Grandpa went home," she replies. "We were getting a little worried about you. Haven't heard from you all day."

"I went to see a lady."

"Oh, you mean Tess? Dana told me all about her."

I chuckle. "No. I went to see the lady in the harbor, the Statue of Liberty. Something I never did before."

"I've never been there, either. Good for you. How was she?"

"Magnificent."

"Are you hungry? We made some shrimp creole."

"Mmm, maybe later. I got to make a couple of calls."

"You alright?"

"I'm fine. A little tired. Did Detective Laszlo call?"

"No."

"Did you and Dana have a good day?"

"Boy, did we! First, we went to the mall, where we had lunch and bought a few things. Then we did some shopping in the supermarket. We even had time to bring Eddie's truck in for an oil change."

"Sounds like you guys had a busy day."

"Actually, I'm so glad I decided to spend some time with my daughter. She's such a bright girl, and fun. I can't wait to see what we do tomorrow."

Tess, too, says she was worried when she didn't hear from me, and she tried calling me several times. I tell her where I went, adding that I decided to travel "incognito," with my phone turned off to the world.

"Do you do that often?" she asks with teasing curiosity.

"No. I never did it before, and I'll probably never do it again. I needed some time to think."

"And did you think some good thoughts?"

"Yes…maybe."

"Want to talk about them?"

"Not now. What are you doing tomorrow night?"

"After I feed and bathe my child, post my bills, and write my novel, nothing."

"Good, I'll see you tomorrow. I'll bring some Chinese. Oh, by the way, you made a great friend in Dana."

"She's a sweetheart."

"So are you…and she's spending some time with another sweetheart, her mom."

"Oh, she came! That's wonderful. When? For how long? Why didn't you tell me?"

"She arrived yesterday. I don't know how long she's staying, probably a few days. I didn't tell you because I was away, trying to figure out who stole Eddie Dvorak. I'll tell you all about it tomorrow."

The call to Laszlo begins pretty much like the others. "Where've you been?" he asks. "I've been trying to reach you."

After I explain where I went, I ask him whether there are any new developments.

"I paid a visit to Melinda in the hospital," he replies. "The medical staff is not too optimistic. She's remains in a coma, and her chances of coming out of it soon are still iffy. She took a pretty vicious beating. It looks like she put up a brave fight for her life, but the attacker must have surprised her and probably used both a blunt instrument and fists. I talked to her mother, and she told me that Melinda dated a guy named Raymond Loesch a couple of times. So I contacted Mr. Loesch—I got his name from a phone directory I picked up in Melinda's apartment—and he said they were just friends, and they met in school. More important, he just returned this morning from a long trip to his sister's place in Arizona, and he said he hasn't talked to Melinda in over a year."

"So I guess that's that," I say, sighing. "Is there somewhere we can talk?"

"There's a diner on Route 17, near Mahwah."

"I think I passed it. Meet you there."

Later, in a quiet booth at the diner, I unload my idea. "Okay, this is not the theory of relativity," I begin, "but here's a theory on what may be behind the Eddie Dvorak abduction. As you pointed out early on, this doesn't smell like a ransom or kidnapping case. I think we both can agree this isn't an alien or family abduction. And it doesn't exactly feel like an act of terrorism. Don't you think we would have heard from the terrorists by now? So what is it? No one we spoke to seems overly concerned about Eddie—he'll be alright, he just needs some time to recharge his batteries. Only one person was worried, Melinda, and we know what happened to her. Another thing we kept hearing from several people we interviewed: Eddie has strong feelings against the government. On my way to see the Statue of Liberty, I was listening to the radio, and an idea began to take shape."

"Oh, oh, here it comes."

"No, no, hear me out. This is interesting," I continue. "Speaking of conspiracy, I think Eddie is, or was, part of one, an anti-government group, one of hundreds in the country. I don't know if it has a name, but, if it's anything like the others, it's strongly opposed to the current world order and believes it can dramatically change the way the government is run. Some of these groups even have militias. I'm not sure why, whether it's for fun and games or to accomplish their goals by force."

"So how does Eddie's abduction fit in?"

"I'm not sure. That's the big question. And if he's a member of such a group, why would they whisk him away in the middle of the night?"

"Because he did something they didn't like," Laszlo contends.

"That makes sense."

Laszlo pulls on his chin with his hand. After taking a sip of coffee, he says, "I think it's time for another trip to the trucking company. How's seven-thirty tomorrow morning for you?"

"See you then."

Chapter 24

Next day, as we're about to enter the trucking firm's headquarters, Detective Laszlo spots Waldo Cameron in the parking lot. Waldo, who looked nervous when we first interviewed him, seems to be in a big hurry today.

"Let's nail him for a short talk," says Laszlo.

"Hey, Waldo! Waldo!" I shout.

He turns, waves slightly, but keeps on walking away.

"Wait up!"

He stops, mumbling something under his breath.

"Whew, what's the hurry?" says Laszlo, slightly out of breath.

"Busy, very busy. Got to pick up some tools now."

"Have you heard from Eddie?"

"No," he says sheepishly. "Why would he call me?"

"Because you're his friend," says Laszlo.

"Yes, that's true. I'm his friend, but no, he didn't call me. Like I told you, he's probably off somewhere, alone, dealing with some personal issues."

Laszlo says nothing at first. He just stands there, eye to eye with Waldo. Finally, the detective says, "We understand you're a member of an organization that's opposed to the government and wants to change it."

"WHAT?" says the tall, lanky mechanic, his eyes wide open. "I don't know what you're talking about. I don't know nothing about an organization like that."

"What about Eddie? Does he belong to an anti-government group?"

"I don't know. That's his business. You should ask him when he comes out of hiding."

"Waldo, please. We're trying to help your pal before anything bad happens to him. Please tell us where he is," I say.

He's pale and trembling slightly now. "Look," he says, "I'm just a working stiff here trying to make a living for my family. Talk to Mr. Jackson."

Laszlo hands him his card. "In case you remember something you think we'd be interested in knowing."

Wendell Jackson is a little less friendly than he was the first time we met him. Perhaps annoyed is a better description. "If you don't mind, let's make this quick," he says, impeccable in his white designer shirt and crimson tie, "There's a big ship coming in from Greece."

"Sure," says Laszlo. "Are you part of an anti-government group?"

He does a barely perceptible double take, and his response is brief. "Come again."

"I guess what I'm trying to say is, Are you a member of an organization that holds some strong views about how the federal government is being run these days?"

"Oh, that! Never said I wasn't. What's the big deal? People who share some common views like to get together from time to time, and maybe when they get together they talk and have some fun."

"How often do you meet?"

"It varies...when the spirit moves us."

"Does the organization have a name?"

"Gosh, no," he snickers.

"Do you have a militia?"

"A MILITIA? Oh, God, no. We may go hunting in the woods on occasion."

"Where's that?"

"Usually upstate New York, in the Adirondacks. Say, what's this all about, detective?" he remarks peevishly.

"Just routine questioning."

"But what's it have to do with the Eddie Dvorak case?"

"Probably nothing, unless, of course, his abduction is tied to an anti-government organization you might know something about."

I close my eyes, waiting for the explosion.

"I don't know what you're trying to insinuate, Detective Laszlo. Like I've told you before, Eddie is a good guy, and I like Eddie and I'd like Eddie whether we share the same views or not. So, we happen to share the same views in some areas. So what? And we happen to get together for some fun and games and talk a little politics from time to time. So what? Lots of folks do that. I don't care if you call it an anti-government group or a bunch of people who like to talk politics. We like each other and happen to be looking for a good time together. We're also honest to goodness citizens, and if we can also make a difference in this country, that's fine, too. Understood? We're not looking for trouble, sir."

"I didn't say you were, Mr. Jackson. One more question, and we're out of here: How many people in this gathering of like-minded folks?"

He blows out a stream of frustration. "Oh, I don't know. It varies, depending on who's doing what. Less than a dozen, for sure."

"Thanks for your time, Mr. Jackson. Anything to add, Richie?"

"I was wondering. What's the latest on Melinda Childs' status?"

Another subtle double take, along with a sweaty brow. "Terrible thing what happened to her."

"Last we heard she was in a coma in the hospital ICU."

"No change," he says, shaking his head. "What a terrible thing."

"Sorry to hear that, Mr. Jackson. We had lunch with her a few days ago."

"So I heard."

I turn to Laszlo in the car as we head home. "Imagine that. He heard about our lunch date with Melinda."

"I bet he did," says Laszlo, taking a puff on a cigar. "Here's one of his trusted employees secretly meeting with a detective and his associate, and it's witnessed by Mr. Cartwright, the snitch. We didn't learn much about the whereabouts of Eddie Dvorak, but I think we hit a nerve with Mr. Jackson today."

"Boy, did we ever! 'Me, a part of an anti-government organization? We're just a small group of like-minded people who get together from time to time, who happen to dislike some of the things the government is doing, and who would like to make a difference in this country if we can.'"

"I have to trust my instincts here. When he said his little group of like-minded folk is not looking for trouble that worries me."

"Yeah, it make me wonder. What are they planning?"

Chapter 25

The Foothills of the Adirondacks: As the senior vice-president of a trucking company, fifty-six-year-old Wendell Jackson does well for himself. But the truth is he doesn't need the job, thanks to his profitable real estate and stock holdings.

His most prized possession, more so for personal than business reasons, is a mansion that's stood guard over the beautiful lakes and valleys in the foothills of the Adirondack Mountains for more than ninety years.

As a youth growing up in the mansion, Wendell heard the stories of how his ancestors cleared the grounds, laid the foundation, and built the venerable house and accompanying structures. The stories usually begin with Louis Jackson, Wendell's grandfather, who bought a piece of land in the lower Adirondacks after returning from World War I and slowly, with the aid of his family, began building on it. Part of the first structure, a log cabin, can still be seen on a pathway leading into the nearby heavily wooded area.

At first, the mansion was used exclusively by Louis and his wife Mary for a growing family. In time, as most of the children got older and moved out and after Louis and his wife died, it became the sole possession of Wendell's father, Foster Jackson He eventually married and raised his own family on the property.

Over the years, members of the other Jackson families kept returning to the mansion for vacations and holidays, and for a while Foster opened the place to outsiders, but that didn't last long. A demanding man with strict principles, he couldn't tolerate any misbehavior or raucous nonsense from visitors.

Throughout the years, but especially during the height of its popularity, the mansion had a lot going for it. It was a magnet for anyone looking for a little peace and quiet, like taking a stroll through the woods, reading a book by the swimming pool, or tossing a fishing line in one of the many nearby lakes. The mansion was also the jumping off point for more adventurous pursuits like hunting, jogging, ice-skating, skiing, or boating in the Hudson. For other thrill-seekers, it served as the transportation hub for anyone needing a ride to Saratoga Racetrack not far away.

The mansion, which never had a name of its own though it cried out for one, now serves a different purpose, as foreshadowed by the thick layers of pine, spruce and oak trees butting up against the sides of the main building. Its decline is evident to neighbors and travelers, but for those using the property now, the mansion and surrounding grounds hold a new, sinister purpose.

Wendell and his wife, Constance, regularly visit the mansion, sometimes inviting friends or co-workers to join them. All the other Jacksons, it seems, have either died, moved away, or built their own getaways, relegating the old mansion to the relics heap.

To Wendell, seeing the aging house lose its luster is sad and depressing. He still remembers the old days when they were begging to get into the place. But those days are gone. In his mind, the old mansion now has a higher, more important purpose, as the planning base for one of the most significant events in the history of our country. *Wait three more days.*

Inside a doomsday shelter built underground, another man has a different view of the nearby mansion and surrounding property. To him, the Jackson estate is pure evil. Abducted and imprisoned in a small compartment of the long metal bunker less than eighty feet from the mansion, Eddie Dvorak bravely holds on but is terrified and desperate, and he feels so helpless.

What keeps Eddie going is the hope he'll someday be freed and reunited with Dana, his strongminded, beautiful teenage daughter. But he's worried. *Who's taking care of my child? Her mother may be able to spend a few days with her, but how long can she stay? I'm sure she'll want to get back to her family in Florida. Forget about the next-door neighbors. One is always calling the cops on me; the other is never home. I hope the priest who moved in across the street will continue to lend a hand. He seems like a decent guy. I should have stayed in touch with my dad. How he loved Dana!*

A rifle slung on his shoulder, a man slides the small viewing panel in the door to one side and tells Eddie to face the wall. The man opens the door and places a food tray on a metal table bolted to the floor. "Eat, you'll need the energy," says Larry Noble.

"Did Jason contact my daughter again?" Eddie asks.

"Is that all you want to know? 'Did Jason contact my daughter again?' Why don't you ask me about the weather or the Yankees or Mets for a change?"

"Well, did he? Did he contact her again?"

"No."

Eddie sighs. "So what's the weather like?"

"Ah, it's lovely out there. Spring is everywhere."

"Do you really think it's going to make a difference?"

Larry's eyes narrow. "What are you talking about, Eddie?"

"I'm talking about the video messages I made under duress and Jason delivered to my daughter: 'Tell the police to back off.' 'I just need a few days to work out some issues.' Do you really think those videos are going to make a difference?"

"All we need is three more days."

"You're crazy, Larry, you and the rest of the group, especially your high and mighty leader. Do you realize what he's trying to make you do?"

"It's the only way we can change what's happening to this country."

"And you'll all kill yourselves in the process."

"If we die, you die, Eddie."

"I'm already dead. Don't you see that?"

Larry shrugs, then reaches into his back pocket. "Here's your magazine. Give me the old one." They trade magazines through the slit. "Believe it or not, we almost had a companion for you in there."

"Who?"

"A girl, no less," he says with a heckling laugh. "Your friend, Melinda Childs."

"Please don't tell me you hurt her…or worse."

"No, she's alive." Then, almost in a whisper, he adds, "barely."

"What did you say?"

"Eat up! Like I said, you'll need your energy." Larry slams the slit shut and walks up the concrete steps to the surface.

Eddie pulls a stool up to the table and looks around. It's a room of bare essentials, including a cot, a sink, and a toilet—all made out of an aluminum alloy of some sort. His captors bring him food twice a day, give him a change of jumpsuits whenever they see fit, and trade magazines with him once a week or so. Eddie stirs the stew with a plastic fork before he snaps the fork in half, gets up, and throws himself on his cot. *Larry's right. I should eat,* Eddie tells himself. *I need the energy, but for what, for when, I don't have a clue. Besides, I can't eat this slop.*

Eddie, a vocal critic of the actions and inactions of the government, had been the leader of the group until recently when Wendell Jackson took control. To a few members of the group, he deserves better than average treatment, even though he never chose to turn his frustrations into violent action, as Wendell wants every member to do.

That's why Eddie is here in this tomb. He refuses to go along with the group's plan under Jackson to assassinate our Congressional leaders—and nothing can make this U.S. Navy veteran change his mind. Not now.

Above ground, Larry joins Ponti, Fergie, Russ, and Jason, who are inside the large shed next to the garage on the western side of the mansion. Time for another munitions check. Ponti, designated by Jackson to be squad leader in charge of munitions, insists on at least one review a day of the weapons and explosives right up to the launch of the attack.

Larry attempts to tell the guys about his conversation with Eddie, but Ponti, a brawny man with the sense of humor of a bowling ball, would have none of it. "Cut the horseshit, Larry," he growls. "We got a lot of work to do here."

"How many times do we have to check this stuff?" asks Larry.

"Don't mock me, man. We'll do it as many times as we need to. And tomorrow we'll review our strategy for the actual attack, all day if necessary, until we get it right. In case you haven't heard, Larry, there's a war coming."

The old mansion at the foothills of the Adirondacks contains many parts, and except for Wendell Jackson and perhaps his wife, no one alive has seen them all.

An enormous oak door serves as the main entrance to the house. It opens to a foyer offering the visitor three choices: A large dining room on the left, a staircase leading to the upstairs rooms, and an expansive living room on the right. A fully equipped, modernized kitchen, breakfast area, pantry, and spare room take up the rear of the main floor.

On the second floor, a hallway splitting away from the main staircase leads to the master bedroom and guest rooms, all with tall casement windows and most with baths. Also on the floor is a sitting parlor for quiet reading and writing.

On the top floor, a sprawling, wooden attic holds odd pieces of furniture along with other treasures from the past such as china, tools, clothing, sculptures, and paintings—dream pickings for anyone with an eye for valuable, old things.

As Ponti pointed out yesterday, this is an important day for the group. Commander Jackson will be reviewing the strategy for the attack on the convention center.

The main gathering place for the meeting is the basement, a huge cavernous area with a ceiling almost as tall as those found in the upstairs rooms. The center of attraction is a magnificent fireplace lining the back wall. The fireplace, constructed of beautiful, large rounded rocks that look like they were harvested from the ocean, rises high and wide over the room like a cathedral altar.

The eyes of those seated in the basement this morning are trained on Wendell Jackson, who's looking over some papers at a lectern in front of the fireplace. Seated in an easy chair next to him, his wife Constance checks over the agenda one more time. Everyone is waiting for the arrival of the last two "warriors", as Wendell prefers to call the group members.

Finally, Waldo Cameron arrives. After making apologies for his lateness, he takes the first empty chair he spots. Wendell raises his head from the papers and, arms crossed, gives Waldo the once-over. He wonders how the young man will handle himself in combat. He always looks so worried and nervous.

"Welcome, Waldo," says Wendell. "Any trouble getting here?"

"No, sir. Sorry I'm late."

"How's the family?"

"They're good."

"Did you sign all those papers I gave you?"

"Yes."

"Please leave them with Constance. Make yourself comfortable. There's coffee and sweet rolls on the side table. Help yourself."

"Thank you."

Wendell turns to Constance and whispers, "I hope he appreciates what we're doing for his family."

She shrugs her shoulders.

The last of the warriors arrives. While Mildred Jordan will not be part of the attack squad, she will be working with Constance at "headquarters"—the mansion—on "coordination and communication issues," as Wendell laid out.

Mildred is a late bloomer in the group. She became a member while attending several meetings with Eddie Dvorak, her boyfriend at the time. Even as she and Eddie began drifting apart, she continued to go to meetings. When Wendell sought her help in covering up Eddie's abduction, she obliged without any reservations. She had become attracted to Wendell as he stepped into the top leadership role. "Tell them he went away to work out some issues," he told her. "Embellish if you like. We can't have Eddie walking around, revealing our business. Right?"

"Good morning, Mildred," says Wendell as she takes a seat. "Get comfortable. Have some coffee. I think we can begin now."

For the next two hours, he outlines the plan for the attack on the conference center near Lake George where the leaders of Congress are about to meet. Ironically, the conference is designed to break the roadblocks to solving hotly debated issues such as immigration, gun control, and health care. It's ironic because the reason Jackson's group is shifting into a more violent mode is the unwillingness to work together in Washington, D.C. Obviously, Jackson and his group don't think the conference will accomplish much, if anything.

Wendell presses a remote, and a screen slides down from the ceiling. "Thanks to Dimitri Cooper here, we have some new photos of the conference center. As you're all aware, Dimi is a waiter at the center. Let's give him a hand for his bravery in taking these pictures."

After acknowledging Dimitri, Wendell clearly and slowly takes the group on a pictorial excursion of the conference center. The center is conveniently situated less than ten miles from the mansion—a major reason why Wendell could not pass up this long-awaited opportunity to unleash his bold plan of attack. He pays particular attention to the breakfast room, where the leaders will be gathered on their first day.

"Remember, no one fires a shot until we get word from Dimi that everyone is present and seated for breakfast."

Mildred raises her hand. "Suppose someone takes ill and doesn't go to the breakfast room?"

Constance mumbles something conveying her annoyance with the question.

Wendell ignores his wife and says in a mild, controlled way, "How likely is that to happen, Mildred? But if that happens, I'll give you the nod when to go. We'll all have transmitters and receivers."

"Gotcha, Wendell...I mean, commander,"

He continues, "I'm sure you all understand our mission. It's to take out our so-called government leaders before they can do any more damage to the country. In a moment, I'll show you recent photos of those leaders. I want you to remember—and never forget—what they look like. After all, they are our targets. Right?"

"RIGHT!

"We'll have an assortment of weapons to carry out our mission, including assault rifles, small arms, and grenades. After four weeks of training camp, you should all know your assignments inside out. Remember, absolute secrecy is crucial to the success of our mission. Any questions?"

Silence in the room.

"Good. You'll each find a small duffel bag under your chair. It contains a bullet proof vest, headgear, goggles, canteen, Tylenol, eye drops, and a few other things. They're yours to take home with you when this is all over. Larry and Jason, would you please see me up front? The rest of you, get up and stretch, if you like, but stick around. There's a surprise for you coming up."

Constance turns to Wendell and, with a concern that magnifies the wrinkles around her eyes, says, "Are you sure you want to do this?"

"Yes," he replies decisively.

There's an audible gasp when Eddie Dvorak is led into the basement about ten minutes later. Most of the group members have not seen their one-time leader in weeks. His hands cuffed behind his back and his ankles shackled, Eddie looks pale and shaky in a black jumpsuit that's obviously too big for him. He stares straight ahead with bloodshot eyes as he's led to stand next to Wendell.

"Hi, Eddie," says Wendell, looking neat and comfortable in a light-blue blazer and open-collared tan shirt. "Would you like a chair?"

Eddie shakes his head. Raising his voice to a level where it begins to crack, he says, "I'd like to go home...now. You have no right to hold me prisoner."

"There's good reason to retain you, and you know what that is," Wendell says confidently. "But I have a proposition for you. Join us in the fight, and you can go home to your beautiful daughter."

"Never."

"Okay, what do you want to do?" says Wendell, standing akimbo. "Do you want to do nothing as our so-called leaders in Congress continue to promote their special interests over the real needs of the people?"

"No. I've given it a lot of thought."

"You have?" says Wendell, a smug tone in his voice. "Tell us what you've concluded."

Constance shoots a disbelieving look at her husband.

"Violence is not the answer," Eddie says. "I love this country too much to see it torn apart by the destructive actions of a few. This is a unique country founded on sound principles of freedom, equality and the right of people to disagree. Too many brave men and women have limped home with torn bodies and minds they received trying to preserve those principles. There's got to be a better way to get our country back on course without killing our leaders. And, yes, they are our leaders, for good or for bad. We voted them into office. We can vote them out of office. Think what you're about to do."

A hush engulfs the group. Are those tears in Waldo Cameron's eyes. Larry seems bewildered. Constance is shaking her head with this I-told-you-so look on her face. A sardonic grin crosses the face of Dimitri, a giant of a man who, at Wendell's order, had smacked Melinda Childs around—probably harder than he should have once she began fighting back—to keep her in line after she spoke to Detective Laszlo and Richie Bianchi at a restaurant.

"Beautiful words," says Jackson.. "But only sticks and stones and guns can make the difference. Don't you think so, guys?"

Wild applause.

"See, they agree with me," says Jackson, wearing a victorious smile.

Eddie clears his throat. "Tell me something, Wendell," he says, "what's your end game?"

"What do you mean, end game?"

"What are you going to do when this is over…if you survive the attack?"

"I haven't given it much thought?"

"I hear you've already booked plane tickets to your little retreat in the Bahamas?"

Wendell throws darts at Mildred, who decides to search for something on the basement floor, while Constance searches her husband's soul with squinty eyes.

"I haven't made any firm plans," he says almost under his breath.

"What about your surviving warriors? What plans have you made for them?" Eddie asks.

"They're always welcome to stay here at the mansion. It's up to them, whatever they want to do. But enough of this crap. Let me repeat my original question. Will you join us?"

Eddie shakes his head "No! Never!"

"Take this weasel back to his hole in the ground!"

Chapter 26

Wendell Jackson may have his little gatherings of like-minded people to talk politics, as Detective Laszlo and I learned the other day. I'm having a few friends over tonight for no special reason except, perhaps, because my house finally looks like a home. While I'm in the supermarket picking up the makings of a nice, simple dinner, I suddenly hear someone calling my name.

"Richard! Richard Bianchi!" says this paunchy man whose face I can't place. "It's me, Russell Donovan. Remember me? We were in the seminary together."

"Oh, yeah!" The memory of a skinny, scared, ruddy-faced young man gradually takes form in my mind.

"I left after the first year."

"Sure, Russell. We used to eat at the same table, and sometimes we'd walk in the garden and talk. I remember. We had some pretty deep conversations."

"We did. We had such high hopes and dreams. What about you? I figure you're assigned to a parish somewhere in the city now."

"I was, until about two months ago. I've taken a leave of absence. I'm not sure I want to continue my active ministry."

"Oh. That's got to be tough after all these years."

I agree with a nod.

He continues. "I wish I could give you some advice about lay life. The only thing I can tell you is that it's got its highs and its lows. Right now, I'm in one of those lows. I'm out of work, and I have a wife and three kids. My wife Sissy is working in Macy's, thank God. Sometimes I ask myself, usually late at night when I'm lying in bed, whether I made the right move leaving the seminary. You know what? All in all, it was the right move for me. I would have been an awful priest."

"Oh, no. You would have been a good one, Russell. You just chose a different way to do God's work."

He laughs. "Thanks for that, Richard."

We talk a little more about getting together soon, exchange phone numbers, and go our separate ways. I don't know about the three kids, but could that be me in a few years?

Dinner at Bianchi's is set to start at five-thirty. Guests include Dana and her mom, Elsie; Tess and little Simon; and Dana's best friends, Hugo and Angie.

Grandpa wanted to come, but he had volunteered to oversee a bingo meeting in his church basement. I also invited Detective Laszlo—nothing fancy, chicken with pasta—but he was attending a security planning meeting for the cavalcade of Congressional leaders headed up to Lake George. His job will be to secure the northern New Jersey leg of the procession as it moves into New York State.

I thought this would be a good time for a party. All the boxes are emptied and their contents put away, my favorite pictures and prints are on the walls, and curtains are hanging in the windows (thanks to some guidance from Tess). All in all, the place looks pretty domesticated, if I may say so.

More important, we need this little time for some R&R. Although we have theories that, sort of, make sense, the investigation is stalled. Dana is feeling low again after spending some enjoyable days with her mom, and I suspect Elsie would like to return to her family in Florida soon.

As we sit around an oak table I recently bought to replace the rickety picnic table I had been using, all eyes are focused on Simon. Watching the toddler eat pasta from a bowl is an unforgettable experience for everyone, especially the teens, who can't stop laughing. There isn't a part of his body he hasn't fed, despite Tess's best efforts to redirect his food to the proper orifice. It's wonderful seeing Dana laughing so heartily. It's a lot easier on the ears than hearing her scream, as she did when Grandpa collapsed.

Later, we gather in the living room. Simon steals the spotlight again by doing somersaults, which are really head-presses on the rug. "That's enough, Simon," says Tess. "You're going to throw up on this lovely rug." When the laughter dies down, he stops the acrobatics and snuggles next to his mom on the sofa and gradually falls asleep.

"Mind if we use your basement, Richie?" Dana asks.

"No, go ahead. Not much down there, except for a couple of old lounge chairs."

"That's perfect. We just want to hear some music," she says, holding up her IPod.

The three teens move to the basement, where they continue their laughter spree and listen to rock. They seem to enjoy each other's company. Hugo is a quiet, pleasant boy who's fond of Dana and vice versa. I remember when I first met wide-eyed Angie. She was so worried about what happened to Mr. Dvorak and the blood on the carpet. She proved to be a good friend when she asked her parents to open their home to Dana.

Tess and Elsie settle into a calm, relaxing conversation, while I listen in. Tess answers Elsie's questions about what it's like raising a toddler in New York City—"Thank God for grandparents and taxis"—and Elsie offers some insights about bringing up two little ones in Florida—"I wish the supermarkets, doctors, and Grandma Mendez were closer, but I don't miss the snow, except around the holidays."

Now I'm the target of interrogation, and the big question: "How are you doing, Richie?" asks Elsie. My stomach does a flip, like it used to when I was called on to prepare a special holiday sermon.

"I'm doing," I stumble along. "Lay life, it's different. I like it, most of the time. I'm getting a whole new perspective on living on my own.

There are some rough spots, but there are the good times, like what we're doing tonight. It's great. Moving was the hardest thing I've done in years, but, as you see, it's coming together, and…"

My phone sounds off.

"Saved by the buzz…It's Detective Laszlo." I get up and continue the phone conversation in the kitchen. "What's going on, detective?"

"Nothing much. Still at the meeting. Did you get any calls tonight?"

"No, not really. Why do you ask?"

"I got a couple of calls in the space of two or three minutes about an hour ago, and all I heard was breathing, and then 'Click', the phone went dead. I tried tracing the calls, but I couldn't get anything."

"Hmm, that's strange. I wonder…"

"My hunch is someone is trying to tell me something about Eddie Dvorak."

"You may be right."

"I was trying to set up another meeting with Wendell Jackson, but he's away on business. I did a little probing into his background. Age: Fifty-six. Married twice. No children. He's loaded, mostly from real estate and stocks. Even so, he likes working for the trucking company. It keeps him grounded, according to an interview in one of those society magazines. He thinks most of our economic problems are coming from those 'rascals in Washington,' and that's a quote, from the same article."

"Interesting. I guess we sit and wait until he gets back, unless you have another idea."

"I'll think about it. How's your party going?"

"Terrific. You missed a memorable meal."

"Remember me for the next one. Call me if you hear anything."

Chapter 27

Early next morning, Dana phones and asks me to come over to her house "right away." She doesn't say why, and I don't ask. When she opens the door to let me in, she's trembling and holding something, apparently a photograph. She ushers me into the living room where Elsie has this far-away look in her eyes, seemingly searching to understand it all.

"We found it," says Dana as I sit down.

I shoot a questioning glance at her.

"The fireplace. We found the fireplace," she says as she hands me the photograph.

Sure enough. There it is, the magnificent fireplace. Exactly as it was in the video. "This is terrific." Elsie's nodding in agreement, her eyes glistening with joy.

"We were going through some old photo albums, my mom and I, and there it was. I can't believe it. Like, we must have gone through hundreds of photos, laughing and having a good time, before we came across these photos. They're from a trip my dad and I made about four years ago. I was eleven or twelve at the time, and it was for only four days."

"Now, the big question: Do you remember where it was?"

"Check the back of the photo."

I turned the photo over and read the hand-written notation:

Wendell Jackson's Mansion
Upstate New York, August 2012

I leap out of my chair. "Wow! Let me have all the photos from the trip. I've got to show them to Detective Laszlo. We've got to get moving on this."

"Want me to come?" asks Dana.

"Yes. Why don't you both come along?"

I begin mumbling to myself. "Got to tell him we're coming…he'd better be in the office. Is this all of them?"

"All we could find," says Elsie.

"Put your shoes on, Dana. Let's go."

Police headquarters is housed in a long, sand-colored brick building not far away from the main highway links in Bergen County. Detective Laszlo, in shirtsleeves, eagerly greets us at the reception desk when we arrive and leads us down a long corridor.

We finally enter his office. The walls are covered with photographs, memos, citations, and framed letters. Obviously, this office belongs to someone who's occupied it for some time.

"What's up?" he asks as he motions for us to sit down in chairs set up for us. He settles into a swivel chair behind his cluttered desk.

We show him the photographs. Eyebrows arched, he examines them carefully as Dana explains what they are. "About time we caught a break in this case," he says. "First things first, let's try to get the exact location of that mansion." He snaps up the phone. "Mary, would you see if you can find the exact address of a mansion owned by a Wendell Jackson in upstate New York? He's an executive at World-Beaters Trucking Company in Elizabeth, New Jersey. Like always, use your discretion, and call me as soon as you have a positive ID. Thanks."

He turns to Dana. "What do you remember about the place?"

"Like I told Richie, I was only eleven or twelve at the time, and the trip was a short one, about four days. The man who owned the mansion was my father's boss at the trucking company. My memory is a little fuzzy about some things, but I remember the place was very old, enormous, with lots of rooms, big rooms with tall ceilings, and we were not allowed to go into certain rooms because we might break things."

As she's talking, Laszlo is taking notes. "Go on."

"There were four or five kids there, including me. I think the other kids were also children of people who worked at the trucking company. I never saw them after that. It was hot, so we played outdoors a lot. They had an in-ground pool, and we'd go in there, and we played in the woods nearby. I remember they had a large garage separate from the house, and we were told not to go in there, but we did. And, oh, yeah, they were building something underground at the time, and that was another no-no, but this time we stayed away because they built a fence around the building site."

Laszlo interrupts her. "This thing they were building underground, do you know what it was?"

"I'm not sure. It was pretty long and wide, with rooms, but I never got a good look at what they were doing."

"This thing they were building, was it a shelter or bunker?"

"Yeah, like that."

"Tell me about the garage. How large was it? Was it big enough for one car, or two cars, or more?"

"I'd say it was big enough for at least two cars."

"How far were the woods from the house?"

"Not far. You could easily walk to it, and the woods were very thick. That was one place we stayed away from at night."

"Were there any houses nearby that you recall?"

"No. The mansion stood out by itself, like a fairytale castle."

"Anything else you remember about the grounds around the house."

"Not really. No, wait. There was one other building. I think they called it the shed. It was pretty big for a shed. Gosh, everything seemed big to me. That was another place we had to stay away from. They said we could get hurt if we went in there."

"Okay, now tell me about the fireplace. Where exactly was it?"

"In the basement, a huge basement. We used to go down there to play at night. Once it rained, and we played there all day. Mr. Jackson made a fire that day, and we toasted marshmallows."

"Sounds like you had a fun time," I say.

"We did, but it was over so fast. I guess that's why I couldn't remember it right away."

Laszlo's phone buzzes, and he quickly answers it. "Hi, Mary...You got it? Great. Where is it? Hmm, interesting. Send it to me. I want to check out the town and surroundings. Thanks."

"Well, we have a location," he says after hanging up. "The mansion is in a little town not far from Lake George. Beautiful area." He turns to Elsie. "We haven't had a chance to talk. If it weren't for you and Dana, these photos would still be in their albums somewhere in a drawer or closet. Is there anything you want to add?"

"I'm so proud of this girl...I wish I had her memory."

"I second that. Now if you'll excuse me, I need to make a few calls and talk to some people. After that, I'm on my way to upstate New York. They'll have to get someone else to take my place along the Congressional caravan route to Lake George."

Chapter 28

After driving Elsie and Dana back home, I call Detective Laszlo and plead my case to go along with him. I figured he'd buck me on it. "Absolutely not," he says, his voice rising to a level I had not heard it reach before. "Too dangerous."

"Come on, chief. I've come this far with you," I remind him.

"I'm not a chief."

"Okay, detective. I'd like to see this thing through. And you know me by now: the man with this insatiable curiosity about everything."

"I don't know how many people are in that mansion, and there may be shooting."

"Good reason to bring a priest along," I say with a smile in my voice. "No kidding, I hope and pray Eddie is there, and, if he is—God knows what shape he's in—he may need to see the face of a friendly neighbor."

"Boy, you really have a way with words. Okay, but…"

"I'll stay out of the way."

"You'd better," says Laszlo. "You're either very brave or very nuts, Richie. I'll swing by in about twenty minutes. Bring an overnight bag. I hope that's all it takes."

By the time I let Elsie and Dana know where I'm going, change into what I call my "cowboy clothes"—boots and jeans—and pack my carry-on, Laszlo arrives. We're off.

From the start, it's obvious this will not be a joy ride, and in no time we're on the New York Thruway streaking upstate. When his phone buzzes, I almost jump out of my boots. He turns on the speaker and answers. "Hello, who's this?"

Almost whispering, this voice replies, "Waldo. Waldo Cameron."

A wide-eyed Laszlo puts on this surprised look. "Oh, hi, Waldo. What's up?"

"I can't do it," says Waldo, his voice laced with fear. "Call me a coward, call me a rat, call me what you like. I can't betray my country or abandon my family."

"Where are you, Waldo?"

"Right now, I'm in the woods, all by myself. Less than two-hundred feet away, they're plotting the worst crime in our history."

"Who's plotting what crime?"

"They! Them!"

"Please, Waldo, tell me who they are."

"I can't talk loud, I can't talk long," he says, like he was short of breath. "I think you knew all the time. I'm talking about Wendell Jackson and the group. They plan to kill the leaders of Congress."

"Wait a second, Waldo." Laszlo pulls off the highway and onto the shoulder. He gives me a pad and pen and hand-motions for me to take notes. "Okay, go on."

Waldo continues, "They're planning to kill all of them tomorrow morning at a conference center near Lake George, less than ten miles from the mansion."

"We know about the mansion and the conference, Waldo."

"Then you know what they're planning to do."

"No. We didn't know that. Listen to me carefully, Waldo."

"I'm not a coward. I'm not a rat."

"Right. You're not. You're a brave young man. Now listen to me. How many people are at the mansion now?"

He pauses. "I think ten—eight men, two women."

"What kinds of weapons are they planning to use?"

"Everything—assault rifles, small arms, grenades, you name it, and we've been training for more than a month how to use them."

"When is this attack set to take place?"

"At the breakfast session the day after they arrive, as soon as we get the word from Dimitri."

"Who's Dimitri?"

"He's our inside man. He's a waiter at the conference center."

"Got it." Going out on the limb, Laszlo asks, "Where are they holding Eddie?"

I hold my breath, and I have a feeling where he might be. So does Laszlo, I'm sure.

After a long pause, Waldo replies: "In the bunker, near the mansion."

"Who are the two women?"

"Wendell's wife, Constance, and Mildred, Eddie's old girlfriend."

"That figures."

"What?"

"Never mind. Waldo. I want you to get away from there."

"I can't. They're always checking. Lucky I'm out here now. I told them I was going to get some wood for the fireplace."

"Okay, sit tight. Act like nothing happened. Mingle, talk, be yourself. We'll get you out of there."

"I don't know about that, detective."

"You want to see your wife and kids again? Do what I say."

"Okay."

"Remember, sit tight, Waldo."

They hang up.

"Wow! Now what?" I ask.

"I need to make some more calls. You better drive, Richie. Let me have those notes."

I can't help but feel this country is facing a conspiratorial crisis it hasn't seen since Lincoln was assassinated, and I'm a front-row witness to it. Me. Richie Bianchi. A one-time parish priest trying to figure out what to do with the rest of his life. A man deeply in love with a lovely, caring woman. A neighbor trying to help a family caught up in a terrible crisis.

No, I'm more than a front-row witness. I'm a part of it. And that scares me, but not enough to make me want to go home.

I listen attentively, sometimes offering a comment, as Detective Laszlo speaks to one law enforcement supervisor after another.

Chapter 29

The Finals— Game Two: Dana's doorbell never stopped ringing all morning. Now, about an hour before game time, friends and neighbors continue to come by and express their support for the Owls. Many of the well-wishers live on Dana's block, but a surprising number are from other areas. Elsie is flabbergasted but pleased and proud of the attention swirling around her daughter and the team.

Game time. Players line up for the opening faceoff. To Dana, who's reunited with line-mates Ernie and Hugo today, the Ice Storm players seem to be all business as they strive to even the series.

Hold on to your helmets!

Right off the bat, the Ice Storm try to slow up the Owls by grabbing, holding, or hooking them, causing Coach Fenda to explode with angry protests calling for penalties to be handed out to Ice Storm players. None is assessed, however.

Halfway through the first period, in a tangle of sticks and bodies and skates, Dana finds the puck and carries it into the Ice Storm zone. The only one in her way now is Jesse Woods, whose persistent, clawing style of defending has been giving the Owls fits up to now. Somehow she manages to get around him and get off a shot, and the puck sails past the goalie's glove and slams up against the back boards, an innocent play that usually doesn't result in a goal. But this time the puck bounces directly back out onto Dana's stick, and she slaps it into the net.

Score: Owls, 1; Ice Storm, 0.

The Owls celebrate like it was an overtime goal, while the Ice Storm players shake their heads in disbelief. It obviously didn't start the way they expected. After a brief meeting with their coach—Felix Fontaine, a savvy hockey mind with one of the winningest records in the Northeast leagues—the Ice Storm resume their hit-grab-hold play. Apparently, the coach believes the intimidation tactics are working, despite the goal by the Owls star player.

In the locker room, between the first and second periods, Coach Fenda praises the players for keeping their cool. "We've seen this stuff before. They're just trying to scare us into making mistakes. This is the time we…"

"I hear you," says Lenny, interrupting him, "but you know what, coach? I'm getting sick and tired of their crap. I say it's time we answer back. A good knee to the groin…"

"And then what? You sit in the penalty box. Right now we're winning. We're in the driver's seat."

"But, coach…"

"Trust me, Lenny, you start gooning it up with those guys, we lose. This is the time we turn the other cheek."

As the second period begins, the Ice Storm are checking the Owls every chance they get, with an elbow thrown in for good measure. By now, the Owls fans have had enough, and their boos, along with Coach Fenda's protests, are starting to have an effect. Twice, Ice Storm players are called for penalties. Now, while the Owls are unable to score with the player advantages, they manage to keep the other team trapped in its end and eat up precious time.

Six minutes to go in the period, and the Owls are still leading, 1-0. But then Lenny is hit in the gut with the butt end of an Ice Storm stick, and he responds with a butt-end of his own. The stricken Ice Storm player crumples to the ice, apparently in tremendous pain. Lenny is assessed a major penalty, five minutes in the box. The Ice Storm butt-ender gets nothing but a helping hand off the ice and a brief visit to the locker room.

As expected, the Ice Storm mount a ferocious power play,

shooting pucks from every angle, but so far they're either missing the net or Matteo and his teammates are blocking the shots. Finally, half way through the penalty, the Ice Storm start making better passes and picking their shots more carefully. Positioning himself at the side of the Owls net, Mario "The Dog" is gifted with a rare rebound and slips the puck past Matteo.

Score: Owls, 1; Ice Storm, 1.

Because Lenny was given a major penalty, he stays in the box for the full five minutes even though the other team has scored. Right away, it's obvious the Ice Storm continue to press the attack. Their strategy is simple: Throw the puck into the Owls end, then swarm all over the defenders to prevent them from getting the puck out of their zone. Once, the Owls manage to bring the puck out clearly and take a long shot at the Ice Storm goalie, but the puck is easily turned away. Then an Owls defenseman loses the puck in his skates, and it's picked up by Percy McBride, who buries it into the Owls net just before the penalty to Lenny ends.

Score: Ice Storm, 2; Owls, 1.

Shaking his head from side to side, Lenny skates dejectedly to the Owls bench and sits down at the far end and buries his head in his arms. Coach Fenda side-steps over to him and pats him on the shoulder. "Stop blaming yourself, Lenny," he says. "We play as a team, no matter what happens."

Lenny looks up at the coach with reddened eyes.

"It's okay, Lenny. We still got a chance," says Dana before she jumps back onto the ice.

About twenty-five seconds left in the period. Still time to make a play. Dana and her line-mates make a valiant effort to even the score. Hugo has a chance to hit an open side vacated by the Ice Storm goalie, but in his eagerness he shanks the shot, and the puck meanders off to the side boards. The groan from the stands is audible and long.

It's very quiet in the Owls locker room. Time to nurse wounds.

Time to reflect. Time to pray. Normally Coach Fenda has a lot to say between periods. This time he doesn't say anything. He knows what his players are feeling. He knows they know what they have to do.

As the Owls return to the ice for the third period, they jump on every opportunity to carry the play. But the Ice Storm have their own ideas about what they need to do: Build an impenetrable wall in front of their goalie. Frustrate the Owls at every turn. Take advantage if the opportunity to score presents itself. Above all, defend, defend, defend.

By the "Oohs" and "Aahs" coming from the Owls fans, it looks like the strategy laid out by Coach Fontaine is working. Dana and her linemates are getting shots, but they might as well be shooting from New York City. And when they're close enough to get off a good shot, Ice Storm goalie Jay Rivers is right there to make the save.

The Owls are running out of gas and time. Less than two minutes to go. Coach Fenda pulls Matteo and replaces him with another forward, Lenny, who immediately sends the puck sliding deep into the Ice Storm end of the ice. Players on both sides converge in a desperate attempt to take possession of the puck. Once again, Mario "The Dog" is in the right spot at the right time. He steals the puck and lifts it clear of everyone and down to the other end, just missing an open net.

Seven seconds to play now. Another scramble by the Ice Storm net. The puck squiggles into the corner. Dana collects it, sees a narrow opening between the goalie's pads and the goal post, and shoots. The puck pings off the goal post as the horn sounds to end the game.

Many of the Owls fans had expected the team to finish off their opponents today. The mayor already had plans in motion for a big parade down Main Street the following day, but there's still one more game to play in the championship round. Dana is sobbing as she passes by her mother, who's been sitting behind the bench. Elsie has a smile of pride on her face.

Chapter 30

After arriving in the Adirondacks, Detective Laszlo meets with local police, state troopers, and FBI agents and briefs them on on the plot by Wendell Jackson's group to attack Congressional leaders at the conference center near Lake George. In an overcrowded room at police headquarters, he reports the raid will be launched tomorrow morning, as Waldo Cameron informed us.

The law enforcement team now working on the case is quite a bit larger than the original squad, and for good reason. The mission has grown from rescuing Eddie Dvorak to rescuing Eddie Dvorak *and* preventing the assassination of government leaders. A raid on the Jackson mansion this evening could accomplish both goals.

When Laszlo finishes speaking, Lionel Hunter, chief of the local police, outlines a plan of action, which with a few tweaks is a go.

Basically, it calls for a three-pronged attack. The FBI agents will storm the mansion through the front door. Under cover of the wooded area behind the mansion, some state troopers will force their way into the rear of the building while others will investigate the garage and shed. Local police, led by Chief Hunter and Detective Laszlo, will secure the bunker where Eddie is supposedly being held.

The police chief knows the exact location of the bunker. "I used to drive by when they were building that damn thing," he recalls. "I don't know. I suppose it could come in handy someday. I hope not."

I'll be riding in a modified police van, which is designed to hold any prisoners we take. Driving the van will be police officer Gregory Nichols, a serious young man who'd like to be part of the attack squad rather than "the chauffeur" (his description) of a police vehicle. He's also instructed to keep an eye on me and make sure I don't get too close to the mansion.

Time to move.

To hide our identity, we travel in a broken line to the mansion using different vehicles made for public or commercial use except for the police van. As we get closer to our destinations, we split up or slow down before reaching our assigned positions. Two vans carrying FBI agents proceed down a side road, then turn onto a long, curved driveway leading to the front door, while the state police squad, as planned, slip into the wooded area behind the house. The local police follow the FBI vans. Our van pulls in behind the local police.

From my position, I have a pretty good view of the mansion. I'm immediately impressed by the beauty, size and majesty of the old house against the twilight sky. I want to visit it and roam through it and listen to the stories it tells, which is highly unlikely to happen under current circumstances. The mansion is an imposing building that requires the same care one would give to a grand old lady. It would be a shame if it were blown to pieces in the battle that could erupt at any moment now.

FBI agents exit the vans and, like leopards on the hunt, slink across the large lawn to the front of the house. Not far away, a small group of local police officers led by Chief Hunter and Detective Laszlo dash toward a nearby concrete structure and vanish from sight as they descend into the bunker.

An FBI agent checks the scene inside the mansion through a front window. "One woman sitting on a couch watching TV," he reports almost in a whisper. I'm expecting the agents to ram the door with a tree trunk or something or blow up the door with explosives, but that's not what happens. One agent, who appears to be the leader, lifts the knocker on the venerable old door and gives it three raps. At first, no one responds, and agents are ready to move to step two—ramming down or blowing up the door—which would be quite a sight, considering this massive door has weathered many storms.

Someone, probably the woman on the couch, opens the door, but barely. Apparently she wants to see who's knocking. Next, the door is suddenly pushed wide open, and now all of the agents pour into the house with the force of a fire hose.

I get out of the car and take a few steps closer for a better sight line and crouch down. Officer Nichols is not happy with my maneuver. "Where do you think you're going?" he grumbles. I smile and say, "Right here. This is as far as I'm going. I'm fine, Gregory, really."

A middle-aged woman lying on her back on the floor, while the team leader hands out orders and commands. "Who's in the house?" "Where are they?" "You two, check upstairs." "Talk to me, lady. Who's here, where are they?" The woman on the floor mumbles something, "Joey, Regis, Frankie, check every room on this floor." "Talk to me some more, lady." "You guys, check the basement."

An agent leads another woman by the arm into the room where the team leader is standing.

"She was in the kitchen texting someone?" says the agent.

"Who are you?" the leader asks.

"Mildred. Mildred Jordan."

"Anyone else in the house?"

"No, only Constance and me."

"What happened to the men who were here?"

Constance sits up now and in a barely audible voice says, "My husband's at a business meeting."

"What about the other men, ma'am?"

"I don't know what you're talking about," says Constance. "All I know is Wendell will be mad as hell when he hears how you barged into our home and knocked me over."

"Who's Wendell?"

"My husband, Wendell Jackson. His family built this house."

Mildred starts walking across the room.

"Where're you going, ma'am?"

"I want to get a tissue," she says, pointing to a nearby bureau.

"No, don't move."

She keeps going.

"Stop! Now!"

She walks faster.

He fires two rounds from his rifle into the bureau.

She stops and crumples to the floor, wailing.

He walks over to the bureau, opens the drawer, and pulls out a pistol. "Is this what you're looking for, ma'am?" He shakes his head. Turning to the other agent, he says, "Take them to the van, Joey. We need to have a talk with them later."

After the agent handcuffs the women, he leads them out of the house. As they pass by me, Mildred and I come face to face. This doesn't seem to be the time to acknowledge we know each other, even with a nod of our heads. We just stare at one another. I see pain in her pitiful eyes crying for help. I also see anger and hate.

The raid lasts less than an hour. Now that it's over, what do we know we didn't know before? There was no one in the mansion except Wendell Jackson's wife and Mildred Jordan. There were assault weapons and explosives in the shed, which were seized by the police. Finally, Eddie Dvorak was not in the bunker, as we were told he'd be.

I'm glad no one was hurt but disappointed we didn't find Eddie or catch the would-be assassins. I'm sure Detective Laszlo feels the same way, and he's probably a little embarrassed, as we all gather on the big lawn in front of the mansion. "That's what that guy Waldo Cameron told us—there were eight men and two women in the mansion and the attack was set for tomorrow morning," he explains.

"I don't know where they all went, but just looking at those explosives, whoever was here was up to no good," says P. J. Kaminski, leader of the FBI team.

"Yeah, and what did they do with Mr. Dvorak?" Laszlo wants to know

"Most likely, they took him with them, wherever they went," says Chief Hunter.

"Or worst," Laszlo adds.

"Obviously, they changed plans," says Kaminski.

"Clever son of a bitch, that Wendell Jackson," Laszlo says. He checks his watch. "The Congressional leaders should be arriving at the conference center in less than an hour, maybe less. I think we should alert Security at the conference center about what happened here."

"And we should send the troops back to Lake George, in case those mansion boys decide to pay a visit," says Police Chief Hunter.

"Right," Laszlo says. "I'll head there myself, especially since there's a good chance they took Mr. Dvorak with them." He turns to me. "What about you, Richie?"

"Whenever you're ready…"

He nods his approval. "Let's go."

I guess I've earned my combat stripes.

Chapter 31

Lake George is only about ten miles away, but by the way Detective Laszlo is driving we'll be there in less than five minutes.

A part of me wants to tell him: *Slow down. What's your hurry? Do we really want to be caught in the middle of a fire fight? Shouldn't we stop now and wait until the dust settles? Do they really need us there to help resist an attack? Probably not. I'd only get in the way.*

But I really want to convey this message: *Move it, detective! We both know what our mission is now. It's to find Eddie Dvorak and bring him home safely to his daughter. And if Wendell Jackson and his group are holding Eddie while they stage a violent attack on our government leaders, then we've got to be there. Only, hurry! Hurry!*

The sky has darkened. Less than a mile away from the conference center, I hear what sounds like firecrackers going off. "Hear that?" says Laszlo. "That's gunfire. I'd recognize it anywhere." Ahead of us, the sky lights up after a short, low boom. "That's a small explosive igniting," he adds.

The closer we get the louder the gunfire becomes and melds with the piercing sound of police sirens. The few people on the streets seem to sense trouble in the air and are hustling toward home or shelter. There's a look of intense fear on their faces, anticipating the worst scenario—the scourge of our age: *Is this our time for a terrorist attack?*

"I think I know a good location for us," Laszlo says. He reaches into his inside jacket pocket, pulls out a pamphlet, and hands it to me. I turn on the overhead light and open the pamphlet. It's a traveler's guide to the convention center.

"Where did you get this?" I ask.

"Chief Hunter gave it to me. He thought it might come in handy. Turn to the centerfold."

The centerfold shows an overhead view of the convention center, complete with the main building, outdoor swimming pool, tennis courts, and surrounding grounds.

"There, in the upper right hand corner next to the parking lot, is an area marked *Daytime Talks and Moonlight Walks*."

"I see it."

"Looks like a perfect place to observe what's going on. It's a wooded area overlooking the parking lot, with lots of evergreen trees, a duck pond, and walking paths."

"Right."

"Here's what we'll do. I'll stop a little past the conference center and walk back to the wooded area. Then I want you to drive a mile or so down the road, Richie, and wait for me there."

"No. I'm going with you. We've come this far together."

He takes a deep breath and lets it out, full-force. "You can be a handful sometimes, padre. Here, take this," he says, reaching down and retrieving a small revolver holstered to his leg. "In case you're wondering what it is, it's a gun. For your protection. It's loaded and ready to go.'"

I take hold of it and turn it over a few times.

"Just aim and pull the trigger," Laszlo says, sensing I'm no gun expert.

"The bishop should see me now." I shove the gun in my pants pocket.

When we get out of the car, Laszlo opens the trunk and grabs two flashlights and hands me one. Next, he picks up a pair of night vision binoculars, which he drapes around his neck.

We move into the wooded area, which is dimly lit by a lamplight here and there. On a normal day I bet this would be an ideal place for some serious meditation or contemplation. Laszlo leads the way, walking along one of the dirt paths, careful not to make any noise or shine his flashlight straight ahead of us or upwards. As we reach the last line of trees, he tells me to crouch down and crawl "unless you want your head shot off." Seems like an excellent suggestion. We're soon at the end of a grassy area overlooking the parking lot. Below, an intense fire fight is in progress.

While some of the lamplights in this part of the lot have been shot out, many are still working and offer a pretty clear view of what's happening. Men in black jumpsuits, apparently the ones who evaded capture at the mansion, are behind cars and trucks firing their automatic weapons at two or three troopers behind a short brick wall under a canopy at the front entrance of the building. Another officer is lying face-down on a bed of new-born tulips along the edge of the driveway. I want to run down and lift him out of there, but Laszlo, apparently reading my mind, puts a hand on my shoulder. "Be still," he says. "Later."

Where is everyone? I mean, where are all of our government protectors? It's a slaughter down there. Two brave officers have set up a line of defense at the front door after they got word an anti-government group bent on killing the lawmakers might be headed here. Could we have gotten here sooner than our main force?

Laszlo draws his revolver and is about to take aim when a couple of state troopers appear on the roof of the main building and begin firing at the militants. One of the jumpsuits, a giant of a man, loads a bomb into a mortar. The missile is sent flying toward what I think is its intended target, the roof, then veers off and explodes in a clump of trees on the side of the building. The attacker quickly makes an adjustment and fires another round. This one falls on the roof, exploding near where the troopers had been positioned. Rising out of a cloud of smoke, a trooper returns fire and strikes the mortar man in the forehead, sending him crashing to the ground like a felled oak tree.

Tess tells me curiosity is my fatal flaw, and I laugh when she says that. But she's right. What I have witnessed so far today, in this short time, should satisfy my insatiable curiosity for a long time. Or will it?

I cannot forget our mission: Find Eddie and bring him home. My eyes scour the parking lot for anyone or anything that could lead me to him. Unexpectedly, I spot someone I recognize. I borrow Laszlo's night vision binoculars to be sure. He's holding up the rear of the invading force, and he seems to be looking at me as I'm looking at him. It's Wendell Jackson, armed with an assault rifle. He ducks when a bullet hits another one of his fighters and that man collapses on the hood of a car.

I whisper to Laszlo, "I think I spotted Wendell. He's behind that red Highlander in the last row." As I'm talking, it looks as if the cavalry is finally arriving. A squad of FBI agents enters the battle from the opposite side of the parking lot. I'm no military expert, but I'm hoping this means the tide of battle is about to turn in our favor.

Laszlo takes a good look through the binoculars. He nods. "Yup, that's him. Stay put." Startling me, he gets up and dashes back into the woods. I'm waiting for him to return…ten minutes…fifteen minutes. No sign of him. I rise and run into the woods after him. Laszlo is probably taking a trail that will lead him to an area right behind where Jackson was last seen.

I'm not sure where I am when I exit the woods again, but the parking lot is still in sight, only from a different angle, further away from the main battle zone. Here, all the lamplights seem to be intact and lit. A man with a rifle comes into view and strides away from the battleground toward a van in the corner of the lot. Apparently, Wendell Jackson has had enough of war or knows the battle is lost and has decided to beat it out of here.

At the van, Jackson leans his rifle against the fender and rips off his jumpsuit and throws it on the ground. Next, he picks up his weapon and hurries around to the driver's side, where he meets someone he probably didn't expect to meet. "Drop the weapon and turn around," says Laszlo, his revolver pointed at Jackson's torso. I think this is a good time to show myself, and I run over to assist the detective in any way I can.

Laszlo raises his anxious eyes skyward when he spots me. "Geez, I thought I told you to stay put."

"When you didn't come back right away, I got worried," I explain. "Besides, I thought you could use some help."

"Okay, you want to help? Pick up his weapon and keep it pointed at him, while I check out the van. If he moves, shoot the bastard. Understand?"

"Sure," I say, sure I can't shoot anyone. I think Laszlo understands that. My initial reaction after picking up the weapon is hardly the excitement of holding it. *Boy, this thing is heavy!*

Laszlo motions for Jackson to give him the car keys. Jackson does, and Laszlo opens the door. "Oh, my God!" he shouts when he turns to his right. He dashes to the rear of the van and pops open the trunk. "It's Eddie," I shout. Folded in the trunk, like a sack of dirty old clothes, he's shackled and anchored to a chain bolted to the floor of the car. His eyes are shut tight, and he's still in the black jumpsuit he wore in the video.

As Laszlo bends over to check Eddie's vital signs, Wendell Jackson makes a dash for the wooded area less than a hundred feet away. I drop the rifle and follow, in close pursuit. I may not have engaged much in team sports, but I always could move fast when I had to. Just as Wendell is about to step into the wooded area, I lunge at him with both hands and bring him crashing onto the parking lot pavement. I lean over to examine him. He's moaning and bleeding from a scrape on the side of his forehead, but he's alive, thank God!

Laszlo finally catches up to me. "Nice tackle," he says, puffing.

"Thanks."

"Why didn't you shoot him like I told you?"

"I thought it would be easier to run after him and tackle him. Besides, I don't know how to use the gun."

"Great! Remind me to teach you sometime."

Wendell's eyes are open now. Laszlo leans over and cuffs him behind the back. After lifting him to his feet, he says, "If you try running away again, I won't have any trouble shooting you." Struggling to contain his rage, he then reaches into Wendell's pocket and pulls out his keys. "Come on, let's go."

Back at the van, Laszlo unlocks the shackles and checks Eddie's pulse. "He needs medical help right away."

"There's a hospital down the road," I remind him. "We passed it on the way."

"Yeah, I remember. Now hurry, go get my car."

"What do we do with this guy?"

"Don't ask," Laszlo replies. "Just go get the car, Richie, and bring it here."

When I return less than fifteen minutes later, Laszlo carries this sliver of a man out of the trunk of the van, like he was a sleeping child, and gently places him in the backseat of his police car. Then, shooting an icy look at the leader of the jumpsuits, he says, "You're under arrest, Mr. Jackson. Now it's your turn to wear shackles."

After reading him his rights, he calls Chief Hunter and asks him to arrange to have someone pick up Jackson at the hospital and lock him up until we figure what to do with him. Hunter, glad Eddie was found and the leader of "those mansion boys" was arrested, obliges, loud and clear. "Not to worry, detective. I'll have someone at the hospital when you arrive."

Chapter 32

After examining Eddie, the medical staff at the hospital concluded he'd been knocked out by a combination of drugs that hasn't been determined yet. But the early signs are favorable, and Eddie seems to be gradually coming out of it.

The hospital has been treating several casualties of the fire fight. The toll, as far as we can determine from the hospital staff, is five dead, including two state troopers and three militants (Dimitri Cooper, Ponti Fawcett, and Russ Cowell), and two wounded. Jason Biddle and Larry Noble surrendered, and, of course, Wendell Jackson was captured. We ask to speak to one of the wounded, Waldo Cameron.

Waldo's injury is not life-threatening, but still bad enough to need hospital care under police guard. He was nicked by a ricocheting round in his shoulder. He does not appear surprised when Detective Laszlo and I enter his room. "I knew you guys would be here sooner or later," he says. He seems less nervous than the last time I saw him. Probably because he's under protective custody.

"I tried to call you again but couldn't," he explains to Laszlo. "After I spoke to you, he decided to change the plan of attack."

"By 'he', you mean Wendell Jackson," says Laszlo.

"Right. Just like that, he changed his mind. 'We're a go for tonight, when all the Washington biggies arrive, not tomorrow morning,' he told us. Why? 'Too much can happen between now and then. Too many people can talk and ruin everything. Besides,' he said, 'the element of surprise will be more on our side if we attack now.' I tried to sneak away, so I could tell you, but I couldn't. He and his henchmen were everywhere. The next thing I knew, we're packing our gear and piling into cars and vans and on our way to the convention center."

"Do you think Jackson got a tip from someone?" I ask.

"It's possible. But he's just a suspicious guy. Doesn't trust anybody."

"So, what happened when you got to the convention center?" Laszlo asks.

"Well, we never expected to meet the resistance we met. Somebody must have tipped them off. We took cover behind the cars in the parking lot and started firing back."

"Are you saying you personally fired at the security police?" Laszlo asks.

"No! I didn't aim at anyone. I pretended."

"Did you fire your gun?"

"No…yes. What would you do if a fully armed man named Wendell Jackson was right behind you? But I didn't aim at anyone."

"Really?"

Waldo becomes his old nervous self. "Look," he says, "I'm telling you the truth. Remember, I was the one who called to tip you off about what they were planning to do. I didn't shoot at or hit anyone."

"What did Jackson hope to accomplish by taking Eddie Dvorak with him to the convention center?" asks Laszlo.

"I don't know. I only know Wendell likes to cover all the bases. Maybe he planned to use Eddie as a bargaining chip, or it's possible he planned to put the blame on him if things went wrong, as they did. There's one other possibility."

"What's that?"

"Eddie was always popular with the guys, and Wendell, let's face it, may be strong and tough and rich, but he doesn't have Eddie's character and…what's the word?"

"Charisma?" I suggest.

"Yeah, charisma. I think Wendell brought Eddie to the convention center because the boys look up to Eddie and trust him."

I'm curious, as usual. "Why was Eddie abducted in the first place?"

"That's easy," says Waldo. "Eddie didn't want to go along with the plan. That became very clear at the brotherhood meeting at Eddie's house."

"Tell us about that meeting," said Laszlo.

"Well, it started off fine. A few drinks, something to eat, some friendly conversation. It was just the guys, and we were all having a good time, and Eddie was the perfect host. Then we got into politics, and Wendell, sort of, took over and began talking about the convention center meeting and how this was our big chance to finally do something, to stop the craziness in government in its tracks, especially since the meeting was going to be held so near our command center, the mansion. I mean, it wasn't something we hadn't heard before, but he said it was time to get ready."

"Then what happened?"

"It seemed like all heads turned toward Eddie, waiting for him to say something. At first he didn't say anything, but slowly he began to speak. Once again, he made it clear he was against the plan. 'It's treasonous; there's got to be a better way.' But Wendell persisted, and pretty soon they were going at it head to head, and, finally, Wendell got up and said, 'Let's go, boys. We know where he stands with us.' And we all got up and left."

"So what are you saying? Except for Eddie, you all agreed with the plan?'"

Waldo looked down at his hand and made a fist. "At the time, Yes. Wendell was afraid Eddie would rat us out. So, later, he had three of his heavyweights—Dimitri, Ponti, and Larry—go back to Eddie's house, abduct him, and lock him up in the bunker. Wendell was our leader now, and he was so sure our plan would work."

"One other question," said Laszlo. "What do you know about Melinda Childs? I'm sure you're aware what happened to her."

There's a long pause, and he sighs. "Damn Dimitri Cooper! He was supposed to deliver a simple message to her: 'Keep your mouth shut.' But he went overboard when she started fighting back."

"Who sent him to deliver the message?"

"Who do you think? Wendell got nervous when she had lunch with you guys."

"You mean to say that if she didn't fight back, she wouldn't be lying in a hospital fighting for her life."

Waldo shrugs. "Dmitri is, or was, a crazy dude."

Another moment of silence. Laszlo says, "Just for the record, we caught up with Wendell Jackson in the parking lot. He was about to hop into his van during the heat of the battle and drive away. I guess he thought the war was lost."

"It figures."

"He's in police custody now. Did you know Eddie was unconscious and shackled in the trunk of Jackson's van?"

"No. I heard they were bringing him, but I didn't know… Geez, in the trunk of the van?"

"Yeah. Where do you think Jackson was headed when we bagged him?"

Waldo shakes his head, uncertain. "The word was he was planning to go to his place in the Bahamas after it was over…with Mildred Jordan, Eddie's ex."

"Well, I guess he has to change his vacation plans. We'd better go and see how Eddie is doing, Richie."

"Be well, Waldo." I have one more question. "By the way, does that snake tattoo on your arm have any special significance?"

"It was Wendell's idea," Waldo explains. "He thought the group should have a secret symbol of our own, but no name, and somebody came up with a snake that's ready to strike. I think it was Constance."

Chapter 33

It's almost midnight now. Even so, it's pandemonium in the ER waiting room. Reporters are pleading with the hospital staff for information about the dead and wounded, about anyone and anything connected with the attack at the convention center.

On the TV overhead, a cable newscaster is reporting on the latest bit of news in this major international story. It seems the leader of the band of militants has been captured and is sitting in an upstate New York jail, awaiting possible charges on a long list of criminal activities, including the attempted assassination of government leaders, the killing of state troopers, and the abduction of a man who refused to go along with the assassination plot.

Detective Laszlo shakes his head. "Can you believe this?"

"No. Do you think they realize Eddie is here?"

"Someone here knows something, I'm sure. Let's get out of here before they leap on us."

"Excellent idea." We head for the front door. "Don't know about you, but I'm hungry, and we need to find a place to stay for the night," I suggest.

As we exit the hospital, we cross the street and enter the parking building. A casual glance to the rear confirms the feeling I've had since we left the hospital, and I relay my suspicion to Laszlo. "I think someone's following us."

"Keep walking, like nothing's happening," he says. "A man or a woman?"

"A guy, a young man in gray pants and a wrinkled light blue blazer."

"Right out of the pages of *GQ*, I'm sure."

"His hair is sort of spikey, and he needs a shave."

"Boy, you're good," says Laszlo. "When I say 'Move', back as far away from me as possible."

"Got it."

As we approach the car, Laszlo reaches inside his jacket and shouts "Move!" I do what I was told. Laszlo has both hands on a revolver aimed at our pursuer. "Who are you? What do you want?"

The man gives the universal surrender sign, hands high in the air. "Don't shoot! It's me, Dougie Hoffman, freelance reporter. You may not remember me, detective, but I met you when I was covering the story about the two four-year-olds who went missing in Paramus Park."

"Yeah, I remember. What do you want? "

"I was wondering...Can I put my hands down?"

"No. What are you doing here?"

"I've been vacationing in Lake George for a couple of days, and I heard about the shooting at the convention center, so I ran to the hospital, you know, to see if I can get a story, and I saw you, detective."

"So what?"

"I was wondering...I heard on the news about the guy from Jersey who was abducted, and about the man under arrest who is believed to be the leader of the gang that abducted him and raided the convention center. I was wondering, since you're from Jersey, whether you have anything to do with the abduction case."

"Put your hands down, Dougie."

"Thanks."

"Call me next week. Maybe we can talk. Next time don't sneak up on me. Now get out of here."

Dougie doesn't need to be told twice. He quickly exits the parking garage.

"These guys are swarming all over the place," Laszlo groans. "Personally, I don't like to BS the press. It'll only come back to haunt you."

I'm impressed by Laszlo's coolness under pressure.

"You know, I was going to be a reporter myself at one time. Even worked for a community paper for a short period," he suddenly confesses.

"Obviously, you didn't pursue a career in journalism.'

"I decided against it. Too damned hard."

"By the way, what happened to the four-year-olds?"

"It took us an hour or so, but we finally found them. After walking away from the picnic area without telling their parents, they decided to go hang out by the pond, or a little lake in the park. When we spotted them, they were throwing rocks at the ducks in the water."

"That must have been scary for everyone."

"Especially the ducks…I should have nailed the parents for not keeping an eye on their kids."

Just another side of this giant of a man I didn't know.

Luckily, we find a place to stay and, right next door, a place to eat. Neither is very fancy, only convenient, and we're tired and famished. The menu in the all-night eatery is quite extensive, including everything from shish-kebab to stuffed clams, but I play it safe. I order a Western omelet. Laszlo orders the late-night special—two burgers, fries, side salad, cherry pie, and coffee.

Ravenous. That's the only way to describe our behavior after the food arrives. There's no such thing as table conversation at this point. After devouring my omelet and home fries, I eye the other burger he hasn't touched yet, but there's no chance I can swipe it faster than he can grab my hand. I order some cherry pie and coffee.

"You should have ordered the late-night special. It comes with everything," he says with a slight air of superiority.

I agree with a grunt and a nod. Time for a check of my poor, neglected phone. Tess called me three times. I'll call her back later. Other callers include my mom, Dana (twice), Gustav, and the Bishop's office.

As if I brought it back to life by checking my messages, my phone vibrates. I answer it quickly. "Oh, hi, Dana."

"I tried reaching you a couple of times. Are you okay?"

"I'm fine. I got your calls. Sorry I wasn't able to get back to you right away. It's been crazy here."

"Is it true what they're saying—my dad is in the hospital?"

"Yes. Detective Laszlo and I brought him there right after we found him."

"How's he doing?"

"The nurses say he's coming along. He's been through a lot."

"I know. I've been glued to the TV. I can't believe what those people were going to do, and what they did, and some of them were in my home."

"Well, you know your dad didn't want any part of what they were planning, and he stood by his beliefs."

She starts sobbing. "I'm so proud of him…and I love him so much."

"And I know he loves you, Dana. How's your mom doing?"

"She's good. I don't know what I would have done without her, and she was so worried about Dad, too."

"Listen, Dana, I got a lot to tell you when I get home. Tomorrow we'll check on your dad and see how he's doing. I don't want to make any promises, but I'm hoping the hospital will release him, but we'll see. Now you get some rest, okay?"

"Okay. Thank you, Richie."

"Sure."

"And thank Detective Laszlo for me, too."

I relay her message to Laszlo.

"She's a sweet girl. Eat your cherry pie, Richie."

Later, in my little, no-nonsense motel room, I put in a call to Tess. It's late, but I want so much to hear her voice again. After two rings comes this long, low "H-e-l-l-o" I hardly recognize.

"Tess? Is that you?"

"Sure is."

"You sound so different."

"What do you expect me to sound like at two in the morning? Vivien Leigh?"

"No, but—"

Her sense of humor apparently never sleeps.

"How are you?" she asks "I've been worried sick. I tried calling you several times, but then stopped. I figured you went incognito again or you're very busy."

"It's been unbelievable here. Oh, Tess, you wouldn't believe it."

"The newscast said the leader of the crazies—Wendell…what's his name?"

"Jackson. Wendell Jackson."

"They said he had Eddie abducted because he didn't go along with the assassination plot and hid him in an underground bunker until last night, when they attacked the convention center."

"That's right."

"According to newscasts, he was locked up in the trunk of Wendell's van during the attack. Why would they do that?"

"There are several theories."

"Okay. What are they?"

"Now who's curious? I'll tell you all about it when I get back."

"Did you hear what happened to the leaders of Congress during the attack?" she asks.

"No, what?"

"They were diverted to another hotel. They're spending the night at a Holiday Inn."

"Perfect. They'll probably get a lot more accomplished there."

"Yeah, and I think the breakfast is complimentary…When will I see you again, Richie?"

"Here's the plan, Tess. Laszlo and I are going to the hospital tomorrow morning, and we'll see how Eddie is doing. If they say he's good to go, we're taking him home. If it's a no-go, we may have to hang around here another day or two."

"Lake George is lovely."

"Yeah, but I'd rather be home. When I get back, I'll call you, and we'll do that night on the town we never finished."

"Sounds like a pretty good plan."

Chapter 34

An Owls Practice Session: After talking to Richie early this morning, Dana didn't feel like practicing for the final game of the championship series. She wanted only to sit by the front window and wait for her dad to come home from the hospital. However, after some gentle persuasion from Elsie, she changed her mind, and they headed off to the ice rink, a platter of home-made cookies in mom's hands.

What makes this practice session so special? It's one of the last times these young players will be with one another as a team. Most of the Owls players have been together for at least two years; a few, for even a longer period. During that time, they've come to know each other's strengths and weaknesses, not only as hockey players but also as human beings. And in the coming weeks they will decide whether they want to continue playing hockey and move onto the next level or call it quits and focus on something else like their school studies, jobs and career opportunities, or romance/love interests.

Their final game of the season may shape the future of some of these young players as they move into their late teens and plan the paths they will take into their twenties and beyond. And the feelings are mutual. Ice Storm players will be facing many of the same decisions as the Owls in the coming weeks.

Dana is excited as she enters the ice rink for practice today. Elsie, her mother, is with her, and her father is coming home from a harrowing experience

During the free play segment of the practice session, pucks are flying all over the place. Elsie is dazzled by the speed and dexterity of the players as they stick-handle through a maze of cones. In the excitement, Dana finds time to introduce her mom to as many teammates as she can corral.

"This is Lenny," says Dana. "He's one of our best players, and one of our toughest."

"Hi, I hear you made some goodies for us," says the tough guy.

Elsie smiles. "Yes. I hope you'll like the cookies."

"They're delicious," says Dana. "I sampled a couple on the way here."

"Don't let Dana fool you," says Lenny. "She's the star of the team. I'm probably second or third best. Matteo, our goalie, is probably right up there."

"Do you want to be a professional hockey player someday?" Elsie asks Lenny.

"Not necessarily," he replies. "Between you and me, I'm a pretty good hockey player, but I don't think I'm good enough to play professionally. My mom said I should go into sales. What do you think?"

"I did some selling in my younger days," says Elsie. "It's fun. But if you get disappointed easily, I wouldn't recommend it. There are plenty of things out there you can do. Give yourself a chance to poke around and see what's out there and what really interests you."

"Thanks for the advice. And this guy here," he says, pointing to Titus, drifting over, "is a pretty good player, too."

"Hey, Titus, meet my mom," says Dana.

"Oh, hi," he says shyly.

"Titus, what a great name."

"Everybody tells me that. I'm not sure I like it."

"It's wonderful. I think it's of Greek or Roman origin."

"Well, I guess I'll keep it. You like hockey?"

"I wish I understood it better," she replies. "It's beautiful to watch you guys skating around. Looks like you're having a lot of fun out there."

"Oh, don't use the 'fun' word around here," he says with a slight grin. "Coach takes practice very seriously."

The whistle blows, and Coach Fenda gathers the team around him at center ice.

"You don't have to stay for this," Dana tells her mom.

"I'm staying. Now go practice," she says.

Coach Fenda's voice is loud and strong. "The big game is only days away. I want you to really hustle today, like you're going to do in the game. No slackers, no drag-asses, no fakers. Skating drills first, then passing and shooting drills. I want a good hard practice on the power play, and we'll finish with a full-ice power skate. Okay? Let's do it, guys."

The players line up for the skating drills. Elsie is impressed by the speed of the teenagers, but she doesn't understand what they're doing and why. Same with the passing and shooting drills. She decides to go down to the little snack stand for some coffee. After she picks up her order, she returns to the stands. Her eyes are on the players on the ice, but her mind is drifting in another direction. *She's gotten so tall. Where did all the time go? I missed her so much. She's so graceful and smooth, the way she skates. I have to find a way to spend more time with her, and I want her to get to know her brothers better. I can't wait to see those guys. I'm not going to let them get away from me, like I did with Dana.*

Coach Fenda comes skating over to Elsie, disrupting her train of thought. "So you're Dana's mother."

"Sure am."

He extends his hand. "Sam Fenda, the Owls coach."

"I know. So nice to meet you."

He takes a deep breath and says, "Listen, I know you live in Florida. I think it's really thoughtful of you to come up here and spend some time with Dana. She's a terrific hockey player, and a tough one, but she's taken the ordeal with her father pretty hard. I'm glad things are finally looking up. Maybe we'll see Mr. Dvorak at the final game."

"Let's hope so. Eddie's a decent man who didn't deserve what happened to him, and he's done a great job with Dana."

"That he has. Excuse me while I get back to the team. Will we see you at the game?"

"You bet…and good luck."

A tall man in a baseball cap slides onto the bench not far from Elsie. He turns to her as he unzips his light gray jacket. "How do they look?" he says, an ashen look on his face.

Elsie is reluctant to respond at first, but he seems sincere enough. "They look great to me," she says

"Your son play on the team?" he asks.

"No…my daughter does."

"Oh, you must be Dana's mom. Hi, I'm Harold, Hugo's father."

"Of course. I'm Elsie."

"Dana's a terrific player, the best." In a serious, almost somber tone, he continues, "I'm a little worried about the upcoming game. That's why I'm here today. I left work a little earlier today, so I can see how they're doing. I've seen every game they've played so far. I don't like the way they played the last game."

"I'm no hockey expert, but they look pretty loose and confident today."

"That's just it. Maybe they're too loose and confident. They need to play desperate hockey. I bet the Ice Storm will."

Hugo comes skating over to them. "Hi, Mrs. Mendez. Hi, Dad. What are you doing here today? Shouldn't you be at work?"

"I got off early today. I thought I'd swing down here to watch you guys practice."

"And what do you think?"

"You look great."

Parents! Elsie is left pondering their role.

Chapter 35

With help from Detective Laszlo's contact in the Security Department, we manage to enter the hospital next morning through a special side entrance, and that's a big break for us. The media, with their TV trucks and cameras, are jammed in the area outside the main entrance awaiting a press briefing by the hospital staff.

By now, Eddie is out of the ER and in his own private room on the third floor. Our security guard leads us up the stairwell to it. At the door, we're stopped by a police officer, who lets us pass after talking to our security guard.

As we're about to enter the room, Eddie is sitting up in his bed, listening attentively to a doctor explain the steps he should take for his continued recovery. We stop and wait for a break in their conversation. Eddie, far from looking like his old self, gives a weak wave and a slight smile when he spots me. I wave back, still hesitating at the doorway.

The doctor turns around, and says, "Come on in, gentleman. I'm about finished here."

We introduce ourselves. He's Doctor Pendleton, a resident connected with the hospital's drug rehab program. Both Laszlo and I stare at him with the same question on our minds.

"I guess you're wondering if he can go home," says the doctor. "Well, over all, Eddie is doing pretty well, considering what he went through. I'd like him to stay another day or two to be on the safe side, but Eddie wants to go home now."

Eddie sits up straighter in bed. "Like I said, doctor, there's not much I can't do home that I'm doing here." He shoots an inquisitive glance at Laszlo.

"Detective Laszlo here has been working on your case almost from the beginning, Eddie," I explain.

"I heard about you, detective. I did manage to pick up some information in the bunker."

"I feel like I've known you a long time," says Laszlo. "Welcome back, Eddie."

"Thank you. I'm grateful to be back."

"How are you feeling?"

"I feel fine." Turning to the man in the white jacket, he says, "Really, I'm fine." His eyes misting, he adds, "Geez, it's been more than a month since I last saw my daughter, doctor. It's just the two of us. I heard, through the grapevine, that her mother is visiting now, thank God, but that's only temporary, I'm sure. She's got to get back to Florida and her two little boys."

"What's your daughter's name?"

"Dana. She's sixteen."

"I have a three-year-old. Her name's Nancy."

"Dana plays ice hockey on an all-boys team."

"Is she a good hockey player?"

"She's very good, or so they tell me."

"She's the best player on the team," I interject. "I saw her play."

"I'm not a big hockey fan," says Eddie, "but she's playing in a major regional tournament now." He turns to me with a questioning look in his eyes.

"Her team has made it to the finals," I add. "One more win and they're the champs."

"Wow, that's quite an accomplishment," says Doctor Pendleton. After taking a moment to reflect on what he's about to say, he adds, "Okay, Eddie, go home, but you have to promise me you'll take care of yourself— eat well and build yourself back up, rest, and relax."

"I promise."

"I'll leave instructions for when you get home, and please arrange to see someone as a follow-up."

"I will. Thanks, doctor."

Both Laszlo and I break out into wide smiles. "We'll keep an eye on him," I say.

In the next hour or so, while the nurses are preparing the paperwork, I run out and pick up some clothes for Eddie to wear home. Jumpsuits are out.

Laszlo's driving, I'm sitting next to him, and Eddie is in the back seat. If Eddie feels like talking, we listen. Otherwise, it's a relatively quiet ride.

I can only imagine what Eddie is thinking after being imprisoned for more than a month. It must be strange seeing people doing normal things, like driving someplace, playing basketball in the schoolyard, cleaning up the yard. He's taking it all in as if he had never observed such wonders before.

Occasionally, Eddie would shake his head and mumble something. Once I thought I heard him say "crazy bastards."

When I asked him, "What's that, Eddie?" he said, "Oh, nothing. Just talking to myself."

I wonder if that's something he picked up in the bunker.

The ride home takes more than four hours. As we leave the New York Thruway and enter New Jersey, Eddie becomes excited when he recognizes more familiar sights along the way.

"My God, we used to come here for pumpkins around Halloween."

"Ah, Paramus Park! My favorite mall. I love the Chick-Fil-A there."

"Well, what do you know? There's The Honey Comb."

He slips into his silent mode again. Obviously, passing the place where Mildred worked brought back good memories that turned sour during the past few months when their relationship fizzled. Her recent involvement with the anti-government group must have been especially troubling. Her presence at the mansion with Jackson's wife suggests she may have been actively involved in the plot, but that's for the police to determine.

A few minutes later, almost out of the blue, Eddie says, "I guess I'll be looking for a new job."

"Who knows? But if you have to look, I'm sure you won't have any trouble finding another job," says Laszlo.

"I hope you're right, but I'll miss the people at the trucking firm, especially my friend Melinda."

"Melinda Childs?" says Laszlo.

"Yes, do you know her?"

"Of course. We had a chance to meet her while we were trying to find out what happened to you. In fact, we had lunch with her. Lovely lady, and she thinks very highly of you."

"I'll have to give her a call when I get home."

Laszlo shoots a glance at me, then says, "Something you should know, Eddie. She's in the hospital now... in a coma."

"Oh, God! What happened?"

"She was badly beaten up in her apartment almost two weeks ago."

"Who did it?"

"Don't know for sure, but we have some ideas."

"I bet he arranged it."

"Who?"

"Wendell Jackson."

Laszlo nods.

Eddie heaves a long sigh, shakes his head. "What happens to all those people?"

"What people?" Laszlo asks.

"Jackson and the rest of the gang, or the ones who survived."

Laszlo scratches his head. "Well, basically the federal judicial system and the U.S. Attorney take the lead now. The case is presented to the grand jury, which will decide whether the defendant or defendants should stand trial. I think there are some serious charges here, don't you think?"

"Yeah."

Finally, Laszlo turns onto our street and pulls up in front of Eddie's house. Not surprisingly, Dana is looking out the front window, waiting for her dad to arrive. Suddenly, she's no longer there, and the front door swings open, and she's running down the pathway. Eddie is hardly out of the car when Dana flings her arms around her dad and smothers him with kisses. Tears in his eyes, Eddie is trying to prevent himself from falling with his daughter in his arms. Laszlo and I do all we can to hold up both of them.

Elsie and Gustav are still standing in the doorway, witnessing this special moment. At what they feel is the right time, they hurry down the pathway to join the celebration. Gustav, his eyes glistening with joy, wraps his long arms around Eddie. Throwing back his shoulders, the Vietnam War veteran salutes his son, "I'm so proud of you, Eddie." Last, Elsie gives Eddie a warm, gentle embrace. "Thank God…thank God you're alive," she says.

"Oh, Elsie, thank you for being here," Eddie whispers to her.

At that, Mrs. Tufts, the Dvoraks' sometimes vexing next-door neighbor, opens the front door, sticks her head out, and utters in a loud, but gracious voice, "Welcome home, Eddie. I'm so proud of you. The whole town's proud of you." She looks like she's about to cry as she turns around and goes back into her house.

Wow, just when you think you know someone…

Chapter 36

Later, as we prepare to sit down for dinner, a crowd begins to gather outside the house. I sneak a peek out the side window. If the TV van parked across the street and the cameras in the hands of some of the people are any indication, the onlookers consist mainly of reporters along with some curious neighbors. At the moment, the crowd is small and under control, but scenes like this tend to grow fast once the word spreads.

I wish Detective Laszlo hadn't left so soon after he arrived. He said his wife Norma was worried about him, and that's understandable with all that's happened in the past couple of days. But if he were here, maybe he could advise us on how to deal with the press. I decide to call him.

"First of all, eat your dinner," he says in his usual direct style. "I'll call the precinct and make sure you get adequate police security. I'm sure they're on their way now. Sometimes it helps if someone goes out and talks to the reporters and asks them to back off. Above all, make sure Eddie follows the doctor's orders. I'll call you later."

As advised, we eat our dinner, valiantly trying to make conversation. When we're almost finished, I tell everyone what Laszlo suggests and volunteer to act as spokesman.

"No you won't," Eddie insists.

"What do you mean?"

"I'll talk to them."

"Do you really want to go out there, Eddie?"

"Yes. Let them see what they did. More important, they ought to know what they were planning to do."

A silence around the table. Outdoors, a chorus of anxious voices is rising in the night.

"I'm worried, Eddie," says Elsie.

"I'll be fine."

"They'll probably ask a lot of questions," says Grandpa.

"I can handle it."

"And they can be pretty rude sometimes," Grandpa adds.

"I'll answer the best way I can."

Now the noise level outside is louder than ever.

My final argument: "Remember what the doctor told you."

"I'll be alright. There are some things a person has to do for himself."

"Do it, Daddy! We'll stand behind you," says Dana.

A late-March wind has made this night a little colder than usual for this time of the year. Eddie leads the way out of the house to the curb, where a large group of journalists and others are gathered. Some people, probably neighbors used to seeing this young, vigorous man, wince when Eddie comes into view and begins to speak.

"Good evening. I'm Eddie Dvorak, I've been locked up in an underground bunker for more than a month. Yesterday, I was taken out of the bunker, injected with drugs that knocked me out, and placed in the trunk of a van."

His voice is low and a bit raspy, forcing most people in the crowd to stop talking and listen. If anyone's still talking, they're harshly hushed up.

Eddie swallows deeply, continuing: "If you're wondering why I was taken away from my family, it's because I refused to go along with a plot to get our country back on track by assassinating some of our most important government leaders. The ones behind that plot were afraid I'd tell someone about it. And I would have, if I were given the chance. This may sound corny, but I love my family and my country too much."

"Do you consider yourself a hero?"

"No."

"Why not?" someone asks.

"Why not? Because I did what most people in this country would do if they were in my place."

"Where do you stand in the political spectrum?"

"I'm angry, that's where I stand. I don't like a lot of the things happening in Washington, especially the bickering, infighting, and petty politics. That's where I stand. But I don't believe the assassination of our leaders is ever the answer. There's got to be a better way."

"Which is?"

"Like them or not, they are our leaders. We voted them into office, we can vote them out. And we should stand up and express what we believe."

"How well did you know the plotters?"

"Some of them were my friends. I even had them over to my house on occasion. We had some good times together. It was only recently they began talking about taking violent action, and…"

"Who's they?"

"I don't think this is the time or place to name names. Sorry. To continue what I was saying, I just couldn't go along with what they wanted to do, and I told them so, and I tried to change their minds. But they wouldn't listen to me."

After a moment of silence, this question: "Why did they lock you in a car trunk and take you to the area where they attacked the convention center."

"That's something you'll have to ask them." Straining to speak as loudly as he can, he adds with all the emotion he can muster, "You know, those law enforcement officers who lost their lives defending our leaders are the real heroes of this tragic story. Now, if you'll excuse me, I got out of the hospital a few hours ago and I'm getting hoarser by the second. I've got to get back into the house. Doctor's orders. Thank you and goodnight."

A couple of more questions are tossed into the night, but Eddie waves them off and heads back inside, proudly followed by his family and me.

Later that night, Tess called me on the phone. "I think he did a great job," she says, referring to the way Eddie handled himself at the press conference, which got wide coverage on TV.

"I agree."

"I mean, the man went through a lot, and it showed."

"I offered to act as his spokesman, but he wanted to do it on his own."

"That was brave of him. I'd like to meet him someday."

"Sure. How about Saturday? And if you're up to it, we can go to the final game of the hockey tournament."

"I'd love that. Uh, did you forget something?"

"No…if you're talking about our date. I'll pick you up after you get out of work tomorrow. I have one stop to make before I see you."

"That's fine. Where are you going?"

"The Bishop's office."

"Oh. That should be interesting."

Chapter 37

To be honest, I'm uneasy about my meeting at the Bishop's office in the city. I can't say exactly why. I'm sure I won't be coerced into staying the course or flogged for even thinking about discontinuing my priestly ministry. So, why? I suppose it's because the church has been my home for so long, the place where I grew into a man-priest and where I was schooled, sheltered, and nurtured to do God's work, and now I'm thinking of leaving that life. Of course, there's some guilt, too—probably more than I realize. How can I exit the priestly ministry when my church needs all the help it can get?

I am greeted in the reception area by Monsignor Gosselin. From the different occasions when our paths crossed, I remember him as an extremely bright young man. Originally from the upper West Side, he has strong academic credentials, including a deep knowledge of canon law. The monsignor is a low key but genial guy with a reputation of being on the fast track in the hierarchy.

He leads me down a long hall and into his office and gestures toward a tall, leather chair. "Please sit down, Richard."

I notice a large, ceramic crucifix on the wall behind his desk. "That's remarkable!"

"Thank you. I found it in a small workshop in Rome," he explains. "It was quite an ordeal getting it home, but it was worth it."

"How long were you in Rome?"

"Three years."

"I've been there twice, but only for brief periods…too brief."

"I know what you mean. So, Richard, how are things going with you? I understand you're living in New Jersey."

"Yes, I'm renting a house. I think I'm finally settling in. Moving was quite an experience. I forgot what it was like."

"I'm sure. What's the church like in your town?"

"It's very nice. Physically, it's sort of like a large chapel. It's not that old. I think it was built in the early sixties. The pastor, Father Doyle, is a sweet man, but he has his hands full. Like lots of other churches in the state, it's going through a major restructuring phase now. A couple of years ago, it closed its elementary school."

"We're going through a similar process here in the city."

"Yes, I know."

"Sad, isn't it? These are tough decisions we have to make, and they're upsetting everyone. So, how are you spending all your time these days?" he says, changing subjects with a sigh.

"Besides unpacking?"

"Yes," he replies with an easy smile.

"I've made friends with some of the neighbors." I tell him about Dana and, after a little hesitation, recount my first meeting with her in the snowstorm.

I've never seen the monsignor laugh so hard. "She sounds like a bright, refreshing teenager."

"She is. And she's the star of an all-boys hockey team. They're in the finals of a major regional tournament now."

"Wow."

"You might have heard about her father, Edward Dvorak. He was abducted from his home, then locked up in an underground bunker for refusing to go along with a plot to assassinate a group of Congressional leaders."

"Oh, yes, Dvorak, Edward Dvorak! I've been following that story. Brave man. I watched the TV interview outside his home."

"I was there, standing behind him."

"Oh, my. That's amazing."

"He's a brave man. He went through quite an ordeal."

"My goodness. And I'm sure it was God's will that you happen to be there to help that family…Listen, if you don't mind, Richard, let me get right to it. Have you come to any conclusions about whether you want to continue your ministry?"

"Yes. I can't say I've thought about it every single moment. Life goes on around me, and I like to reach out and help people whenever I can. But that doesn't mean I stopped thinking about my own future. As you know, Monsignor, I've been a priest for eleven years, and, add my years in the seminary, I've spent almost half my life in the church. It's meant so much to me. The church has been my home, my strength, my provider. Most of all, it's been my teacher. It taught me how to do the Lord's work, which I plan to continue doing…not as a priest, but as a lay person, working with the church whenever possible."

"So, you're saying you cannot continue living the life of a priest?"

"That's correct."

A long pause. "I was hoping you'd continue your ministry."

My eyes turn to the splendid crucifix on the wall. "Believe me, this is the toughest decision of my life, but it's what I want to do."

"What about your plans for the future?"

"I wish I could tell you I have something specific all lined up. I don't. But I plan to use whatever skills I have, after years of working with adults and teenagers in crisis situations, to help people make better lives for themselves."

"Is marriage part of your plans?"

"Yes, if Tess will have me. All I know is we love each other deeply."

"As you know, there's a process involved when a person is released from his priestly duties and responsibilities and moves into the so-called lay world. It's called laicization. Celibacy is certainly one of those responsibilities requiring a dispensation."

"I'm aware of that. The process can take a while to complete."

"For the record," Monsignor Gosselin continues, "a priest released from his duties can no longer function as a priest, and that means he no longer will be called 'Father' and he can't celebrate Mass, confer the sacraments, or be a part of the ministry within a diocese or religious institution. Also, he can't hear confessions except in one situation: Every priest is obliged to hear the confession of a Catholic in danger of dying. I'll give you some materials on all of this to take home."

"That would be helpful."

"Now, if you don't mind waiting a few minutes, I'll see if the Bishop is free. He's been at meetings all afternoon on this restructuring business. Would you like some coffee or tea?"

"I'm fine."

About fifteen minutes later, Bishop Browne sweeps into the room, followed closely by Monsignor Gosselin. A man of high-octane energy and enthusiasm, the bishop is not one to rely on formality except in the exercise of official religious functions or ceremonies.

"Hey, Richard, how're you doing?" he says.

As I spin around, about to rise out of my chair, I almost lose my balance. "Oh, fine, your excellency. Nice to see you again."

"Please, don't get up," he says as he pulls over a chair and places it next to mine. His broad smile quickly disappears as he sits down. "Monsignor told me about your decision."

"It was probably the most difficult decision I've ever had to make."

"Are you sure you want to do this?" he says, glancing at the monsignor, who's back behind his desk.

"Yes, I've given it a lot of thought."

"I'm sure you have," he says with a slight grin. "And I'm not going to muscle or pressure you in an effort to change your mind. But there have been occasions where a person who left the ministry wants to return. And if you ever want to talk about any such matter, please, please, Richard, feel free to call me anytime."

"Thank you."

"I want you to know we think highly of you, Richard. You've been an excellent priest, especially when it comes to working with young people of all persuasions, and that will be a growing concern of ours in the future, especially since we have such a diverse population. I hope, once you receive the necessary dispensations, you'll be able to help us educate and guide these young people."

"I'll certainly consider it, your excellency. Thanks for your confidence in me."

The bishop seems saddened, but I'm buoyed by his overall reaction.

"I wish we had time for lunch or something, Richard, but…let's plan on getting together soon." He shoots another look at the monsignor, who jots down a note on a small pad. "Be well, Richard, and God bless you."

Chapter 38

There's time before Tess gets home from work and it's a beautiful spring day, so I decide to walk crosstown to her apartment. Besides, it will give me a chance to review what just happened. All in all, I think it went well, considering I'm about to leap into a whole new way of life.

How quickly Monsignor Gosselin was able to pick up what I found so difficult to put into words.

"So, you're saying you cannot continue living the life of a priest?"

And my stiff reply:

"That's correct."

The monsignor didn't need to tell me what a priest can and cannot do when he leaves the ministry. But his words are still ringing in my ears:

"A priest released from his duties can no longer function as a priest, and that means he no longer will be called 'Father'...

"He can't celebrate Mass, confer the sacraments, or be a part of the ministry within a diocese or religious institution...

"He can't hear confessions except in one situation: Every priest is obliged to hear the confession of a Catholic in danger of dying."

Clear enough.

As I'm about to reach Fifth Avenue, I recall the Bishop as he pulls up a chair and sits next to me. He has some kind words for me.

"You've been an excellent priest, especially when it comes to working with young people..."

And he makes a generous offer.

"I hope, once you receive the necessary dispensations, you'll be able to help us educate and guide these young people."

I'm open to the idea: It's certainly worth considering once I receive "the necessary dispensations."

On Fifth Avenue the crowds thicken. Looming in front of me now is Saint Patrick's Cathedral, that spectacular sand castle of holiness built on the bedrock of Manhattan. Ever since I can remember, Saint Pat's was a special place to visit, even for a boy growing up a few blocks away on the West Side. I decide to stop by the beautifully renovated cathedral for a visit. Not to say farewell but for some quiet time to ask for some guidance as I continue my life journey.

In my eagerness to enter the church, I accidentally bump into a woman coming out the front door. She's with a burly guy carrying two shopping bags from Fifth Avenue's most venerable shops.

"Hey!" she says, piqued. "Why don't you watch where you're going?"

All eyes turn on me. "Oh, I'm so sorry," I say, and I mean it.

"Yeah," says her burly friend, punishing me with his angry mug. In an aside meant for universal consumption, he says, "Asshole!"

I make believe I didn't catch what he said, but I'm certain his crude comment was heard as far away as Second Avenue. I'm boiling inside me, but I decide against making a comeback I learned in my old neighborhood and move cautiously past the couple and into the church. I slip into the first empty pew I can find and bury my head in my hands and quietly begin to sob. Someone pats me on the shoulder. I look up at an old man with rheumy eyes. "Are you alright, young fella?" he asks with a noticeably Irish accent.

"I'm fine, thanks."

"One of those days, eh?" he says.

"Yeah, I guess."

"Well, you're in the right place now. Would you like a tissue?" he says, reaching into the back pocket of his corduroy pants.

"No thanks, but that's kind of you. I'm fine now."

Welcome to the lay world.

A bouquet of springtime's best flowers in my hand, I enter Tess's apartment. She wraps her arms around my neck and kisses me with her warm, welcoming lips. "Boy, you look beat," she says, never one to mince words.

"It was quite an afternoon. Here, these are for you," I say, thrusting the flowers at her.

"Thanks. They're beautiful," she says. "Come on in and sit for a while and tell me all about it. My mom is minding Simon, so there won't be any interruptions."

After she places the flowers in a vase, I tell her all about the meeting at the Bishop's office. I skip the incident at Saint Pat's for now.

She heaves a huge sigh of relief. "That sounds like it went well," she says when I finish. "I'm glad for you, Richie."

"What do you think about the Bishop's offer?" I ask her.

"Is that something you'd like to do?"

"Yes, but I'd like to give it some more thought," I reply. "I may want to do something completely different."

"Like what?"

"I don't know. I'll tell you when I find it."

"Okay. Do you still feel like going out for dinner?"

"I don't know. Do they deliver around here?"

"Sure. What do you feel like eating?"

"I don't know."

"Boy, aren't we decisive tonight?"

"Ah, hell." It's not that I was never embarrassed before. "Let's go out to our favorite restaurant. I'll tell you a funny story when we get there."

Chapter 39

Late afternoon, the day before the big game. We're gathered at the Dvoraks for a private party—Dana, Eddie, Elsie, Angie, Hugo, Grandpa, Yank, and me. Later, the town will hold a rally for the Owls at the high school football field.

It's like someone turned on the switch. Dana, the once nervous, worried teenager, is calm and relaxed, and I've never seen her smile so much. I'm sure she's happy her family and friends are all together, whether she's about to play a championship game or not. Most important, her mom and dad are here, together, and when was the last time that happened? Yes, Mom! The woman who fell out of her life to take care of her addictions and raise a new family. And, yes, Dad! Her seemingly last link to family whom she thought she might never see again after he was yanked from their home.

Dana seems to be gaining more confidence in herself as she buzzes around the living room, making sure everyone is well fed and having a good time. "How about another sandwich, Grandpa?" "Eat something besides potato chips, Hugo." "Angie, you eat like a bird." "Can I make you another cup of coffee, Mom?"

She's especially concerned about her dad, who seems to be gaining strength with each passing day, but slowly. "Dad, stop staring at your food. Eat up. It's very good, and it's good for you."

He shakes his head and stabs a floret of broccoli. "I can't believe I'm here ...in my home...with the people I love."

"I know, Dad, but it's important you build yourself up, like the doctor told you."

"I will...I am...Look, watch me eat this broccoli. Hey, all you're doing is giving orders to everyone. Eat something yourself. You're the one playing the big game tomorrow."

I can't help smiling. It's as if the dynamic duo are back at it again. Meanwhile, Elsie gets up and walks into the kitchen. I follow her. She pulls a pack of cigarettes and a lighter out of her bag and starts for the back door.

"Mind if I join you?" I ask.

"Not at all. You smoke, Richie?"

"No. Incense was the closest I came to it."

She laughs. "It's an old habit that was hardly discouraged when I joined AA."

"Yeah, I know what you mean. I've sat in on few meetings. It was like the London Fog."

She laughs again, opens the back door, and walks outside. Yank and I are right behind her.

It's a clear, cool night, and I find an old stump to sit on while I pet Yank. "So, you're leaving on Sunday morning. You must be happy about that."

"I can't wait to see my two little guys again, but I'll miss my teenage girl. It's amazing how much she's grown and matured. I'm so proud of her."

"Do you think you two will connect more frequently in the future?"

"Now you're sounding like a priest."

"That happens to me sometimes."

"Well, the answer is yes. I want to see her more often, and I hope she can come visit me in Florida whenever she can. It's sad, but that's the way it is. I'm so delighted the way she's developing. Eddie's done a wonderful job, but I'm a little worried about him. That was a terrible experience he went through."

"Yes, it was, but he's a tough, courageous young man, and he loves his daughter so much."

"Yes, he does, and it shows."

My cell sounds off. "Excuse me," I say and walk to the back of the yard. It's Detective Laszlo, and he asks me if I want to take a ride with him next week.

"Where to?"

"To see Melinda Childs. I understand she's out of the coma."

"That's good news. Sure, I'll go. Should I ask Eddie to come along?"

"I'll leave that up to you. I have no problem with that. I don't expect to drill the poor woman with a lot of questions."

"Okay. I'll get back to you."

As I turn around, Elsie is gone, back in the house.

"Come on, Yank, let's go join the party."

Later that evening, Elsie and I slip into the first empty spaces we can find at the high school football field. Eddie and Grandpa decided to pass on the Owls pre-game rally; it's been a long day. On a patch of artificial turf facing the aluminum stands, the high school band is playing a series of rah-rah tunes that set my feet and hands in motion, offering. I hope, some rhythmic accompaniment. As the music is playing, the team, in orange jerseys, lines up next to the band. I'm thrilled to spot Dana, front and center among the boys. Nearby, a microphone is waiting for a master of ceremonies, who turns out to be Josh Cimmaron, an original Owl and one-time junior hockey coach.

"Good evening, everyone, and welcome," he begins in a voice booming with confidence. "Do you know why we're here tonight?" Although some people in the stands offer a few replies, he's not really expecting any. "That's right. Our very own Owls! You won't find a better amateur team in the region. And the proof will be in the pudding tomorrow afternoon when the Owls face off in the final game of the regional championship hockey series. Isn't that right, folks?"

Folks agree with something that sounds like "YYYEEEEAAAAHHHH!" And Cimmaron adds his own tagline: "Let's go, Owls!"

BREAKAWAY

Which is picked up by the folks in the stands : "LET'S GO, OWLS! LET'S GO, OWLS!"

"As an original Owl, I'm so proud of this bunch of players. And we owe a lot of their success to their fantastic coach. Let's hear it for Coach Sam Fenda."

Coach Fenda, dressed in a blue blazer, rose-colored shirt (tieless), and tan slacks, walks slowly up to the mic and waits for the cheering to die down.

"We wouldn't have come this far without you, our wonderful fans, but we're not done yet. We got one more mountain to climb, and it won't be easy. This team we're facing tomorrow is a good team."

Loud boos in the stands.

"No...no...let's be fair. Give them their due. But our Owls are a pretty good team, too. Right?"

Resounding cheers, applause, and whistles.

He continues: "The players here have worked hard to be where they are, and they deserve the recognition they're getting. If you don't mind, I'd like to introduce each one of them to you. First, say hello to our wonderful goalie, Matteo Bautista."

Matteo steps forward and waves to an appreciative crowd. Coach Fenda goes on to introduce the other players. When Dana is asked to take a bow, she receives a thunderous ovation from everyone, which brings one of those Broadway smiles to her face.

With the introductions complete, Coach Fenda concludes: "Like I said, we're not done yet. We won't be satisfied until we complete this tournament with a victory, and with your support we'll win tomorrow. So, join me one more time, folks:

"LET'S GO, OWLS! LET'S GO, OWLS! LET'S GO, OWLS!"

"Thank you. Now, let's hear it for one of our biggest fans, Mayor Midge Larkin!"

Curly-haired Mayor Larkin cuts a young, dashing figure in a neatly pressed navy blue suit and designer white shirt (with tie). "Good evening, everyone. What can I say that hasn't been said already? For the next few minutes, sit back and listen and enjoy while our talented school band plays a few songs you might remember, ending with a song special to all of us in this fine community."

Over the next ten minutes or so, the band plays a medley of popular songs that live happily in our memories, from "Somewhere Over the Rainbow" to "Everything's Coming Up Roses". Despite an occasional sour note, the music overall is easy on the ears and well received. The final song in the series, it turns out, is the high school song, which brings a tear or two to some of the long-time residents in the stands.

"Well, how'd you like that, folks?" Mayor Larkin gushes. "Let's hear it for our fantastic high school band."

More resounding cheers.

"Well, that about does it. We've had a lot to cheer about tonight. And they'll be a lot to cheer about tomorrow. Goodnight, everyone, and God bless the Owls! And God bless America!"

Suddenly, bolts of lightning fill the sky, and the rain comes down hard and fast. "Where did this come from?" Elsie asks as we make a run for it. "I hope it's not an omen," she says. I shrug, trying to keep up with her. Somehow we can't help laughing as we finally plunge into my Passat, soaking wet.

Chapter 40

*T**he Finals—Last Game:* The stage is set. The stands are overflowing with gung-ho fans on both sides. Anyone who can't get into the ice rink can watch the cable-cast of the game at home or at their favorite pub or they can listen to the game on a local collegiate radio station.

Press coverage is unprecedented for a regional amateur hockey game. Reporters from community newspapers all over northern New Jersey along with freelancers and sports staffers from big-city publications are curious to see what the fuss is all about. Most of the college recruiters and pro-hockey scouts have been here since the finals began, some longer. They're expected to wait until the last game is over before they render their final recommendations to their athletic directors.

Why all the excitement? It's hard to say. People may want more amateur sporting events that are closer to home, with their purity, simplicity and affordability. Perhaps it's time to turn up the spotlight on local or regional amateur sports events that capture the enthusiasm, spirit, and competiveness of teenage athletes in pursuit of their dreams. That there's only one female player could be a point of pride or contention or both, but that aspect of this tournament is also attracting a lot of interest. Of course, the abduction and rescue of the father of one of the players also caused public interest to soar.

Once again, Mayor Larkin is sitting, front and center, soaking in the attention. Sitting next to him and his son is tonight's guest of honor, Edward Dvorak, father of the Owls' star player and a national hero for refusing to go along with a plot to kill Congressional leaders. Seated next to Dvorak are Elsie Mendez, his former wife;

his father, Gustav; and a couple of friends, Richard Bianchi and Tess Tessalone.

After librarian Phyllis Gurth sings the national anthem and the teams line up for the opening faceoff, this burly, scruffy man in the side stands shouts, "Hey, Dana, why don't you go play with the girls?" A moan of disapproval of that remark ripples through the entire rink. Dana, who's waiting for the puck to be dropped, is more shaken than outraged and lets out a heavy sigh. The girl's father snaps his head around to locate the boomer, who lets out another blast, "Get out of boys' hockey, girlie!"

Eddie zeroes in on the heckler in the last row of the stands behind him. "Shut your big, fat mouth, boy!" he shouts up at him.

"Take a walk, sailor!" the agitator yells back.

Dad jerks himself out of his seat, ready to tear up to the top of bleachers. Richard Bianchi wraps his arms around Eddie's waist to hold him back, while Mayor Larkin starts dialing someone, probably Security. Within seconds, two guards are hustling up the steps, and after a brief conversation they seize the loudmouth and lead him out of the ice rink.

Finally, the puck is dropped, and the game begins. Dana tries to stop the puck, but it squirts between her skates and winds up on the stick of an Ice Storm winger. He, in turn, passes the puck to Mario Cane. "The Dog" carries the puck into the Owls zone and takes a high, hard shot. Owls goaltender Matteo catches the puck with his glove hand and holds onto it for a whistle, giving his teammates time to regroup. At the same time, Coach Fenda makes a line change.

An embarrassed Dana shakes her head when she reaches the bench.

"Ah, forget about him," says Hugo. "He's outta here now."

Coach Fenda puts a reassuring hand on her shoulder. "You can play with anyone, Dana. You're that good. Now forget about that jerk. Let's play some hockey."

From the start, it seems like this will be one of those games—lots of highs and lows, as reflected by the crowd sounds, but little or no scoring. Both teams have come to play a more defensive game today. On the Owls' side, Big John Mason and his partner on defense, Gussy Grant, prove exceptionally skilled at blocking shots with their bodies and poking the puck out of harm's way with their sticks. Stepping up their physical play, the bigger Ice Storm defense corps is breaking up plays with crushing body checks and cross-checks without regard to gender. Twice, Dana leads rushes into the Ice Storm zone only to be rammed into the boards, and not one penalty is called. Obviously, the refs are letting them play, which is another way of saying they're not calling penalties they should be calling. The first period finally ends.

Score: Owls, 0; Ice Storm, 0.

Physically and emotionally spent, Dana tramps off the ice with her head down. "Way to go, team! Way to go, Dana. Keep it up, guys!" her dad says as she walks by.

Dana shakes her head in frustration. "I wonder what game my dad is watching," she says to Hugo.

"Ah, he's just trying to cheer us on, Dana."

After giving the team a chance to unwind, Coach Fenda moves to the center of the locker room and stands there, not saying anything. When the rustling and murmuring stop, he speaks:

"Well, that was fun, wasn't it? I suppose it was great if you like old-time hockey. I don't, and I don't think you do. But I'm not ready to turn the other cheek. And I don't think we should go ballistic, either. I have a solution, and I think we ought to try it, unless you have a better idea. It's called S-P-E-E-D. Use your speed. Move those feet. Go like the wind around and over and through those guys. They can't hit what they can't catch. Got it?"

It's like the light bulb went on.

"And one more thing: I need you defensemen to move up on the play, and you forwards, keep an eye on the defensemen. Size up your options. If a defenseman is in the clear, give him the puck. And if you defensemen get a chance to shoot, don't wait for anyone to tell you. Shoot!" He takes a deep breath. "We can do this. Remember, we're a team of six players on the ice, not five, not four, not three, not two or one, but six! Let's do it."

As the second period begins, the Owls appear more confident and committed. In the first shift, they manage to get two good shots but are denied by the Ice Storm goaltender, Jay Rivers, who at six foot, three inches tall—and widely built, to boot—fills up most of the net. As the game opens up, Matteo, the Owls goalie who's no match in physical size to his counterpart on the other end, is busy making one spectacular save after another.

At one point, Matteo kicks the puck out to the neutral zone where it's picked up by Dana, who stick-handles past two Ice Storm players and moves into the zone in front of the net. She shoots, and the puck hits the right goal post and bounces out onto the stick of onrushing Owls defenseman Gussy Grant. In one motion, he slams the disk into the wide open side of the net.

Score: Owls, 1; Ice Storm, 0.

Out on the ice and on the bench, Owls players are orbiting in a galactic celebration of the goal by Gussy, assisted by Dana. They're beaming with team pride, while the Ice Storm can only stand by, enviously watching the other team celebrate, waiting for their time in the spotlight. The stands, or at least those parts occupied by Owls fans, are rocking. The guest of honor and his family and friends are a tangled mass of happy people when the Owls take a one-goal lead.

Now there's still plenty of time left to play, which causes some of the more cautious and knowledgeable hockey fans to temper their celebration. But don't bother to tell Mayor Larkin to cool it. He'll continue to reach out and shake as many hands as he can reach, win or lose.

Before the second period ends, the Ice Storm manage to take several close-in shots at Matteo, crowding the net area with bodies while they probe for a rebound. But the Owls goalie survives the late-period surge by the Ice Storm as the buzzer sounds for the close of the period. The score remains: Owls, 1; Ice Storm, 0.

Coach Fenda is pleased with how his team played in the period. At the same time, he reminds everyone the Ice Storm are one desperate and hungry team who twice before in previous tournaments finished second best. "We must continue to take the play to them with our speed. I want shorter shifts and fresh bodies out there all the time. Of course, it would ease things a little if we score one or two more goals. But remember we have the lead. Play smart out there."

Lenny stands up. "I just want to say, 'Thanks, coach. You always manage to hit the nail on the head for us.' Now let's rock and roll over these guys."

Dana gives him an odd look, hoping Lenny has said all he wants.

Lenny, however, has something to add: "Notice how their goalie… what's his name?"

"Rivers," someone replies.

"Yeah, Rivers. Notice how that big guy flops down on nearly every shot we take. Well…"

The coach clears his throat. "Thanks, Lenny. Now let's all gather around me here for a moment of silence before we head back out there."

As the third period begins, one of the Ice Storm defensemen takes a run at Dana as she rears back to take a slap shot and sends her careening into the boards. For several moments, she just lies there, without moving. Finally, she's helped to her feet and guided off the ice and to the locker room. The Ice Storm player who hit her is assessed a four-minute penalty and a game misconduct.

With a one-player advantage, the Owls stand a chance to increase their lead at a critical point in the game, but there are a couple of major stumbling blocks in their way. First, the Owls' best scorer is in the locker room, tending to an unspecified injury to her leg. Second, without Dana leading the way, the Owls are having a tough time entering the Ice Storm zone. Again and again, the Owls are turned back before they're able to set up and create a scoring chance.

After the four-minute penalty ends, the Ice Storm dominate the play and create some of their best scoring opportunities. But, thanks to some excellent defensive work by the entire team, especially Matteo, the Owls hold onto their slim lead.

Seven minutes to go…now six…five. Still no change in the score or sign of Dana's return. The Ice Storm continue to press the attack in the final minutes. With three minutes to play, Percy McBride snares the puck behind the Owls net and scores a wraparound goal, sending the Ice Storm team and its fans into a frenzy.

Score: Owls, 1; Ice Storm, 1.

On the positive side for the Owls, Dana is back on the bench. Hugo skates over to her. "Man, do we need you. How're you doing?"

"My leg's still sore, but I think I can still skate a couple of shifts."

Hugo shoots a pleading eye at the coach.

"I'll leave it up to you, Dana," says the coach.

"I'm good," she asserts.

The Owls fans give a rousing "Dana! Dana! Dana!" cheer when she skates onto the ice. Those cheers are soon merged with the roars of the Ice Storm fans as the teams face off at center ice. It's obvious Dana does not have full use of one leg, but she can skate. It's the long strides that give her some discomfort. Hugo and Ernie are both keeping an eye on her. They are just glad she's on the ice with them.

Ninety seconds to the end of the period. Hugo passes to Ernie, who carries the puck deep into the Ice Storm zone. With the shooting lanes blocked, he circles around the Ice Storm net to the left circle. As he does, Dana positions herself on the opposite side of the ice. Ernie passes the puck to her. All in one motion, she swoops up the puck and sends a wrist shot toward the open side of the net. In a desperation move, Ice Storm goalie Jay Rivers reaches out with his glove and makes a brilliant save.

Thirty seconds to go. A faceoff deep in the Owls zone. Coach Fenda sends his two top defensemen onto the ice to complete the line change. The Ice Storm win the faceoff, and the puck is sent back to a defenseman on the blue line, who passes it across ice to the other defenseman. He shoots. Somehow the puck ricochets off two players on its way to the net. Matteo doesn't stand a chance.

Score: Ice Storm, 2; Owls, 1.

With only 12 seconds left, the Owls desperately attempt one more shot, but they run out of time. The Ice Storm erupt into a volcanic celebration. When they come back to earth, they line up for a victory handshake with the Owls players, one of the most gallant gestures in sports.

There are tears in the eyes of Owls fans, tears of disappointment, of course, and pride.

Chapter 41

Early next morning, I'm sitting in the Dvorak's living room contributing to what is sometimes called small talk or idle conversation. We cover a variety of subjects, including the weather forecast (partly sunny in the low-sixties here and bright and sunny in the seventies in Florida), the bagels on the coffee table hardly anyone touched, and yesterday's championship game, without coming to any conclusions except that the Owls deserved to win the game, according to Grandpa.

"I suppose so," says Dana.

"I know so," Grandpa counters. "If you didn't get hurt…"

"I don't want to talk about it, Grandpa. "It's over. We lost."

"But you really won the game, sweetheart," Grandpa insists.

Eddie stares at Grandpa. If his eyes could talk, they would be telling Grandpa to let it go. Enough already!

But Grandpa has more to say. "Another thing: There were at least five penalties they should have called against them."

Dana shakes her head, annoyed, desperately hoping to end this conversation.

"What time is your cab coming?" Eddie asks Elsie.

"Seven o'clock. It should be here any minute now."

I had offered to drive her to the airport. So did Eddie. But she insisted on taking a taxi.

"You have everything?" I ask.

"And then some," she says, waving the palm of her hand at the collection of luggage and carry-on bags by the door. "I think I'm going back with a few more things than I brought."

"Isn't that always the case?"

A horn beeps twice out front, and everyone jumps up at the same time.

Dana rushes toward Elsie and throws her arms around her and starts sobbing.

"Now what did we say?" Elsie says. "No tears. We'll be seeing each other a lot more now, and I want to hear from you whenever you feel like talking, girl to girl."

Dana, who's as tall as Elsie, is sniffling. She nods that she understands and says, "I love you, Mama."

"And I love you, sweetheart," says Elsie, holding back tears. "I'm so proud of you."

"And I'm so proud of you, Mama."

"Come here." Elsie gives her a big kiss and strokes her long, blond hair. "I'll miss you. I'll miss all you guys."

One by one, we say our goodbyes.

"So long, Richie. Tell Tess I enjoyed meeting her, and all the best to you as you explore the next big step in your life."

"Thanks, Elsie. Safe trip, and my regards to Alex."

"So long, Grandpa. You'll always be very special to me, you know that."

"Yeah, that's what they all say. Come back soon, Elsie. We'll play some pinochle."

Eddie and Elsie stand there, staring at each other, not saying anything. They quietly embrace.

"You've been so helpful, Elsie. Thank you, and come back anytime."

"Thanks, Eddie. I will. You should be proud. You've done a magnificent job with this young lady. Please take care of yourself."

The horn beeps twice again.

"I'd better go."

Everyone picks up a bag, and they all walk out and down the path to the taxi.

"Sorry," says Elsie to the driver.

"No problem, ma'am," says the cabbie as he piles the bags into the trunk.

One more kiss all around, and she hops into the back seat. As the taxi pulls away into the bright, crisp morning, we already miss her. I know I do. I laugh to myself when I think about that night when Elsie and I got caught in the rainstorm coming home from the rally.

A little later that day, I'm back in my house, and Eddie calls me on the phone. "You gotta come over here," he says. "You won't believe what's going on."

I rush right over. There's excitement written all over Grandpa's face as he opens the door. Yank is barking like a hungry hound. Grandpa waves me into the living room. "They started arriving not long after Elsie left," he explains, smoothing down his tousled white hair.

"Who started arriving? Where are Dana and Eddie?"

He points upstairs. I bound up the steps, two at a time.

In Eddie's bedroom, Dana is talking to someone on the phone, while her dad is sitting at the computer. "She's been getting messages all morning," he whispers.

"Messages? Who's sending them?"

"The athletic directors of universities all over the country. They're all basically saying the same thing." He picks up one of them and reads from it:

Congratulations on your excellent performance at the northeast regional amateur hockey tournament. We would be delighted to talk to you about your participation in our university's hockey program, one of the best in the country, on scholarship. We will be calling you in the next few days about setting up a time and place for meeting with you and, of course, your parents or guardian.

Dana completes her call and hangs up. "That was Minnesota."

"I'll add it to the list," says Eddie. "I'm overwhelmed. I had no clue this would be happening."

"I can't believe it, either, Dad. And all for playing the game I love."

I give her a hug. "Congratulations, Dana. You deserve it."

"It's as if they all decided to jump on the bandwagon at the same time," says Eddie, scratching his head. "I mean, what do they do, call each other and say, okay, here's a good one, let's contact her?"

"I don't think that's the way it works, Eddie. Seems to me that one school is not going to tell another school, a competitor, about one of its key prospects, if it can help it."

"Yeah, I guess. So what do we do now?"

"Let's see what you got."

"Mostly phone calls," says Eddie, "but also E-mails. Someone even sent flowers with a note."

So far, Dana received a total of twenty bids from universities or colleges in seven states, including Minnesota, New York, New Jersey, Massachusetts, Pennsylvania, Ohio, and Vermont. As we're tallying up the calls and e-mails, Dana receives two more e-mail invitations, one from Maine and one from Colorado.

"Wow!" That's all I can say.

"Now what?" says Eddie.

"Well, I remember a couple of boys from my parish who received basketball scholarships from a bunch of schools. What they did was compile a list of their first preferences and second preferences. Next, they set up a schedule—when they would meet, and where. Some of the meetings were held at home. Sometimes they visited the schools to get a better idea of the facilities. Each of the schools had their own websites, which also had a lot of information. Of course, their parents were very much involved in the whole process and talked to lots of people, good friends, former coaches, anyone they thought could help."

"That sounds like a good plan," says Eddie. "What do you think, Dana?"

"Huh? Sure. I'd also like to call Coach Fenda."

"Excellent idea," I say.

She picks up the phone and starts dialing. "Hi, coach. It's me, Dana." She tells him, in an understated way, about the hockey scholarship invitations she received.

His excitement could be heard a mile away.

"How many did I receive?" She turns to her dad.

"Twenty-two and counting," he whispers.

"Twenty-two," she says.

Again, a whoop on the other end.

She's nodding her head now, repeating what he's telling her. "Matteo also got three calls? From schools in the area? And Big John got a couple of calls, too? Awesome! Yeah, I'll have to give them a buzz… Oh, thanks so much, coach. I couldn't have done it without you. Wait, my father wants to talk to you." She hands Eddie the phone. He congratulates the coach on a wonderful tournament and thanks him for all he's done to help Dana during a very trying time for the family.

How Eddie has changed since I first met him!

They exchange more kind words before hanging up. A puzzled look on her face, Dana turns to her dad and says, "Do you think Mom is home now?"

He glances at his watch and nods.

She dials a number in her memory bank, waits for a response, and says, "Hi, Mama, how was your trip?…That's good to hear…You'll never guess what happened after you left."

Chapter 42

A cramp in my toe awakens me early next morning, and I roll out of bed and shuffle over to the window. Eddie's sitting on his front step looking up and down the street. I figured he'd be anxious to get to the hospital where his friend, Melinda Childs, lies in serious but stable condition, slowly recovering from a vicious beating by one of Wendell Jackson's henchmen.

When I asked Eddie last night whether he'd want to come along with Detective Laszlo and me, he didn't hesitate to respond. "Yes! But please tell me what happened to her, the whole story, Richie," he added. I did. Except for a slight roll of his head, he took it well. He was ready to go to the hospital last night.

I turn on the TV for the weather forecast while I get dressed. It should be a beautiful spring day, so I discard the corduroy pants for my one and only khaki slacks. I really need to do some serious clothes shopping one of these days. After I get dressed, I hustle downstairs to make some coffee and pull out two large mugs.

When the coffee is ready, I make a Solomon-like decision, adding milk to one cup and nothing to the other. Holding the two cups in one hand, I somehow maneuver my way out the front door and walk across the street.

"How do you like your coffee?" I ask. "With or without milk?"

"I take it as black as your hair," he says. "Something I learned in the Navy."

"Thanks for the compliment, but I think you missed a few gray strands."

"Now that you mentioned it... By the way, when will Detective Laszlo be here?"

I check my watch. "Give him another fifteen minutes. He's usually on time."

Eddie moves over, and I sit down next to him. We both stretch out our arms in the glorious morning sun. "Isn't this wonderful?" says Eddie, soaking in something recently denied to him. "I can't believe this is all happening, Richie. Not long ago, I was in a bunker wondering if I'd ever see the sun and my family again, and here I am, sitting on the front steps of my house on this beautiful morning."

"Enjoy it, Eddie...every minute of it."

We slip into a peaceful silence. After a few moments, he turns to me and says, "I understand you spent a lot of time with Detective Laszlo trying to find me."

"Yes, I did."

"What was that like?"

"Everything you'd expect—exciting, frustrating, difficult, shocking, especially at the convention center."

"Are you ready to be a detective now?"

"You know what? The investigative part is interesting, but I'm not crazy about the guns and shooting stuff."

He's wearing a big smile now. From him, that's a joy to see.

The front door opens, and out come Grandpa and Dana in a hurry. She's lugging this enormous backpack, as usual.

"Make way, make way," says Grandpa half-jokingly. "Don't want this hockey star to be late for school." Almost in a whisper, he confides in me, "I taught her everything she knows about hockey."

"So I heard," I say.

"A million times," Eddie adds.

They rush off toward Grandpa's Taurus.

"Wait up!" says Eddie. He trots over to them and gives each a hug. "Have a good day, honey...You too, Dad."

Soon afterward, Detective Laszlo pulls up to the curb, and Eddie and I hop into the car.

"I told you," I boast from the passenger seat in the front.

"Yep. Right on time," says Eddie.

"If that's a problem, I could go around the block a couple of times and come back for you guys," says Laszlo, deadpanned.

"Nah, this is fine," says Eddie. "Let's go."

"I figure you guys might be a little anxious to get going." To no one in particular, Laszlo says, "So what's going on?"

Eddie and I fill him in on the flood of scholarship invitations Dana received from universities around the country.

"That's terrific," says Laszlo. "I read about the championship game in the papers. A real squeaker, and they had some nice things to say about Dana. One reporter said she was the star of the game despite getting hurt toward the end. How is she doing?"

"Fine," says Eddie. "Just a sprain."

"She must be excited about the scholarship invitations."

"She can't believe it," says Eddie. "Neither can I. Someone once told me—I think it was Dana—hockey is one of the fastest growing women's sports in the world. I didn't believe it at the time. I wasn't ready to accept it. But I am now. If she can get a good education while playing a game she loves, that's wonderful, and I'm grateful for all the help I get."

The closer we get to the hospital, the more our conversation takes a more serious turn.

Laszlo breaks the silence. "I called the hospital early this morning to see if Melinda is up for a visit from us, and the head nurse said she was, but keep it short."

"She must have taken a terrible beating," says Eddie.

"She sure did," Laszlo says, "but she fought back like a tiger."

"We were close friends, you know," says Eddie.

"I know," says Laszlo. "She told us. She was worried about you."

"I wish I could have done something to help her."

"How could you, Eddie? They forced you out of your home and

locked you up in an underground bunker."

"Yeah, but—"

I offer my two cents. "If you don't mind my saying so, I think it's best to move on, Eddie."

"Yeah. I'm a little anxious to see her."

"And I'm sure she's anxious to see you."

After checking in at the front desk, we take the elevator to the fourth floor and walk down a long corridor to the trauma unit. After seeing Melinda lying on the bed in her apartment—a battered, bloody mess clinging to life—I'm a little apprehensive. I don't know what to expect.

The shades are drawn in her room, probably because she's not ready for bright light. There are two figures at her bedside. One is standing and leaning over the bed. The other is sitting quietly nearby, arms folded. As my eyes adjust to the dim lighting, the two people at bedside turn their heads toward the door. It's Mr. Childs and, I suppose, Mrs. Childs. We exchange greetings with them.

"Look who's here, dear," says Mr. Childs as he and his wife back away to give Melinda a better view. She's sitting up in the bed, her dark blue eyes straining to see who came into the room. There's a hollowness in her pale face, and her auburn hair is a short, scraggly reflection of those long, wavy locks we saw that day in the restaurant. As she eyes the three of us, but particularly Eddie, she reaches for a stray strand and places it back in place and she straightens her hospital gown.

Despite a couple of small facial cuts which are scarring now, she still radiates a natural beauty and poise.

One by one, we approach the bed. First, Detective Laszlo, who reaches out to pat her on the wrist. Hello, Ms. Childs, how are you? I hope you're feeling as good as you look."

"I'm fine," she says in a soft but clear voice. "I'm so glad you're alright. I heard about the attack near Lake George."

"Yeah, we had a front row seat. It was quite something, but it could have been a lot worse.'"

I'm next. "Hi, Melinda," I say, reaching out and gently hugging her. "I'm so happy to see you again…You look terrific."

"Thank you, Richie…and thanks for the anointing."

"Oh," I say, obviously surprised she knew. "You're welcome. By the way, are you Catholic?"

"No, but it worked," she says, a slight smile creasing her face.

Eddie moves forward next. Without saying anything, he wraps his arms around Melinda, holds her for a few seconds, and kisses her on the cheek. There are tears in their eyes.

"How's my pal?" he says. "I wish I could have done something to prevent this from happening to you."

She shook her head. "How could you have done anything, Eddie?"

"You tried to help me…That crazy bunch, who knew they'd do what they did?"

"But they didn't accomplish what they wanted to do."

"That's right, thanks to you two," says Mr. Childs, putting one arm around Eddie's shoulder and holding Melinda's hand. "And thanks to Detective Laszlo here…and Richie… and those young troopers and police officers who put their lives on the line. It's over. It's time to move on with our lives without forgetting what happened and sweeping it under the rug. I speak for a lot of former service men and women when I say this country, with all its faults, has so much going for it. Let's put our heads and hearts into fixing those things that need to be fixed, and let's put country before politics again, like we did during World War II."

On the ride home, I don't know what anyone else is thinking, but there are a few things on my mind. I was happy to learn before we left that Mr. Adler, the owner of the trucking company where Melinda and Eddie worked, had called Melinda to say he wanted both of them to come back to work as soon as they could. Melinda is planning to move out of her current apartment with the grouchy super to a place closer to where her parents live. Czar, her dog, is doing fine and will go along with Melinda to her new home. Eddie and Melinda set a tentative date—two days after she's released from the hospital—for a night out to their favorite restaurant in Elizabeth.

One other piece of news. On the way back, Eddie gets a call from Dana informing him Mayor Larkin and the town council agreed to hold a parade honoring the Owls, after all. It will be held this coming Saturday.

Chapter 43

I didn't know a soul in this town when I moved into my little rental less than two months ago. Now here I am sitting in this make-shift grandstand, one of the guests of honor at a special parade recognizing this town's exceptional hockey team, my team.

It's really Eddie's and Grandpa's moment, however. After all, Eddie is the father of the team's star player, and Grandpa taught Dana how to play hockey (Ask him, I dare you!). Tess and I, along with Detective Laszlo and his wife Norma, are happy to share the moment. Elsie, Dana's mom, returned to Florida, of course, but she's here in spirit. Whatever she misses I'm sure will be recorded for her on somebody's miracle e-device.

All around us are the parents, siblings, and friends of the players. Mr. and Mrs. Bautista and Matteo's two little sisters, all in their Sunday best, are quietly waiting for the parade to start. Not far away, Hugo's father, who took the Owls loss pretty hard, seems to have recovered nicely. He's sharing a hearty laugh now with Lenny's mom. Big John Mason's towering father is engaged in a serious conversation with Eddie, probably sharing their hopes and concerns about the scholarship invitations their kids received. Mrs. Mason, a short, compact woman with lively brown eyes, is listening intently to what her husband and Eddie are saying while gently rocking an infant in her arms.

"Here they come!" someone shouts. All eyes turn down Main Street. Coming into view now are the parade leaders, including a police officer on a motorcycle, a firetruck intermittently blasting its horn, and Mayor Midge Larkin and members of the town council wearing their best business outfits and smiles and waving to the crowds lining both sides of the street. Behind them is a row of three baton twirlers, each doing her own flipping routine.

Next is the high school band in full uniform. As the bright sunlight reflects off the instruments, it's playing a rousing rendition of the "Gonna Fly Now" theme from "Rocky", drawing cheers from the crowd and chills up and down my spine.

The parade route is lined with people, two or three deep in most spots. Most are probably from town, but I bet many live in neighboring communities attracted by the publicity and coverage of the hockey tournament. Some people are sitting on fold-up lawn or lounge chairs they brought from home. Stirred up by the music, festivity and fun of it all, little boys and girls are darting here and there along the parade route, creating havoc for parents, grandparents and the ever-watchful concerned citizen. Some of the stores on Main Street, including two pizza places, a convenience store, and a deli, are enjoying more business than they expected today. The biggest sellers on this warm day appear to be water, soft drinks, ice cream, and flavored frozen drinks.

Finally, I see them. The Owls. They're all wearing team jerseys and skating around on inline skates. Some are skating on a float decorated to look like an ice rink, with a hockey net, a scoreboard, and side boards. The players in the street are handing out hockey pucks with the Owls logo to kids along the parade route. On the float, Matteo is wearing goalie equipment and stopping easy shots from Lenny and Ernie. Standing at the front of the float, Coach Fenda is flashing a big, proud smile as he waves to the crowd. Next to him is Dana, beaming and waving, holding Yank in her arms.

"There's Dana and Yank!" Tess shouts.

"That's my dog!" says Grandpa.

"He's adorable," says Norma

"You should have seen him when I found him," says Grandpa.

By now, the float has drawn up to the grandstand, and anyone who knows anyone is waving furiously and shouting out a name. It's all happening so quickly, and soon the marchers pass by the grandstand and are heading toward their final destination three or four blocks away. As they do, the band is playing another one of my favorites, "Hit Me With Your Best Shot," which probably has special meaning for hockey players.

Finally, it's over. Everyone agrees it was a wonderful celebration. "Short but sweet, like me," says Grandpa. We say our farewells. I don't know if I'll see many of these people again. Being with them, sharing with them, feeling with them. It's been a fantastic experience. It's not that I won't see him again, but saying goodbye to Detective Laszlo is particularly difficult. We've spent so many emotionally charged moments together. He pulls me aside, away from the milling crowd.

"Listen," he says. "I have a question for you. You don't have to give me an answer now. Just think on it."

"What's that?"

"I spoke to my chief," he explains. "I told him all about you."

"Oh, I hope you didn't get into trouble."

"No, not really, we share a good relationship, the chief and I. I told him how well you and I worked together and how helpful you were in the investigation. He was impressed. Well, he started thinking, and I started thinking, and then we got into this 'What if' thing. What if our department hired you to work with me and other detectives? I mean, we'd have to see how it develops over time. It seems that having someone with your experience, working side by side with the police, would add an important and useful dimension to what we do. This may be pie in the sky, but it may even help build better relations between the community and law enforcement. And I think you'd enjoy the work. I mean, I don't even know if this is doable, but what do you think?"

"Wow!"

"What's 'wow' mean?"

"I think it has potential."

Later, I receive another invitation, this one from the mayor's office. Mayor Larkin would like me to sit in at a karaoke recording session— the one he's committed to do after losing a bet to the Ice Storm town's mayor. I agree.

As he steps up to the mic, Mayor Larkin tells his audience of about fifty people, "Tell me what you think. Honestly." Dressed in a tuxedo for a touch of reality, he cues the recording technician. When the music begins, the mayor puts his body in motion and sings:

"I've got you under my skin..."

All I can say is Ol' Blue Eyes Larkin kept his side of the bargain. Honestly.

About the Author

As a kid growing up on the crowded streets of Manhattan's West Side, Valentine Cardinale played hockey with a team called the Owls (no relation to the team in *Breakaway*). While he toyed with the idea of skating into immortality, he had a more compelling dream he was determined to pursue. He wanted to be a writer.

After graduating from Iona College and Columbia Graduate School of Journalism, he enjoyed a successful career as the editor of leading magazines in the advertising and pharmacy fields before deciding to write fiction.

Breakaway is Val's fourth novel. His earlier works include *One More Dance* (Outskirts Press, 2013), a romantic mystery and winner of a 2014 Pinnacle Book Achievement Award; *The West Side Kid* (iUniverse, Bloomington, IN, 2009), a mystery and a Pinnacle Book Achievement Award winner in 2010; and *The Terranovas: A War Family* (iUniverse, 2005), a family historical saga awarded First Prize, Published Fiction, by the Arizona Authors Association.

For more information, visit Val's website (www.vcardinale.com).